WRAPPED UP IN You

USA TODAY BESTSELLING AUTHOR
NIKKI ASH

*Sometimes the best things in life
come from the unplanned...*

Wrapped Up in You Playlist

Unlonely – Jay

Wave of You – Surfaces

Flowers Need Rain – Preston Pablo & Banx & Ranx

Butterflies – MAX & Ali Gatie

Heaven – Kane Brown

Yours – Russell Dickerson

God Gave Me You – Blake Shelton

Bless the Broken Road – Rascal Flatts

My Wish – Rascal Flatts

Lisa,
I hope this story puts you
into the Christmas spirit.

This one's for you.

Christmas magic is silent.
You don't hear it.
You feel it.
You know it.
You believe it.
-Unknown

Prologue
KELSIE

"MOMMY, *OWIE*."

My precious baby girl stares up at me, tears in her eyes, because her ear infection is causing her pain. She's on antibiotics and has already taken a pain reliever, though it takes time to work.

"I know, Ladybug."

I hold her close and run my fingers through her soft, red curls that are identical to mine. She's sweating a bit from crying, and I kiss her damp forehead, wishing I could make the pain go away.

Nobody warns you when you become a parent about how helpless you'll feel most of the time. I'm her mom. I should be able to fix what's wrong, yet there's nothing I can do to make her feel better. Aside from comforting her the best I can and giving her the medication the doctor prescribed, my hands are tied.

"Daddy," Jordan whines, wanting her dad.

Normally, I'd bring her to our room, since our bed is bigger and more comfortable, but he has exams coming up. He has been studying like crazy the last few weeks. If we're in bed with him, he'll feel obligated to be awake, and he needs his rest. Trent's in his senior year of college, majoring in architecture, and it's by far his hardest semester. Since I stay home with Jordan, I'll nap tomorrow when she does, but Trent doesn't have that same luxury.

I continue to stroke Jordan's hair and run my fingers gently along her soft cheek, until her green eyes—which are identical to my own—flutter closed, and she falls into a fitted sleep. I consider laying her in her crib and going back downstairs to bed, but I'm too tired. I know she'll be awake again soon, needing more pain relievers. So, instead, with my two-year-old snuggled into my chest, I fall asleep on the futon in her room.

IT'S HARD TO BREATHE.

I try to suck in a sharp breath, but my lungs burn, causing my eyes to water.

It's stiflingly hot.

Did Trent turn the heat on too high?

Jordan is crying.

She must've woken up in pain.

What's that smell? Why does it smell like...?

I blink several times before taking in the foggy room. It only takes a few seconds for my sleepy brain to stumble awake. The house is on fire. And the alarm never went off. I glance up and remember a few weeks ago when the smoke detector was beeping, indicating the battery was dying. Trent took it out to stop the incessant beeping, but he must not have replaced it.

"Mommy!" Jordan cries through her coughing fit as I bundle her up in the blankets so I can get us out of here. I have no idea how bad the fire is, or where it started—where Trent is—but thanks to being on the second floor, I have no choice but to get us down the stairs in order to get us outside to safety.

When I open the door, the first thing I hear is an alarm going off. Hopefully this means Trent has called the fire department. *Unless he went out...* Sometimes when he's stressed, he'll go for walks or head to the local bar to have a drink and unwind.

When I step into the smoke-filled hall, I look over the railing and see a glow from downstairs that must be the fire. I release a choked sob, unsure how I'm going to get us out. The house is made of wood. Are the steps safe? Will we fall through? The last thing I want to do is try to run through the flames and risk Jordan getting burned.

I race back into the bedroom and close the door behind us. I'm prepared to jump out the second story window if it means we'll get out, but when I lift the curtains, my heart sinks.

Bars are on the windows. This home is old, one of the

reasons we were able to rent it for cheap in Boston. I remember thinking how the bars gave the home a charming feel, and Trent mentioned it made it safer. He worried about Jordan and me being home alone for hours every day. At the time, I thought it was sweet of him. But now, as Jordan's screams increase and I stand stuck in place with no way to get us out, I wish we had the foresight to have the bars removed. But nobody thinks about their home catching fire...until it does.

"It's okay, Ladybug," I coo, trying to keep my voice calm for my daughter. The truth is, I'm freaking the hell out. The smoke is starting to cloud the room to the point where it's hard to see, and I'm having trouble breathing. Jordan is choking on her cough, and I don't know what to do to save us.

Please, God, let the fire department be on their way.

I open the window, needing the fresh air so I can think. My cell phone is downstairs. I have no idea where Trent is.

"Trent!" I scream, hoping he'll answer, only to be met with silence. "Trent!" I yell again, now in full-on freak-out mode. Jordan picks up on my stress, and her cries morph into panicked sobs.

Despite the window being open, allowing Jordan and me to slightly catch our breaths, the smoke is too strong, and it's causing me to become lightheaded. With her in my arms, I think about what I was taught in school. Stop, drop, and roll sure as hell isn't going to work in this situation. I try to approach the hall again to see if I can somehow maneuver us down the steps, but the flames are too high and hot.

This is the only room up here. There's a bathroom, but it doesn't have a window. It's a small two-bedroom, two-bath townhome Trent rented for us that's close to the college he's attending. His parents are helping pay for it as long as he stays in school.

"Oh, God," I cry, the reality of the situation hitting me. We're trapped, and unless a miracle occurs, this is where we're going to die. As I slide down the wall, holding my daughter as tightly as humanly possible, my thoughts go back to the day I found out I was pregnant with her.

"How could you do this?" my mom hissed. "You have your whole life ahead of you."

"We didn't mean for it to happen," I choke out. "We used protection but—"

"This is why I told you to wait until marriage. Now you'll have to get an abortion, something no woman wants to live with."

Wait, what? *"No." I shake my head. This baby might have been an accident, but I'm not getting rid of him or her. It's my choice to make, and I'm choosing to have my baby. "Trent and I talked about it, and he said it's up to me. Sure, it'll be hard, but we'll get through it together."*

"Kelsie," Mom says, her voice devoid of all emotion. "Getting pregnant at eighteen and having a baby out of wedlock is an embarrassment to this family. What will everyone think? Do Trent's parents know?"

Seriously? Her biggest concern is what her country club friends will think?

"He's telling them right now."

"Your mother and I will not support this," Dad says. "If you go through with having this baby, you'll be cut off. No college, no

trust fund. You will no longer be a part of this family."

"But..." I stare at my parents. They've always been on the conservative side, refusing to allow me to get on birth control because doing so would mean they condone premarital sex. So, I'm shocked they're not only okay with me having an abortion, but they're insisting on it. I knew they'd be upset, but I thought they'd suggest Trent and I get married... "It would mean killing my baby."

"If it's between you having this baby or having a future, we choose you," Mom says. "Your future."

"Well, I'm choosing my baby," I reply, holding my head up high.

"Then, consider yourself on your own," Dad says. "You've already graduated high school, and you're eighteen. If you insist on embarrassing this family, then you're no longer part of it."

"Are you kicking me out?" I gasp.

"I will not watch you ruin your life," Mom says. "You want to destroy your entire future? You will not do it under our roof."

When I ran to Trent, telling him what they said, he pulled me into his arms and told me, "We've got this, Kelsie. It won't be easy, but we'll do it together."

A month later, Trent and I moved into this home. His parents were just as mad as mine, but they said they'd still pay for his college. They refused to pay for daycare, or anything baby related, saying if we were adult enough to make a baby, we were adult enough to care for our baby. So I deferred college and stayed home with our daughter.

As much as I want to say I wish I were in school, the truth is I love spending my days with my precious baby girl. I was always told college was the next step. Before I got pregnant, I was fully prepared to go, but I had no idea what I wanted to do. Honestly, if it were up to me, I wouldn't go at all. I love being a mom and taking care of my daughter, and I'd be okay with being a stay-at-home mom for the next several years.

Sure, many days are hard, with Trent working and going to school and interning at the architecture firm. We're only twenty-one, but most days it feels as though we're an old married couple. Once Trent graduates and has a stable job, things will get easier, and we'll be able to focus more on each other and our future.

As I stare at my crying daughter, I think about everything we'll never get to do with her. We'll never take her to Disney to see the princesses she loves or walk into her first day of school because our lives are about to end, right here, in this home, before any of us has gotten a chance to truly live. My only hope is that Trent got out, that he's safe and can continue to live his life.

"Mama, ouch," Jordan cries, rubbing her eyes. The scared look she gives me has me screaming out for help, even though I doubt anyone can hear me.

"Someone, please help!" I cough out. My throat is scratchy, and my lungs are burning, but I hate the thought of giving up. "Help!" I scream again before nuzzling my face into Jordan's neck.

"I'm so sorry, Ladybug," I cry.

I want to stand and carry her down the steps, consequences be damned, except my body is weak, and it's hard to breathe. My brain is foggy, and keeping my eyes open is getting harder.

"I love you, Jordan," I whisper, needing the last words I speak to my daughter to be words of love. "You have been our entire world since the day we found out—" I choke on my cough, unable to finish my thoughts.

My eyes land on my daughter, her eyes filled with tears, and as I accept our fate, I pray she doesn't suffer. All I ever wanted was to give her life... and now, too soon, it's being taken.

As my eyes close, a voice calls out to me, telling me everything is going to be okay. I'm not sure if it's Trent or my imagination—or maybe it's God welcoming Jordan and me home—but before I can pry my eyes open to see, everything goes black as my brain shuts down.

Beep. Beep. Beep.

The loud beeping forces my eyes to open and take in my surroundings. The white walls and monitors stationed around me tell me I'm in a hospital.

Why am I in a hospital?

Like a flip of a switch, everything comes flooding back.

Jordan having an ear infection.

Me rocking her to sleep.

Waking up to the house on fire.

Unable to get us out.

Screaming for Trent.

Holding Jordan while I prayed for a quick and painless

death.

Only death never came because I'm alive, which means...

"Jordan! Trent!" I scream in panic, pulling the oxygen tube out of my nose and throwing the heavy blanket off my body.

"Jordan!" I yell, padding across the floor toward the door. If I'm still breathing, that must mean my baby girl is alive as well, right? "Trent!" Please, please let them both be alive. I can't be the only one who survived.

Just before my hand lands on the doorknob, a nurse steps inside. "You're awake."

"I need my daughter. Jordan Penelope Monroe. She's two years old and has curly, reddish hair, like mine. She doesn't have the same last name as me because her father and I... Trent..." My heart beats erratically behind my ribcage. "We were waiting until he graduated to get married."

The nurse places a hand on my shoulder. "Take a deep breath. You're having a panic attack."

"I... I can't breathe," I choke out. "I need my daughter and Trent. I need to know they're okay. Please," I beg, "tell me they're okay."

"Kelsie, I need you to calm down."

Oh God. That's not good. I can see it in her eyes. She's preparing to tell me bad news. I stumble back to the edge of my bed, trying to control my breathing so I don't pass out. My throat burns, not helping matters.

"Please," I say, once I'm slightly calmer. "I need to know... Is my daughter alive?" There isn't a world I would want to live in where my daughter doesn't exist. If she didn't make it...

"Yes," the nurse says with a small smile. "Your daughter is alive. You've both suffered from smoke inhalation, but with your lungs being strong, you'll fully recover."

Oh, thank God. "And Trent?" If we made it out, surely he did as well. We were on the second floor, and he was on the first. All he had to do was—

"Trent Monroe didn't make it," she says, slicing through my thoughts—and heart—with a sharp knife.

"He… he didn't make it?" I breathe. "Are you sure? Maybe he got out and wasn't injured, so he didn't have to be admitted."

"I'm sorry," she says, her eyes filled with sympathy. "They confirmed he didn't make it out. He died from smoke inhalation."

"Did he…" I clear my throat. "Did he save us?" I ask, trying to get a grasp as to what happened. How we made it out, but Trent didn't. None of it makes any sense.

"No." She shakes her head. "From what I've heard, a firefighter got you and your daughter out, but by the time they went in for Trent, it was too late. I'm so sorry."

"But he was on the first floor. Why didn't he get out?" I cry, begging for answers while she squeezes my hand, trying to comfort me.

"I don't know," she confesses.

"And you're sure?" I ask again, because my brain just doesn't want to accept it.

"Yes," she says softly. "I'm sure."

Holy shit. Trent is really gone. How can this be? We were just sitting at the table eating dinner. Jordan was cranky, and

I told him she had an ear infection. He pulled her into his arms and held her while we ate, and she lay against his chest, content for a little while.

After dinner, he excused himself to get some schoolwork done, kissing my cheek and thanking me for dinner, like he does every night. I did the dishes and then gave Jordan a bath. That was the last time we saw him.

I didn't want to bug him, so I put Jordan to bed myself. I didn't want to distract him, so I stayed in her room with her. And now, we'll never see him again. Because he's gone. Jordan and I made it. Trent didn't.

In a single moment, Trent's life ended.

I lost my boyfriend, the father of my daughter.

And Jordan... She lost her daddy.

Oh my God. Trent is gone.

"I need to see my daughter," I tell the nurse, needing to hold my baby and comfort her. She's going to ask for her dad. What will I say? How will I tell her that her daddy is gone? She's too little. She won't understand.

My heart aches at the thought of everything Trent will miss out on. Jordan growing up, going to school... And what about us? We never got to get married. We were waiting until we could afford a nice wedding.

"I can take you to see your daughter," the nurse says. "Let me just grab a wheelchair."

She wheels me to a room down the hall, where I find my precious baby lying in bed with Trent's dad, Ron, sitting next to her. Her eyes are squinted, and even though she's sleeping, I can tell from her facial expression that it's a fitted sleep.

But she's alive. Unlike Trent.

A sob breaks free, and Silvia and Ron turn their heads to look at me. Ron shoots me a sympathetic gaze, but Silvia is pissed.

"This is all your fault!" she hisses. "My son's life is over because of you! I warned him he was making a mistake, but he didn't listen. Now look what's happened! He's dead!" She stalks toward me, but the nurse steps in between us.

"Ma'am, if you can't calm down, I will have to ask you to leave."

Ron stands and pulls his wife into a hug. "Shh, Silvia, I know you're hurting—everyone is—but it's not Kelsie's fault. You heard the fire marshal. The furnace was faulty. She and Jordan could have just as easily died."

"Silvia, I'm so sorry," I choke out. "I was upstairs with Jordan, and we couldn't get out. I screamed for Trent, but—"

"It doesn't matter," Silvia says, glaring my way. "He's gone. He was left to rot in the fire, and nothing will bring him back."

Thankfully, Ron insists that he and Silvia go for a walk, claiming emotions are high right now and everyone needs to take a moment.

I climb into Jordan's bed, needing to hold her and feel her beating heart. We spend the day there. And when she asks where her daddy is, I'm forced to tell her that he went to heaven. She doesn't get it and ends up upset, wanting him. She cries herself to sleep while I hold her, thanking God that she's alive. Promising Trent that I'll make sure our little girl never forgets him. Praying that I can be both mom and dad to Jordan...

Later in the day, the doctor comes by and clears me, but because Jordan is only two, he insists on monitoring her a bit longer. Luckily, since I'm cleared, he's able to discharge me so I can stay with her the entire time.

A few days later, she's discharged with a clean bill of health, but as I pack up our stuff, it hits me that we have nowhere to go. I have no money or phone. No home or car... So, I call my parents on the phone at the nurse's station, hoping for once, they'll be understanding.

"Mom," I choke out when she answers the phone. "There's been an accident and—"

"We heard," she says. "Silvia's telling everyone you killed Trent."

"What?" Oh my God. "That's not true! There was a fire and—"

"I warned you what would happen if you chose to have that baby instead of focusing on your future. Now look what's happened."

"Mom!" I hiss. "Stop thinking about your reputation for one second, please," I beg. "I'm your daughter, and Jordan is your granddaughter. We almost died in that same fire. I lost my boyfriend. Jordan lost her dad! We've lost everything." I sniffle back a sob. "And now, we have nowhere to go."

"Do you hear yourself?" Mom says. "You have no money. No home. No job. How do you think you're going to support that child of yours? On love and rainbows? That's not how life works. She deserves better than what you can give her, Kelsie."

"What are you trying to say?" I whisper.

"I think it's time to face the facts. You're not mother material. You're too young. You have no education. No income. If you'd like to come home, we can help you. If you're willing to sign your parental rights over to us, we can help you go to school, and I'll—"

"You want me to give up my child?" I screech, making the nurses look my way. The nurse who broke the news to me about Trent extends her arms to take Jordan from me, and I give her a grateful smile.

"I just lost everything. The man I love, the father of my daughter. My daughter lost the only home she's ever known. And rather than being there for me, *for us*, you want me to give up my daughter too? What the hell is wrong with you?" I hiss. "For so long, I thought maybe you'd come around one day, but I was so stupid. You think I would ever hand my daughter over to you after the way you raised me without an ounce of love or affection? You've lost your mind."

Without waiting for her to respond, I hang up and drop my forehead against the counter, needing a moment to think.

"You can come home with us," a masculine voice says. I lift my head to find Ron standing in front of me. "Trent wouldn't have wanted you and Jordan to be left to fend for yourselves."

"What about Silvia?"

Ron flinches. "It's going to take time...for all of us."

The last place—aside from my parents' house—I want to go to, is Trent's parents' home. Nevertheless, since I have no other option, and my little girl needs a place to sleep tonight, I force a smile on my face. "Thank you. We'll be out of your hair as soon as I get things situated."

"No rush," Ron says. "Despite the circumstances, it will be nice having Jordan in our home. It will be like a piece of Trent is still with us."

One

KELSIE

THREE YEARS LATER

"Do you have any plans for Labor Day weekend?" Marissa asks as we clock out from our double shifts at The Omelet, a local café I've been working at for the past three years. I initially started working nights so I could be home with Jordan, but once she started school, I was lucky enough to switch to the morning shift.

Due to a couple of people quitting unexpectedly, I've taken on a few double shifts recently. I hate having to rely on Silvia to pick up Jordan from summer camp and not spend the afternoon with her, but it's hard to turn down the hours when I'm trying to save for us to get our own place.

"Working all weekend. I think Silvia and Ron are taking Jordan to a barbecue." They might hate me—Silvia more than Ron—but they're good to Jordan. It's the only thing that's kept me living under their roof for as long as I have.

Well, that and the fact that they charge me less for rent than I'd be able to find here in the city—trust me, I looked, and it's crazy expensive. Unfortunately, it still all adds up between paying for Jordan's preschool and summer camp and other expenses like clothes, a cell phone, a car payment, and gas. Ron pays the insurance since it's in his name, which is nice of him, but that still doesn't leave much at the end of the month. I'm saving up slowly, but every little bit is a step closer to getting a place for Jordan and me.

"A bunch of us are throwing a pool party at our place, since it'll probably be the last nice weekend before the cold weather hits. If you aren't doing anything..."

"Thanks," I tell her, grateful to have a friend like Marissa. She understands I'll probably never take her up on her offer but still invites me anyway.

Since I was able to get off a few hours earlier than planned, I hightail it home to surprise Jordan with a trip to the park. I stop at the grocery store on the way to grab a couple of subs, snacks, and drinks for a little picnic.

When I walk through the door, the place is quiet. I'm about to call out Jordan's name, when I hear sniffling and then Silvia's hushed voice. I walk over to the library, where the door is cracked, and find her and Jordan sitting on the couch, looking at the photo album I made Jordan to help her remember her dad. We lost everything in the fire, but thankfully, the digital pictures I took were saved online.

"This is when your daddy graduated high school," Silvia sniffles. "He was so smart. He had a five-point-two GPA."

"What's a GPA?" Jordan asks, glancing up at her grandmother.

"It's grades. One day you'll get grades in school. You want to get good grades so you can go to college, just like your daddy."

"Did Mommy go to college?"

"No," Silvia says. "She got pregnant with you."

"Oh," Jordan says, turning the page. "Look, it's Mommy and Daddy and me in my mommy's belly!" She turns the page again. "That's me being born."

"It is," Silvia says, wiping a tear. "Your daddy loved you so much."

"Don't cry, Grandma. Mommy says Daddy's still here"— she points to her chest—"in our hearts."

Silvia's eyes turn into thin slits. "If it weren't for your mother, he'd still be here."

"Mommy didn't hurt him," Jordan argues. "The fire did! I asked Mommy, and she told me! She said she loves Daddy and didn't want him hurt."

"Yeah," Silvia says, "she loved him so much that she trapped him with a baby and then forced him to work himself into the ground. He died because he was too tired to get out of the fire. The only person your mother loves is herself."

"That's enough!" I step through the doorway, having enough of Silvia spouting hateful things about me to my daughter. Over the years, Jordan's asked me questions that have led me to believe that Silvia has been doing this. I have been hoping I was wrong and chose to let it go without proof. But now, hearing it for myself, I can't even imagine all the horrible things Silvia has said about me behind my back.

"Mommy!" Jordan flies off the couch and into my arms. "Tell grandma it's not true. Tell her you didn't hurt Daddy. The fire did."

I put her down and kneel in front of her, plastering a smile on my face. Despite wanting to destroy Silvia, I choose to be the bigger person for my daughter's sake. "Grandma knows it was the fire, Bug, but sometimes when people are sad, they say mean things."

Jordan purses her lips and looks back at Silvia. "That's not nice, Grandma."

Silvia glares my way, and I know we've reached the end of the road. Jordan is getting older and understands too much, and I can't allow her to live in a home with so much animosity and hostility. I should've moved out sooner, but the truth is I'm scared. I've never lived on my own before and the fear of doing so is what's kept me and Jordan living under this roof for far too long.

"I was thinking we could go to the park," I tell Jordan, changing the subject. "Why don't you go get your shoes on, and I'll meet you by the front door right after I speak to Grandma."

"Yay!" Distracted by the idea of going to the park, Jordan runs out to get ready, leaving Silvia and me alone.

"I—" Silvia begins to speak, but I raise my hand, halting her words.

"Whatever bullshit you're about to spew, don't bother."

Her eyes widen in shock because I've never spoken so rudely to her before. When someone is giving you and your daughter a place to live at a discounted cost, you don't mess with them. With every remark, I've kept my mouth shut, thankful to have a roof over Jordan's and my head.

But now, I've reached my breaking point. I'm no longer the frightened, pregnant teenager or the mourning twenty-one-year-old. And if I keep allowing her to treat me like shit, what kind of example am I setting for my daughter?

"I appreciate you and Ron giving Jordan and me a place to live these past three years, but I can't live under the same roof as someone who hates me. It's not good for anyone, but especially not my daughter. Consider this my notice. Jordan and I will be moving out as soon as possible."

"You have nowhere to go," Silvia sneers. "What kind of life do you think you'll give her working as a waitress?"

"One with love and affection," is all I say before I turn on my heel and walk out the door.

"WILL I HAVE MY OWN ROOM?" JORDAN ASKS AS I PUSH her on the swing. She can swing on her own, but she loves to be pushed, and I love to push her.

"Of course." I make a mental note to find a two-bedroom place. It'll cost more than a one-bedroom place, but Jordan deserves to continue to have her own room and space.

"Can I bring Dots with me?" she asks, referring to the stuffed ladybug I bought her for Christmas a few years ago. She named it Dots and literally takes it everywhere with her.

"Yep, you can take all your stuff." If Silvia even thinks about stopping me from taking Jordan's stuff, we'll have a problem.

"Where will we live?" Jordan glances back at me with a worried expression that no child should ever have. "Grandma said we live with her 'cause you have no money."

I stop pushing the swing and walk around to kneel in front of the swing and hold the chains for support, caging her in. "I know Grandma has probably said a lot of things about me. If something ever happened to you, I would be *so* sad and *so* hurt, just like Grandma is because your daddy died. He was her baby, just like you're mine. But the things she says to you about me aren't true. She's mad at me because she's sad, but that doesn't make it okay. It's okay to be sad and hurt, but it's not okay to be mean."

Jordan nods.

"We moved in with Grandma and Grandpa because our house burned down, but I think it's time for us to get our own place. You're starting kindergarten soon, and it will be the perfect time to move."

Jordan's eyes light up at the mention of kindergarten. She loves school so much. "Can we move somewhere fun, like the North Pole? Wouldn't it be so fun to live near Santa? I could go to Elf school!"

I bark out a laugh at her antics. Christmas is her favorite holiday. It was Trent's and mine as well, so I've made it a point to pass it down to her. Silvia wouldn't allow decorations to be put up or a tree to be in the main house because she said it was too hard with Trent gone. So every holiday season, I take

Jordan to see the decorations everywhere else, and we set up a small table tree with ornaments in her room so Santa will find his way to Jordan.

"I don't know about that," I say, pulling out my phone and clicking on my maps app. I zoom in on Massachusetts since I can't afford flights, so wherever we move will have to be within driving distance. Handing it to Jordan, I say, "Pick a place, any place."

She grins, excited to be part of the process, and takes the phone from me. She's learning to read, so she sounds out several cities, then she shakes her head, not liking the names of any of them.

"Ch-r-is," she says, her brows furrowing in frustration. "What does that say?" She points at the word, and my heart stutters, because what are the odds?

"It says Christmas."

Jordan's eyes grow big. "Christmas? Like Santa and presents and reindeer and Elf school?"

"Christmas Valley," I say, giving her the full city name.

"Wow, do you think Santa will be there?" she asks, in awe of the thought.

"Maybe."

"I bet he's there," she says. "Him and the elves."

"But there's a chance he's not," I warn her, not wanting her to be disappointed.

"But it's Christmas! Santa *has* to go there."

I chuckle. "Is that where you want to live? Christmas Valley?"

"Yes!"

"All right, Ladybug, then Christmas Valley it is."

TWO WEEKS LATER

"I know it isn't big," Gertrude says as she gives Jordan and me a tour of the adorable two-bedroom, two-bath home. I already saw the pictures online, did a virtual tour with the real estate agent, and signed the lease, but Gertrude insisted on giving us a tour herself when we arrived.

She has explained that she's lived here with her husband for the past thirty years. Since they never had children, they never felt the need to move. Her husband passed away a few years ago, and she's now decided to move to an assisted living facility because the home feels empty without him. Gertrude wasn't ready to give it up yet, so instead she's renting it out.

"It's perfect," I tell her as Jordan heads to the room that will be hers. With us living independently for the first time ever, I didn't want a two-story home. The memories of the fire are still too fresh, and I'd be worried I wouldn't be able to sleep if either of our rooms were on the second floor.

Instead, our rooms are across from each other. The master has an en suite bathroom, and Jordan's bathroom is right next to her room, doubling as a guest bathroom—not that we'll be having company anytime soon, what with my parents and I not on speaking terms and Trent's mom pissed that we moved out. There's a decent-sized living room for Jordan to play in, an updated kitchen, a single-car garage, and a wraparound wooden porch. There's also a screened back porch, with a nice-sized yard that's been fenced in. The home is adorable, and it's clear Gertrude and her husband took care of it.

I can't believe I lucked out finding this place. I thought for sure, once we arrived, we'd find out we'd been scammed—which would've sucked since I'm almost positive Silvia would've told me to go fuck myself if I asked her to move back in.

After I told her I had found a place, her pettiness reared its ugly head. Not only did she tell us nothing would be leaving the home that she purchased, but since I would no longer be living under her roof, she said I'd be responsible for making the car *and* insurance payments. I could've argued, but it would've been a waste. I really need a vehicle, so I was just thankful that she let me take it at all. I know this was her way of punishing me, hoping I would break and ask to stay, but that didn't happen.

Instead, I packed Jordan's and my things and loaded the vehicle. It was a little over an hour's drive. I worried I'd made the wrong decision the entire way, but as we passed the town sign that read: *Welcome to Christmas Valley—Population: 6,494*, I couldn't help but feel like this was a fresh start for both of us.

"And this is the master bedroom," Gertrude says when we enter the room. It's painted a soft gray and furnished with a whitewash wood queen-sized bed, two matching bedside tables on either side, and a dresser with a mirror facing the bed.

"It's wonderful. Do you know when the furniture will

be removed?" I noticed the living room and dining room furniture is still there, but it didn't click until I saw her bedroom furniture. I don't have the money to buy us bedroom sets, but I plan to get both of us a bed and a dresser from a second-hand store.

"It's staying," she says, shocking me. "When you mentioned not having any furniture and having to find some once you moved in, I figured you could use it. The place I'm moving to is furnished. I was just going to donate all of this." She waves her hand in the air like it's no big deal, and my heart swells at her thoughtfulness. She has no idea what this means to me. How much money it will save me. I hate the thought of owing anyone anything, but...

"Are you sure?" I choke out, trying not to cry in front of this woman. She might think I've lost my mind and rescind her offer. And there's no way I'll find anywhere else to rent for this cheap.

"Yes, my dear," she says sweetly. "If there's anything you don't want, you can donate it."

"Mommy, come see my room!" Jordan yells.

I cross the hall to her room and find her on the bed, bouncing on her knees.

"Did you buy this?" I ask Gertrude as I take in the beautiful white wicker bed with pink and white polka-dotted bedding—with matching curtains. There's no way this was the bedding she had in here. This is bedding only a little girl would pick out.

"I'm taking my bedding with me." She shrugs. "Didn't want your little girl to not have sheets. It was on sale."

"Gertrude," I breathe, unable to hold back my tears. "This is all too much."

"Nonsense," she says. "Consider it a housewarming gift." She pats my arm affectionately. "When my William and I started out, we had nothing. But our family and friends came together and helped us make it a home. Now it's my turn to do the same. I hope you create as many wonderful memories here as William and I did."

Wetness fills her eyes, and I pull her into a hug.

"Thank you. This home will be filled with love."

"Oh, I know it will, dear. I can already feel it."

After showing us the rest of the home, we go over the electricity and utilities, and then Gertrude takes off, leaving Jordan and me to our new home.

"I love it here, Mommy," Jordan says, staring out the window.

"I do, too, Ladybug."

"Can we go for a walk?" she asks. "Maybe we'll see Santa or his elves."

"Sure," I tell her, loving that she's excited for the next chapter in our book. And who knows? The town is named Christmas Valley. Maybe we will find Santa... or his elves.

Two

KELSIE

TWO MONTHS LATER

"MA'AM, YOUR CARD HAS BEEN DECLINED."

Shit. I clear my throat and paste on a smile, trying to hide my embarrassment. In my rush to get the groceries and get home to make dinner, I forgot to double-check my bank account.

"How much is it?" I ask, not wanting to hold up the line. I have cash from my tips, and I can just pay with—

"Forty-one dollars and thirty-two cents."

Whoa, okay, there's no way I have that much cash. I glance at the line of people behind me and quickly count my cash. Twenty-six dollars. Shit.

I glance at the items, trying to figure out what's not a necessity.

"Can you put back the cake mix and icing, please?"

"Mommy, no," Jordan whines. "That's supposed to be—"

"Jordan, not now," I hiss, feeling everyone's eyes on us.

"Thirty-four dollars and seventy-eight cents," the cashier says.

"Mommy," Jordan cries, upset over me putting the cake mix and frosting back. "The cake is important. Please. Da—"

"Jordan, stop," I say, giving her my 'mom voice' that rarely makes an appearance.

Tears prick her eyes, and I hate myself for not being able to give her everything she wants and needs. But if it's between feeding her dinner and making a cake, I have to choose dinner.

I look in my purse for any hidden bills, but of course, there aren't any. "Umm, can you put back the..." I look at the groceries, trying to figure out what else we don't need, when my eyes land on the fruit snacks. They weren't on sale, but Jordan begged for them because a little girl in her class had them in her lunch box today. There's shampoo and conditioner. I need to wash my hair, but... "Can you put the conditioner back, please?"

The cashier nods and swipes it back across the scanner. "Thirty, twenty-three," she says with a look of sympathy.

Someone in line sighs, and I cringe. "Umm, I'm sorry," I mutter as hot tears fill my lids. I should've paid better attention. It's just been a rough couple of weeks.

Jordan caught the flu, and I had to take off work to be home with her since I didn't have anyone else to watch her. Then, she passed it to me, forcing me to take *more* time off work—which meant having no money coming in for almost two weeks.

And to top it off, the anniversary of Trent's death is coming up, along with his birthday. My brain is a scattered mess, and money is tight. Despite my rent being reasonable, Jordan starting at a new school meant needing school clothes and supplies. It also took longer than I thought to find a job, and by the time I finally found one—at a cute café called "The Busy Bean"—my savings had dwindled down to nothing, leaving us living paycheck to paycheck.

"Here, I got you," a masculine voice says from behind me.

I glance back and I'm met with the most mesmerizing eyes. They're hazel, but the brown, green, and gold are brighter than I've ever seen. So full of life.

He extends his hand with the five-dollar bill as I quickly take in his features. Messy brown hair, strong, stubbled jawline, and a tan that's uncommon for northerners due to the months of frigid winter. But what holds my attention is the soft smile splayed upon his lips. It's not a look of pity or sympathy, just a genuine smile, silently telling me *it's okay*.

I want to shake my head and tell him *thanks but no, thanks*, but I also really want to end this embarrassing ordeal, so I nod in appreciation and take it from him, then hand it to the cashier.

"Mommy, can we get the cake mix, please?" Jordan hiccups as tears flow down her cheeks.

To the outside world, she looks like a spoiled five-year-old who wants cake, but what nobody standing in this line knows is that the cake is a tradition. We make one every year in honor of Trent. He died four days before his birthday, and he loved vanilla cake with chocolate frosting.

It used to drive Silvia crazy because she chose to mourn his death and birthday by crying and being angry, spouting horrible things at me. But that's not how I want to raise my daughter.

After we have cake, I open the photo album I made for Jordan and go through the pictures of the three of us. Retelling stories she was too young to remember, so she'll never forget how much her dad loved her.

"Not today," I tell her, taking the change from the cashier.

"But Daddy loved that cake," Jordan sobs, shattering my heart.

"Thank you," I mutter to the man behind me, refusing to make eye contact. This entire situation is embarrassing enough as it is.

I push the cart out of the store as Jordan continues to cry silently, her shoulders shaking and her eyes puffy and red.

"Ladybug, I'm sorry."

I lift her out of the shopping cart and place her on her feet so we can start our trek home. Two days ago, the vehicle Ron and Silvia let me take was towed away since I was late paying them. When I called to tell them, not realizing it was Silvia who had it towed, she informed me that being late in the real world meant having a car repossessed. I tried to explain that Jordan and I had been sick, and without getting paid for almost two weeks, I was a little behind on paying the bills. She didn't want to hear it.

Not having a car means having to walk everywhere. It's not too bad now, in the high forties, but it'll only get worse. Unlike Boston, Christmas Valley doesn't have public transportation. Thankfully, the home we're renting is only five blocks from the center of town, where almost everything is located—the store, the café I work at, and Jordan's school.

I put the cart in the corral, and we begin our walk home with our bags in hand. We're a block or two away from the store, when I hear, "Ma'am, ma'am!"

I glance behind me and spot the teenage boy, who had been bagging the groceries, sprinting my way.

"Whew," he says, his hands resting on his knees to catch his breath. "I didn't think I was going to catch you." He extends his hand, holding a plastic bag in front of me.

"Oh, did I forget something?"

"Um, kind of." He smiles shakily as I take the bag from him and look inside it: cake mix, frosting, and conditioner.

"Who did this?" I ask, my lids filling with tears.

"Mommy, the cake mix for Daddy is in there!" Jordan screeches in excitement. "Thank you!" She wraps her arms around the boy's legs, and he chuckles, patting the top of her head.

"Actually, it wasn't me," he says with an awkward shrug.

"Oh. I didn't buy these," I tell him, attempting to hand the bag back since there's obviously been some sort of misunderstanding, and the last thing I want is to be accused of stealing.

"I know," he says. "But they're paid for."

"By who?"

"Umm…" He looks at me uncomfortably. "I think it was supposed to be anonymous."

I think about who could've done it. The woman making

the annoyed noises wouldn't have bothered. It could've been the cashier, but... "The gentleman behind me," I guess. The same man who gave me the five dollars.

"Yeah." The kid nods.

"That was very nice of him. Do you know how I can find him to thank him?"

The kid raises a brow. "You don't know who he is?"

"We're new here. Only moved to Christmas Valley a couple of months ago."

"Ahh, that makes sense. His name is Pierce Adler. He works at the fire station."

"Oh, do you know which one?"

He chuckles. "There's only one." He points in the direction of downtown. "You can't miss the two-story red-brick building."

After thanking him for running the bag to me, Jordan and I head home, and then we spend the rest of the day making the cake and looking through the photo album.

"Mommy," Jordan says with a yawn as I tuck her into bed. "We should bring the fireman a piece of Daddy's cake since he saved it. We can pay it...next?"

I smile at my daughter, so proud of the little person she's growing up to be. On our way home, I explained to her that the firefighter who was in line behind us paid for the items, saving the day and that one day when we have the money, we'll pay it forward and help someone else who's in need.

"Pay it forward," I correct her. "And we can do that." I lean over and kiss her forehead. "How about tomorrow?"

"Okay! And can we get a tree too? Thanksgiving is soon,

and we need a tree to decorate."

I open my mouth to correct her and tell her that the holidays are still a bit off, but when I click on my phone to see the date, I realize she's right. Thanksgiving is just around the corner. Which means we're going to need to get a tree soon if we want to continue our tradition of decorating the tree after we eat Thanksgiving dinner. Just like I used to do with my grandma when she was alive and then with Trent and Jordan once she was born.

The only problem is, while Jordan was taking a bath, I looked at my banking info and learned that I was in the negatives—hence my card being declined. I forgot about the check I wrote to Jordan's school for the field trip they're going on. Then the electric and water bills went through. Luckily, the check cleared, though everything else bounced, leaving my account not only in the negatives but also with overdraft fees to boot.

Being an adult is hard. My entire life, I had everything taken care of for me. Even when Trent and I lived together, he handled the checking account and bills. And when I moved in with Silvia and Ron, I paid them. When I told Silvia I was moving out, she said I'd never make it on my own, but I didn't fully understand what she meant until now. The bills add up, and what I make is barely enough. Because I had to take off when Jordan and I were sick, I fell behind on everything when I already didn't have any wiggle room, which means...

"I'm so sorry," I tell my daughter, my voice cracking with emotion as I wonder for the first time if my mom was right. Maybe I'm not fit to be a mom. "I don't have any money right now for a tree."

Not only do I have no money, but the electric and water bills are now late—thankfully, they can't shut it off during winter, but I don't want to get behind and owe more money. If something were to happen, I don't even have a credit card in my name that would save us. I guess it's a good thing Silvia took back the car I was driving because there's no way I could afford that payment, plus the insurance and gas.

As if Jordan can sense I'm about to break, she simply nods and wraps her tiny arms around me. "It's okay, Mommy. Maybe I can make us a tree with my paper and markers so Santa can find us."

Santa... Gifts...

I haven't even gotten through Thanksgiving yet.

Three

KELSIE

"Wow! That's the biggest firehouse I've ever seen," Jordan says when we arrive at the fire station.

It looks like those classic fire stations you see in the movies—two-story, red and gray brick. American flag blowing in the wind. It's beautiful, just like everything else in this town. I wouldn't be surprised if a Hallmark Christmas movie was filmed here. If one hasn't been, it should be.

We're heading up to the entrance when an adorable Dalmatian puppy comes flying around the corner and lavishes Jordan with kisses, making her giggle.

I'm so busy watching my daughter and the puppy that I don't realize someone has joined us, until a deep, masculine voice says, "Cinder, come here, girl."

I spin around and find the gentleman from the grocery store standing behind me. His hazel eyes lock with mine, and a heat I haven't felt in years warms my insides.

"Sorry about that," the gentleman says.

What did the bagboy say his name was again?

"I'm Pierce."

Yes! That's it.

"And that's my pup, Cinder."

"What's a Cinder?" Jordan asks, scrunching her nose in confusion while the dog runs in circles around her, wagging its tail.

"Cinder is a piece of burnt coal," Pierce explains.

"You named your puppy after something burnt?" Jordan asks, staring at Pierce like he's lost his mind.

Pierce chuckles. "Burnt coal is used for heat," he says. "I'm a firefighter, and she's my fire dog. And"—he leans forward like he's about to tell her a secret—"Cinder is short for Cinderella."

"Like the princess?" Jordan gasps, her eyes going wide in excitement.

"Yep," he says. "My niece helped me name her." He glances at me and whispers, "Cinder sounds cooler, so I'm sticking to that, but if my niece asks, it's Cinderella."

He winks playfully, and I can't help but laugh.

"And who might you be?" he asks, looking between Jordan and me.

"I'm Kelsie," I tell him. "And this is my daughter, Jordan."

"It's nice to meet you," he says, grinning, and for a moment, I get lost in him.

Today, his eyes are so bright in the sunlight, they're practically sparkling. He has a single dimple on his left cheek that was covered before by his scruff at the grocery store. It's visible now, though, because his facial hair is trimmed neatly.

My eyes glide down his face, to his navy-blue shirt that's just tight enough to outline his corded biceps but loose enough that what's underneath is left to my imagination— and after years of abstinence, mixed with hours upon hours spent reading romance novels, my imagination is running wild, wondering what he could do with—

A throat clears, popping my fantasy bubble, and my gaze springs back up to Pierce's face, finding a smirk splayed across his full lips. He totally caught me checking him out.

Jesus, Kelsie, get a grip. This guy is so out of your league, and who the hell has time to date anyway?

"Mommy, Cinderella is so cute!" Jordan says, making me look her way. "Can we get a puppy?" she asks through her giggles. She's now on the ground, petting the puppy, who's flipped onto her back and is relishing the attention.

"Not today," I tell her.

She pouts but is too occupied by the puppy to really put up an argument.

"Is there something I can help you with?" Pierce asks, reminding me why we're here.

"Yes," I tell him. "You probably don't remember, but I was in line ahead of you..."

"I remember," he says, his eyes locking with mine. "I'd have to have amnesia to forget a beautiful woman such as yourself."

My cheeks instantly heat at his compliment, unsure if I'm more shocked that he remembered me or that he just said I'm beautiful.

"Thank you," I mutter. "Then, you remember you paid for some of my groceries."

"Mommy, I need to go pee," Jordan cuts in, running over to us with the puppy at her heels. "Really bad," she says, giving me a look that conveys she waited until the last second to say something.

"There's one in the station," Pierce says with a laugh as Jordan wiggles her body, doing the "I've got to go pee now" dance.

Pierce scoops Cinder up, and we follow him into the station. The main area is just as gorgeous as the outside. With sleek gray walls and comfy-looking plush couches, it looks more like a living room than a fire station. As we walk through the room, Pierce puts Cinder into a cage, then takes us past a huge dining room with a table that must seat twenty people. When we enter what appears to be the kitchen, a couple of guys are sitting at the island, drinking coffee and chatting.

"Here you go," Pierce says, pointing toward the door just past the kitchen.

"Thank you!" She runs in and slams the door, making it echo throughout the place.

"Sorry." I flinch.

"No worries," Pierce says. "I have a niece who looks to be about her age. How old is she? Five? Six?"

"Five, with the personality of someone twice her age," I joke.

Pierce laughs, but then his face turns serious. He steps toward me, so close I'm forced to look up at him because he's got quite a few inches on my five-foot-seven self.

"I hope you're not here to try to give me back my money," he says. "Because if that's the case..."

"I'm not," I tell him, swallowing thickly. "As much as I'd like to, right now, I don't have it," I admit truthfully. "But"—I pull out the Tupperware from my purse—"Jordan had the idea to bring you a piece of the cake we made to thank you." I hand him the container, and he smiles at me like I just gave him a million dollars.

"All done!" Jordan says, joining us. When she spots the cake, her face lights up. "I made that cake for my daddy's birthday," she tells Pierce. "Do you like cake?"

"I do," he says.

"It's vanilla with chocolate frosting. Daddy's favorite."

"Looks delicious," Pierce tells her.

"You should eat it now," Jordan says, eyeing the cake. "And if there's a lot, I could have a piece too. And Mommy and Cinderella."

"Jordan," I chide while Pierce laughs.

"That sounds like a good idea," Pierce says. "Let's take it in the kitchen... but Cinder can't have any. She's a puppy and can only eat puppy food."

The guys who were in the kitchen are still there, and Pierce introduces us. "This is Garrett and Wade. They work the same shift as me," Pierce explains. "This is Kelsie and her daughter, Jordan. They brought me cake."

He splits the large piece of cake into three smaller portions, and Jordan climbs onto the stool to eat hers.

"It's nice to meet you," the guys say in unison.

"Are you new in town?" Wade asks. "I don't recall seeing

you before."

"We moved here a couple of months ago," I explain. "We're renting Mrs. Jenson's house over on Holly Lane." Every street name is Christmas or winter related. It's adorable.

"Oh, right," Wade says. "I remember her saying she was moving to a home."

Wade and Garrett both stand.

"It was lovely to meet you," Wade says with a smile.

"I'm sure we'll see you around," Garrett adds before they both excuse themselves.

The three of us eat our slices of cake in silence for a few minutes before Jordan speaks up. "Have you seen Santa?" she asks, taking a bite of her cake.

"Not recently," Pierce says, taking his last bite and throwing the plate and fork away. "Are you looking for him?"

"Well, yeah. I thought maybe he lived here 'cause this is a Christmas place, but I can't find him anywhere. Not even his elves or reindeer." Jordan sighs in disappointment, and I notice Pierce stifles his laugh, keeping a serious face.

"He's around," he says. "Probably busy because it's getting closer to Christmas."

"He's gonna leave to go to the North Pole soon," Jordan complains. "How do I see him before he leaves?"

She finishes her slice and jumps off the stool. I take her plate and mine and throw them into the trash.

"Well, that's simple," Pierce tells her. "He'll be at the Christmas festival."

Jordan's eyes widen, and her gaze swings over to me. "Mommy, can we please go to the festival?" she begs.

"We'll see," I tell her, knowing not to say yes in case I can't make it happen.

"The cake was delicious," Pierce says to Jordan as he walks us back to the front of the fire station. "Please tell your daddy I said thank you."

"Oh," she says, glancing at him. "My daddy's in heaven now. Mommy and I eat it 'cause it was his favorite, and it's mine too."

Pierce's eyes soften in understanding. "Well, that makes you sharing it with me even more special. Thank you."

"Wow!" Jordan gasps, running toward the beautiful tree in the corner. "This is so pretty." She runs her fingers along the bristles. "Why does your tree have decorations already? Mommy said trees don't get decorated till after everyone eats the turkey."

Pierce grins. "This is a special tree," he explains, walking over and plucking a piece of paper off the tree and kneeling in front of her. "It's filled with angels. People take a ticket like this one off the tree to help someone in need."

Jordan eyes the ticket. "Anyone can be on the angel tree?"

"Sure," he says.

"Mommy!" Jordan looks my way. "Can we put a ticket on the angel tree? Then someone can buy us a tree 'cause you said we don't have the money to buy one."

Oh, God. Warmth creeps up my neck and face—and it's *not* the same warmth I felt earlier—as I wish for the ground to open up and swallow me whole.

Without making eye contact with Pierce—because I don't want to see the pity in his eyes—I focus on Jordan. "No,

Ladybug," I tell her. "That's for people who are in need."

"But we *need* a tree!" she argues. "How is Santa gonna find us without a tree? We don't even have a fireplace like Grandma and Grandpa have!"

"That's not what an angel tree is for," I explain. "It's for children who need things like clothes." She looks confused, and I can feel Pierce's gaze on me, so I add, "I'll explain when we get home."

When I look at Pierce, so I can quickly say goodbye, I expect to find a look of pity in his eyes, but he's done an excellent job of hiding it. Instead, he's smiling softly at me, and I don't know why, but somehow, it makes me even more emotional. Like, pity, I can handle. I can think to myself, 'Fuck you, I don't need you to feel bad for me.' Only the look he's giving me... I can't explain it. It's filled with warmth and makes me want to burrow myself into his arms, where I have no doubt I'd feel safe.

"Thank you for the money," I tell him, praying my voice sounds normal, despite the lump of emotion lodged in my throat. "We'll get out of your hair. I'm sure you have work to do."

He opens his mouth to respond, when the door swings open and a little girl with blond pigtails comes running inside. "Uncle Pierce, where's—" Before she can finish her sentence, her eyes land on Jordan. "Jordan! What are you doing here?" She throws her arms around my daughter and the two girls hug it out, giggling.

"Mommy and I made a cake for my daddy and brought the fireman a piece"—she points at Pierce—"'cause Mommy said he saved the cake."

The little girl glances from Jordan to Pierce. "That's my uncle Pierce. He saved the cake? Was it on fire?" Her eyes go big, and Jordan's brows dip in confusion.

"I don't think so, but the oven was really hot, and Mommy wouldn't let me touch it till it was cold."

Pierce and I both chuckle at the innocent conversation between the girls.

"You should come to my birthday!" the girl says, switching subjects so fast I get dizzy. "It's tonight! I'm having a penguin and snowman party! We're going to drink hot cocoa and watch *Happy Feet* 'cause it's my favorite movie ever."

"I'm sorry, Tilly, but I can't go," Jordan says, her voice small. "Mommy said you have to bring a present to parties, and we don't have one."

Jesus H. Christ. This cannot be happening. First, the money, then the tree. Now, of all people we run into, it's Tilly, the little girl in Jordan's class whose birthday party Jordan was invited to. She wanted to go so badly, but I didn't have the money to buy a gift, and it would be rude to show up empty-handed. I hated telling her she couldn't go, but I've seen how people talk about and treat those *beneath them*.

When I was in middle school, I had a friend who went to my private school on a scholarship. She couldn't afford the designer labels everyone else wore, couldn't buy the expensive gifts everyone else bought when we attended the parties, and the parents and students would whisper behind her back.

Christmas Valley seems like a nice place, but it's clear most of the town is on the upper end of the income ladder.

The last thing I want is for my daughter to be made fun of because she couldn't afford to bring a gift to the party.

"My grandma gives me lots of presents," Tilly says. "I can give you one, and then you can go!"

"Really?" Jordan says hopefully. "Can I go, Mommy?"

"Oh, umm..." My gaze flits from Jordan to Pierce, whose face has gone from soft to hard. God, he must think I'm the worst mother in the world.

My thoughts go back to what my mom said after Trent's death as tears prick my eyes: *You're not mother material. You're too young. You have no education. No income.*

"We'll see," I choke out. "We need to go." I take her hand, quickly mutter a goodbye, and rush out before Pierce can catch me crying.

"Mommy, you're going too fast," Jordan complains, yanking on my hand and forcing me to slow down.

"Sorry, Bug," I mutter.

When we get home, I tell her it's nap time. She doesn't always fall asleep, but after school, I have her lie down to rest and unwind after the long school day. I don't usually do this on the weekends, but I need a moment to myself after everything.

Thankfully, she doesn't argue. After I've settled her into her bed and kissed her forehead, I close her door then go to my room. I cry softly into the pillow so that Jordan won't hear—my mother's words playing on repeat.

I'm still crying when there's a knock on the door. Without thought, I rush to open it, in case Jordan's asleep. Only I regret doing so because standing on the other side is none other than Pierce Adler...holding a present.

Four

PIERCE

Auburn hair.

Creamy skin.

Sexy freckles.

Sad emerald eyes.

I watch Kelsie run back onto Main Street from the fire station with her daughter in tow. I knew who she was yesterday when I paid for some of her groceries. It's a small town, and people talk. She's the single mom who's renting Mrs. Jenson's house. From what the women have said, she's quiet and keeps to herself. She works at the café on the corner, "The Busy Bean," and is polite but guarded. Her daughter is in the same class as my niece Tilly, but never participates in the functions or parties. People are curious about where the father is, but nobody's dared to ask, and Kelsie's never shared.

My daddy's in heaven now...

In the three years since my ex and I broke up, I haven't so

much as glanced at a woman. I've been focusing on my career, my family, building my house, and telling myself I need time to get over the wreckage my ex left in her wake.

My parents said I'd know when I was healed and ready to move forward, and they were right. Because as I watch Kelsie and Jordan disappear down the street, it takes everything in me not to scoop them both up and take care of them.

Kelsie's struggling, trying to make ends meet. Doing the best she can with what she's got. And it's clear, despite the lack of money and materialistic possessions, she's a damn good mom. She's giving her daughter everything she has to offer, but I want to provide them with more. Hell, I want to give them *everything*.

I was with Tanya for over seven years, and I refused to take the next step. Even though I've only known this woman and her daughter for a minute, there's no doubt in my mind that I'm going to make them mine.

It sounds crazy. I know it does. But I don't care. Because I can feel it. My dad knew my mom was the one after their first date. They were engaged after two weeks, and they married a month later—and they've been happily married for over forty years. My dad always says, "When you know, you know."

With Tanya, I knew... I knew it was all wrong. That we weren't a good fit. I felt it—the disconnect. Something always felt off.

Now, I feel it again, only this time, it feels right. So damn right. I've heard my brothers talk about it, watched them experience it. The electricity. The connection. The accelerated breathing and pounding of the heart. But until now, I never understood it.

Now, I get it. I felt it the moment our eyes connected at the grocery store, and again while she was here at the station. I'm not going to waste a moment questioning it. Hell no. I'm going to chase it, embrace it, explore it. There's a chance I might be wrong, but I'm going to find out.

"What's got you looking like your head's about to combust?" my brother Beckett asks, strolling into the station. He's the Fire Chief—took over for our dad when he retired a few years ago—but he's off duty this weekend for my niece's birthday.

"A woman," I tell him, not beating around the bush.

His eyes go wide at hearing those words out of my mouth. I was bitter after my breakup. Pissed that I left my home and job for Tanya. Luckily, I went with my gut and insisted we take shit slow, refusing to ask her to marry me. Tanya wasn't thrilled, but I compromised by agreeing to give the city a chance.

Only a few short months after we were there, I caught her fucking the married attorney she was working for, and I knew I'd made the right decision. We fought, then she begged, cried, and swore it was only once and would never happen again. She even tried to blame me, saying I was working too many hours and not giving her enough attention, but there was nothing left for me to say but goodbye.

"Do I know this woman?" he asks.

"Nope, but you will," I tell him with a smirk. "Because I'm going to make her mine."

He barks out a laugh. "Well, I can't wait to see this."

"Daddy!" Tilly yells, running over from petting Cinder. "I need to go see grandma. I gotta get a present from her to give to my friend Jordan so she can come to my party."

"That's sweet of you," I tell Tilly, damn proud of my niece for her big heart. "But you don't need to do that. Jordan will be there tonight with a present."

Beckett looks at us, confused, but I don't have time to explain since I need to get to the store. Luckily, my shift ended a little bit ago, and I'm off for the next four days.

I scoop up Cinder, give my niece a kiss, and tell her I'll see her tonight at her party. Then I take off in my truck to the boutique my sister-in-law Allison owns. She's married to my other brother, Jackson, who runs our family's ranch.

After she helps me pick out two gifts for Tilly—one from me and the other from Jordan—I drive over to Mrs. Jenson's house. There's no car in the drive, but it might be in the garage, so I chance knocking. It takes several seconds, but finally, the door opens, and Kelsie pops her head out. The first thing I notice is that she's no longer in the sexy off-the-shoulder sweater and tight jeans she was wearing earlier. Now, she's wearing a long-sleeved shirt with flannel pants. Still sexy, but in a different way.

My gaze glides up her body, landing on her face. Her eyes are red and puffy, her cheeks tear-stained. She's been crying.

"Pierce, what are you doing here?" she breathes, her sad eyes connecting with the present in my hands.

"Tilly's party is at Snow Hill Park in the community barn at four o'clock." I hand the gift to her. "Dress warmly. It's supposed to be chilly tonight."

"I-I don't understand." Her eyes flit from the present to me. "Why are you doing this?"

I consider telling her everything that's gone through my mind since the moment I saw her in line at the grocery store, but Kelsie reminds me of Tinsel, the rescue horse at my family's ranch. She's timid and scared, and if you don't approach her slowly and carefully, making her feel safe, she'll freak out on you. I don't know Kelsie's story, but I can see it in her eyes. She needs me to approach slowly.

"Because life's too short not to attend a party," I tell her, making her jaw drop open. "See you and Jordan tonight." With a playful wink, I turn on my heel and head back to my truck, hoping my gut is right, and she and Jordan will be there tonight.

Five
KELSIE

HE BROUGHT JORDAN A PRESENT SO THAT SHE COULD attend the party. He went out of his way to purchase a gift and have it wrapped, then drove it over to our house to give it to me. All so Jordan could attend his niece's birthday. He didn't make a big deal out of it, just reminded me of the time and place. He told me life's too short not to attend a party. Then with a sexy wink that went straight to the apex between my thighs, he walked back to his truck, while I watched him, frozen in place, wondering what the hell had just happened.

It isn't until his truck disappears and I glance down at the beautifully wrapped gift that I realize I never thanked him.

Guess we're going to a party...

I let Jordan take a full nap, since we'll be up late. While she sleeps, I get dressed and spend some time reading. When she wakes up and sees the gift, she's beyond excited that she gets to attend the birthday party. My heart sinks at recalling how I told her she couldn't go to begin with, realizing I've allowed my preconceived notions about this town to affect my daughter. The owners of the café I work at are understanding. Mrs. Jenson is beyond sweet, and Pierce is so nice. Even his niece had such a big heart, offering her present so Jordan could attend.

Sure, there will always be people who will judge and make assumptions about me, but I can't allow the fear of what someone might think or say to run our lives. We moved here for a fresh start, yet I brought my past with us. And that's not fair or healthy for either of us.

"Mommy, look at the giant TV!" Jordan exclaims as we walk into the barn where the party is being held. There are blue and white balloons everywhere. Stations for food and drinks and, as Jordan mentioned, a gigantic blow-up screen where I'm assuming they'll be playing the movie.

"Jordan, you came!" Tilly yells, running at full speed toward my daughter.

"I brought you a present," Jordan says, handing the gift to her friend with a proud smile on her face. She didn't ask where I got it, only hugged and thanked me, telling me I'm the best mom in the world.

"Thank you!" Tilly says, taking it from her. "Come get hot cocoa." She takes Jordan's hand, and the two girls run off together.

"I'm glad you came," a masculine voice says, making me jump.

I turn and find Pierce standing there, looking at me with a soft smile.

"Thank you for the gift. It made Jordan's day."

"You're welcome," he says, hitting me with a heated look that warms my insides despite it being chilly outside.

I stare back for several seconds, feeling almost like I'm having an out-of-body experience. I spent years with Trent, was attracted to him and turned on by him. Yet I can't recall him ever being able to pull so many different emotions out of me with just a single look. The thought is both exhilarating and terrifying.

"Pierce, there you are," an older woman says, breaking Pierce's hold on me. "I'm Marta Adler," she says, taking my hand in both of hers and shaking it. "Pierce's mom and Tilly's grandma."

"It's nice to meet you," I say back. "I'm Kelsie Albright. My daughter, Jordan, is running around here somewhere."

My eyes scan the area and find Jordan standing with Tilly, a drink in one hand and a cookie in the other. She's smiling from ear to ear. The visual has me wanting to cry in happiness and thank Pierce again for saving the day... once again.

"Oh, yes," she says sweetly. "You work at The Busy Bean with Dorothy."

"You know her?" I ask dumbly, forgetting this is a small town and everyone seemingly knows everyone.

"Of course. She's a good friend and on the event committee with me." She glances between Pierce and me. "How did you two meet?" she asks, raising a single brow at Pierce.

He barks out a laugh and shakes his head. "Real subtle, Mom."

He snakes an arm over her shoulders and pulls her into

his side, kissing her cheek, and my heart swells at the apparent close relationship between the two of them. I hope Jordan and I will be close like that when she's older—unlike the lack of relationship my mom and I have.

"Kelsie and her daughter made a delicious cake and were sweet enough to share it with me," he says with a wink that only I can see since his mom is tucked under his arm.

His mom looks up at him, a bit confused, but doesn't question him. Instead, she glances my way and smiles. "Well, it's lovely to meet you. I'm sure I'll see you around." She pats Pierce's stomach. "Sara said to tell you that you better grab a cupcake because they're going quickly."

"Mmm," Pierce groans, "Sara is my sister-in-law and Tilly's mom, and she makes the best chocolate cupcakes with fudge frosting in the middle." He removes his arm from around his mom and scoops up my hand. "C'mon, Kelsie, let's grab a cupcake and a sled. You can share with me."

"A cupcake?" I ask dumbly because his hand in mine has my brain going haywire.

"No." He chuckles. "I don't share cupcakes. You'll have to eat your own."

He glances down at me with a playful smirk, then leans in, his face coming so close to mine. I hold my breath, wondering what he's doing. *There's no way he's going to kiss me, right? That would be crazy.*

His five o'clock shadow scratches the side of my cheek, and his lips come so close to my ear that his warm breath causes goose bumps to prickle my skin. "We can share a sled, though," he murmurs. "I promise to keep you warm."

Before I can ask what the heck he's talking about, he's dragging me to the food and drink station. He stocks up on cupcakes and cookies, then hands me a hot chocolate, keeping one for himself.

When we walk toward where the giant screen is, adorable sleds are scattered all over the area. I look around and find Jordan is getting her face painted. Her eyes lock with mine, and I wave so she knows I can see her. She waves back and smiles the most precious smile.

I turn my attention back to Pierce. "You've done so much for Jordan and me, and you don't even know us. Thank you," I tell him, needing him to know how much it means to me. Accepting help from someone isn't easy, but seeing Jordan happy is worth setting my pride aside. "If there's any way I can repay you..." I know he won't let me actually pay him back, but if there's some way I can return the favor...

"You can join me in this sled and watch *Happy Feet* with me," he says, his eyes sparkling in the light. He hands me his hot cocoa for a second, then reaches into the sled, pulling out a cute, fluffy *Happy Feet* blanket. The barn isn't heated, so even though it's keeping the wind and most of the chill out, it's still cool inside.

"This is such a cute party," I tell him, stepping inside the sled and sitting down.

He joins me and takes his cocoa back, setting it in the cupholder on the sled. "Sara is a stay-at-home mom now, but she used to do party planning before she had Tilly. She lives for stuff like this."

"Jordan's having so much fun," I say, glancing at my baby,

who's now getting into the sled with Tilly and another little girl, all three of them talking and laughing.

The movie starts, and the kids all find their seats. Pierce throws the blanket over us, and because the sled is only so big, our legs press against each other.

We watch the movie in silence—aside from the chatter and laughter from the kids—but I can barely tell you what's going on because Pierce's presence is too distracting. I have no idea how we went from him paying for my groceries to us watching a movie together in a sled, but I can't say I'm mad about it. It's been a long time since I've felt the things Pierce has me feeling. And while nothing will come from this, it's nice to decompress from the stress and relax for a little while.

"What's going through that beautiful head of yours?" Pierce whispers, his warm breath tickling my neck.

"This is nice," I admit. "It's been a long time since Jordan and I have gotten out and enjoyed ourselves like this."

I'm facing straight ahead, my eyes on the movie I'm not actually watching, even as I sense Pierce's heated gaze on me. I try not to look his way, but my traitorous brain can't handle it, and I turn my attention to him.

"Go out with me," he murmurs, loud enough for me to hear, yet quiet enough that no one else around us can.

"What?" I ask, having heard him but needing him to repeat himself because there's no way he just asked me out. He's single with zero baggage, has a good career, and what seems like a loving family, while I'm a single mom who waits tables to barely make ends meet.

"Go out with me," he repeats. "I want to take you out

on a real date. One without a sled." He smirks, and a giggle bubbles up and spills out.

Before I can answer him, though, his phone rings, and he pulls it out, checking to see who's calling. "Give me a second," he says. "It's the station."

He presses accept. I don't know what the person is saying on the other end, but he tells them he'll be right there since his brother is off for the weekend for his daughter's birthday.

He hangs up and glances at me, regret in his eyes. "I'm sorry to do this, but I have to go. I'm on call because we have a few guys out this weekend. There's a brush fire in the northern woods because we haven't had any rain. Someone must've set it, and they need me."

It takes a second for my brain to absorb what he's saying, but once it does, everything clicks. Pierce is a firefighter... who puts out fires for a living. I knew this. I've been to his station and seen him dressed in his work uniform, but I didn't fully process it until now.

"Go," I choke out. "I'm good here."

I force a smile on my face, thankful I didn't have a chance to answer his question. I was close to saying yes, though that would've been the wrong answer. Because how the hell could I ever date a man who willingly spends his days risking his life to save people trapped in fires? It's a noble profession, yet also a reckless one.

Pierce looks at me like he can hear my thoughts, but he doesn't have time to question them. "Okay," he says, his tone a mixture of remorse and defeat. "But this conversation isn't over."

"Go," I repeat, unable to agree because the truth is, this conversation was over before it even began. Pierce is sweet, selfless, and sexy as hell. Undoubtedly, I would've enjoyed getting to know him, but that can't happen. Losing Trent in a fire was devastating. Being stuck in a burning house with my daughter and almost dying as well is something I'll *never* forget. There's no way I could ever date a man who has made it his career to willingly risk his life to put out fires like the one that ended Trent's life and irrevocably changed Jordan's and mine.

I spend the rest of the movie wondering if Pierce is okay. If the fire is contained and he's safe. Which only supports my initial thoughts—nothing more can ever happen between Pierce and me.

When the movie ends, I watch the kids sing 'Happy Birthday' to Tilly and enjoy some cake. Once she's opened her presents, I tell Jordan it's time to head home. She's so wiped, she doesn't even argue. After bathing her, she goes to bed, and I'm left lying awake and stuck in my own thoughts, wondering if Pierce is home yet.

I finally fall into a restless sleep and spend the night tossing and turning, trapped in a nightmare. It's awful. Jordan and I are stuck in the burning house all over again, only rather than me passing out, I'm screaming for Pierce to save us.

Six
PIERCE

When I told Kelsie I had to go help out with a brush fire that was out of control, thanks to some teenagers fucking around in the woods and the lack of rain, which leaves everything dry, something changed in her demeanor. A wall of sorts erected right before my eyes. I didn't understand why, and unfortunately, I didn't have time to ask.

My priority had to be getting to the station so I could get changed. When I suit up, everything else has to be pushed aside. My only thoughts on what I'm doing. Every time we get on the engine, we have to be focused. Sometimes it's something simple, like an oven catching fire, but other times, lives are on the line. I could never forgive myself if someone's life was taken because I wasn't on my game and instead thinking about how Kelsie's face went from happy to freaked out, to utterly devoid of all emotion in a matter of seconds.

It's been a long night, but the fire has been contained, and there were no injuries. Thankfully, the kids who were trying to have a bonfire reported it as soon as it got out of control. Had they not, it would've spread closer to the town, and several homes could've been damaged.

After showering the night off, I should lie down and get some shut-eye, but instead, I get dressed and head to the bakery to pick up breakfast and coffee for Kelsie and Jordan. I'd call first, but I never got her number. I hope that since it's Sunday, the girls are home—and I also went by The Busy Bean, and Dorothy told me Kelsie doesn't work weekends.

I knock on the door, nervous and excited to see Kelsie. There's movement in the window, and a second later, the door opens, Jordan smiling up at me.

"Hi, Mr. Fireman."

"You can call me Pierce," I tell her with a chuckle. "Is your mom home?"

"Duh. I can't be alone. She's—"

"Jordan Penelope Monroe, did you open the door?" Kelsie appears, dressed in a cute pajama shirt that reads: *If you really love me, let me sleep,* and matching plaid shorts that are extra short, showing off her creamy, toned legs.

Jordan's eyes go wide. "I looked first! It's Mr. Fireman... I mean Pierce."

"I don't care who it is. You don't answer the door without me. Got it?"

Kelsie raises a brow, and Jordan mumbles back, "Got it."

"Hey," she says, turning her attention to me, her smile sweet but guarded.

"I would've called first, but I never got your number." I

wait a moment for her to say something like, 'Oh, yeah, I need to give it to you!' but when she remains silent, I continue. "I brought breakfast and coffee."

I hold up the bags and Jordan squeals. "Oh! The Busy Bean," she says, recognizing the logo.

"Thank you," Kelsie says, her voice less enthusiastic.

We stare at each other for several awkward seconds. I'm about to hand over the food and drinks because she clearly doesn't want me here, but before I can do so, she widens the door and says, "Please, come in."

It feels a little forced. I should probably decline, give her the food and drinks and let them enjoy their morning, but I need to know what happened, what changed. We've only known each other for a hot second, but before I told her I had to go, she seemed interested and open to spending more time with me.

So, instead, I take her up on her offer and step inside her house. I've been in here before, when Mrs. Jenson needed help moving some stuff she was taking to the assisted living home.

The living room furniture is still the same, so she must've rented it out furnished. But added to the walls are adorable pictures that Jordan's drawn. They're framed, making them look professional, even though they're filled with stick figures and finger paintings.

I set the food and drinks on the table, and Kelsie grabs some plates and napkins. Jordan opens the bags and hands out the coffees to Kelsie and me, keeping the milk for herself.

"Did you have a good time at the party?" I ask Jordan,

making conversation.

"Yeah! I had so much fun. Tilly is my new best friend. She gave me this." She pulls a necklace out of her shirt and shows off a silver chain with a jagged heart that reads: *st ends*

"It's the second half of best friends," Kelsie says with a smile. "Tilly gave it to her last night at the party."

"That's awesome," I tell her, taking a bite of my croissant.

While we eat, Jordan steers the conversation, talking about the party and the upcoming Christmas show they're putting on at school. The entire time, Kelsie focuses her attention on her daughter, avoiding making eye contact with me. It confirms what I thought—something happened last night to make her distance herself from me. My only thought is that she's upset I had to leave unexpectedly for work. Tanya hated the hours I used to put in, but I was trying to move up through the ranks back then. Now, I'm comfortable with my position, and aside from occasionally being on call, I stick to my scheduled shifts.

When Jordan's done eating, she runs to the kitchen to wash her hands, then to the living room, plopping in front of the television and pressing play on whatever show she's watching.

"I'm sorry about last night," I tell Kelsie. Even if that's not why she's being distant, I still feel like I should apologize.

"For what?" she says, quickly glancing up at me before turning her attention to her coffee cup.

"Having to leave the party early. Normally, I only work my scheduled shifts, but I was on call so my brother could enjoy Tilly's birthday weekend."

"You don't have to apologize," she mutters, keeping her eyes trained on the cup. "It's your job." She shrugs it off, but her tone doesn't match her nonchalance. "Besides, it's not like we made plans. I appreciate you buying the gift. You didn't have to do that, but you did, and Jordan had a wonderful time."

With her eyes still trained on that damn cup like it holds the answers to life's mysteries, I stare at her for a few seconds, wondering if I should just throw in the towel and call it a loss. But there's something about her that draws me in.

I've never had to work for a woman's attention. My family is wealthy—despite that wealth not directly belonging to my brothers and me, aside from the homes our parents built for us on our family's ranch—I have a good job, I've been told I'm a good-looking guy, and in high school I played football, which was a woman magnet.

When Tanya and I started dating, it was because she pursued me. She was the one who pushed for us to move in together, and the only reason I moved to the city with her when she took the job there was because she guilted me into it. The truth is, I never gave our relationship my all, and maybe that's why she ended up cheating on me. But as I sit here looking at Kelsie, for the first time, I want to try.

"Hey, Kels..." When she doesn't look up, I gently tip her chin up, forcing her eyes to meet mine. "Last night, I asked if you'd like to go out with me, but I was forced to leave before you could answer. So, I was wondering if you'd like to go out with me one night on a date."

Her eyes widen, and she visibly swallows, staring at me

NIKKI ASH

for several long seconds like a deer caught in the headlights before she finally speaks.

"I appreciate the offer," she says, "but I'm not looking to date right now. Between Jordan and work and hoping to take some classes in the spring, I just don't have the time."

Something in me prickles at her response. It's a solid answer. One I can't argue with, and most guys would take that as their cue to move on, but the sadness in her eyes has me wanting to pull her in closer. If what she's saying is the truth, then it's not that she doesn't want to go out with me, but that she feels like she can't add something else to her plate. Which leaves me only one choice...

"I understand," I tell her. "Then friends it is."

Her brows shoot up, kissing her forehead. "Fr-friends?" she stutters in confusion, obviously not expecting that answer from me. "You want to be friends?"

"Why not?" I say nonchalantly. "I like you and your daughter. I enjoy being around you and would love to get to know you. You said you're not in a place to date, so that leaves friends."

I stand and grab the garbage from the table, then walk into her kitchen, throwing it all into the trash can I saw Jordan use a little bit ago. When I walk back to the table, Kelsie is still sitting there, slowly sipping her coffee.

I sit across from her and lean back in my chair. "Are you ready for the storm?"

This has her snapping herself out of whatever thoughts she was lost in. "What storm?"

"The one that's coming through tonight. They're

predicting about a foot or so of snow."

"Seriously?" she huffs. "That's what I get for not watching TV."

"You don't watch TV?"

"Not really. I enjoy reading. I used to hear the news while in the car, but..." Her voice trails off, and she shakes her head. "Anyway, I need to head to the store. I had no idea." She sighs. "That probably means the café will be closed tomorrow, huh?"

When I nod, she frowns. "Great, another day of missed work," she grumbles, standing. She grabs her phone and checks it, then looks at me. "I got messages from the school and work about the storm. My phone was on silent." She glances at her daughter, whose eyes are still glued to the screen. "Jordan, pause *Beauty and the Beast* and go get dressed in something warm. We need to go to the store. Snow's coming."

Jordan pauses her movie and glances up, a smile splitting across her face. "Snow? Yay!" She jumps up from the couch and runs down the hall to what I assume is her room to get dressed.

"Do you need anything?" I ask.

"No, I'm good."

I nod and stand. "All right, well, I'll let you head to the store then."

"Thank you for breakfast...and the gift...and well, everything," she says, as if this is the last time she'll see me.

"You're welcome," I tell her, not bothering to mention that this is not the last time she'll see me since I have no intention of going anywhere. Once she realizes I'm not trying to take up all of her time—just some of it—she'll be more inclined to say yes to my date.

She walks me to the door, and I itch to touch her in some way, but I refrain. "Take care, Kels. If you need anything, I'm here."

"Thank you," she mumbles, her cheeks tinting the most beautiful shade of pink.

I'm halfway down her street when I realize that if she needs something, she has no way of getting ahold of me because she doesn't have my number. I turn around and head back to her house when I spot her and Jordan walking along the sidewalk.

"Hey," I say when I pull up next to them and roll down my window. "Where's your car?" It's damn near thirty degrees outside.

"Umm, I don't have one," she murmurs, looking at me sheepishly. "It's a long story."

"No, it's not," Jordan argues, scrunching her nose up in confusion. "The man with the big truck took it away and brought it back to Grandma."

Kelsie closes her eyes and shakes her head. "Thanks, kid."

"Welcome!" Jordan says, missing the sarcasm and embarrassment in her mom's tone.

"Get in."

"What?" Kelsie quirks a brow.

"Get in. It's too cold for you guys to be walking. I'll drive you. I was going to the store anyway."

I wasn't, but she doesn't need to know that.

She glances at the road, debating if she should be stubborn, then says, "Okay, thanks."

I get out and help them up, since my truck is lifted. I buckle Jordan into the booster seat I keep on hand for Tilly, then I open the passenger door for Kelsie, stepping up behind her.

"May I?" I ask, not wanting to touch her without her permission. She nods, and I grip the curves of her hips, hoisting her up into her seat.

"You know," she says once I'm back in my truck. "In the books I read, men who drive trucks this big are always overcompensating for other things that are *small*."

She smirks my way, and I'm so shocked by her cracking a joke, it takes me a minute of staring at her before I start to laugh.

"Oh, Kels," I say, shaking my head. "My family owns a ranch. My truck is lifted to go through the rough terrain, but if you need me to prove that I'm not overcompensating, just say the word." I hit her with a flirtatious wink, and she groans, her comment clearly not going the way she planned.

I hang out with her while she pushes the cart—and Jordan—through the store, noticing that she's frugal with what she buys. At one point, I'm almost positive she's counting the cost of each item to make sure she doesn't go over. I wish I could offer to pay so she could buy what she wants, but I've already done that once, and the last thing I want is to make her feel like she's a charity case, when she's not.

I grab a few things to make it look like I was really coming here and then head to a different register, so she doesn't feel self-conscious, telling myself that this thing with Kelsie isn't going to be quick. It'll take time and patience, but I'm okay with that because I have an ample amount of both.

The ride to her house is quiet. Despite her saying she's got it, I help them out of the truck and insist on carrying the groceries.

"Thank you," she says, then rolls her eyes. "God, I must sound like a broken record with how many times I've thanked you the past few days."

"You don't sound like anything," I tell her. "We're friends, right? Friends help each other out."

"Yeah." She snorts out a humorless laugh. "I'll be waiting for the day you need help."

"Never know." I shrug. "Do you have your phone?"

"Umm, yeah..." she says slowly. "Why?"

"So I can give you my number."

Her brows furrow, and her lips form a sexy pout.

"In case you need anything," I clarify. "Remember... Storm...coming through tonight."

She exhales a harsh breath. "Right. Thank you." She chuckles and shakes her head at having said those two words again.

She grabs her phone, and I give her my number, making her promise to call if she needs anything. It's not supposed to be a major storm, but she's new to this town, alone with her daughter.

This time when she walks me to the door, I lean in and kiss her cheek. "Stay safe, Kels," I murmur, hearing her slight intake of breath. She might not want to want me, but the fact is, she still does.

Seven

KELSIE

"Mommy! It snowed! It snowed!" Jordan yells, jumping onto my bed. "I wanna make a snowman!"

Without opening my eyes, I reach for my little snow angel and pull her under the covers, wrapping us up in the warm blankets. "I think we should stay right here where it's warm," I joke, nuzzling my face into her neck and making her laugh.

"No way, Mommy!" She rolls out of the blankets, taking the warmth with her. "We gotta build a snowman before Mr. Fireman takes all the snow."

The nickname she uses for Pierce has my eyes popping open. "Pierce is here?"

"Yeah, he's taking all the snow away," Jordan says, bouncing off the bed and running out of the room.

I quickly put a bra on, throw a hoodie over my pajama shirt, and follow after Jordan down the hall and toward the front door. She swings it open, and in my front yard is none other than Pierce, shoveling and salting my sidewalk and driveway.

"Jordan!" Tilly yells, popping out from around the corner. "I'm making a snowman, but Uncle Pierce said I couldn't knock 'cause you guys might be sleeping."

"I'm awake!" Jordan giggles, throwing her arms around her friend. "Mommy, can I play, please?"

"Of course," I tell her. "Go grab your jacket and gloves, though." She's already changed out of her pajamas and into her snow pants, a long-sleeved shirt, and boots.

"Fine," she replies, dragging the word out dramatically before she runs back inside.

Less than a minute later, she's back, standing before me and ready to be zipped. After zipping her up, I help her with her gloves. Once set, she and Tilly take off into the yard to play in the snow. We got a decent amount—close to a foot, by the looks of it. Definitely enough to have fun on a snow day.

"Hey," I say to Pierce, who has stopped shoveling to look at me.

"Hey," he replies with a half-smile.

"You didn't have to do this, but thank you."

We both chuckle at my overuse of those two words.

"Mommy!" Jordan yells, flying back around the corner with Tilly right behind. "Tilly's grandma has horses, and she's gonna ride them today after helping her uncle take all the snow away. Can we go too?"

"Oh, umm..."

"You guys should come," Pierce says before I can come up with a reason why we can't go. "It's a beautiful day to go riding. You ever been?"

"No," I admit. "I've always wanted to go, but I've never known anyone who actually owns a horse."

"Well, now you do," he says with a smirk. "I have a couple more houses to shovel, but once I'm done, Tilly and I will pick you up."

"You're sure we won't be intruding?"

"Impossible. My family's ranch has an open invitation. Mom always says the more, the merrier."

While the girls play and Pierce shovels, I go inside and make the girls hot cocoa and Pierce and me coffee.

Once he's done, and the girls have built the best snowman ever—their words—he tells Tilly to jump in the truck and then walks over to me. "I should probably get your number," he says with a serious expression.

"Oh, yeah? And why is that?"

"So I can call you when we're on our way."

I bark out a laugh. "We'll be ready. No need to call."

He chuckles under his breath and shakes his head. "You know, friends have each other's numbers."

"I'm not sure we're at that point in our friendship," I joke.

"Seriously? After all the thank yous you've given me, I think I've earned the friendship badge and your number."

"Hmmm." I tap my lips playfully. "Okay, you've earned it."

I pull my phone out of my pocket and send him a text, so he has my number. His entire face lights up when his phone goes off, making my stomach knot.

"Friends, Pierce," I say, reminding him—and myself.

"That's all I can give you."

"I don't know about this."

I glance up at the gigantic horse, having second thoughts. They're beautiful, and the thought of riding them sounded fun, but once you're standing in front of them, they're kind of intimidating.

"C'mon, Mommy, you can do it!" Jordan yells from the horse she's sitting atop, along with Tilly, while Jackson, Pierce's brother who runs the family ranch, holds the rope so the horse doesn't go anywhere. Tilly usually does it by herself as she's been riding before she could even walk, but since the girls wanted to ride together, Pierce has asked Jackson to join us so he could pull them along and ensure they're safe.

Meanwhile, I'm standing next to Jingle Bells—because all the horses are Christmas themed to match the town's vibe—with Pierce cupping his hands so I can use them as a makeshift stirrup. Apparently, he's too cool for a saddle. The whole situation has me wondering if it's too late to chicken out because the horse is tall, and if I fall, it's a long way down.

"Mommy, don't be scared," Jordan adds, making me look her way.

"Jordan, are you holding on tight?" I ask, even though the horse they're riding on has a saddle that the girls are sharing.

"Duh." She rolls her eyes. "Get on!"

Pierce chuckles and whispers, "I got you, Kels," causing

my entire body to shiver, despite how often I tell myself that the most Pierce and I can ever be is friends.

"If I fall off this horse, you're a dead man," I warn, shooting a playful glare his way.

His gaze meets mine, and the laughter that was just in his eyes disappears. "You'll always be safe with me. I promise."

His words slide through my veins like liquid heat, warming my insides. He doesn't know my past and has no idea what those words mean to me, yet somehow, he knew I needed to hear them.

I nod, and he clasps his fingers together again, so I can step onto them and boost myself up. With his help, I swing my leg over and straddle the horse's back. Pierce backs the horse up and uses a nearby hay bale to mount himself up. His muscular thighs slide along the outside of mine, and his arms cage me in so he can take control of the reins. He leans in, and his scent—masculinity mixed with comfort—envelops me. Being this close to him should be awkward, yet somehow, even though I've only known him briefly, his body wrapped around mine feels right.

I push the thought away immediately. He's a firefighter. It doesn't matter how comfortable I feel in his arms. I already lost someone I loved in a fire, and there's no way I could survive losing someone else.

"You good?" he asks, his lips brushing against my ear since my hair is up in a high ponytail.

"Yep," I squeak.

"All right, let's ride."

He lightly nudges the side of Jingle Bells, and the horse

starts to move forward. I look for Jordan and find Jackson's already walking them around the fenced-in area while the girls talk animatedly.

It takes a few minutes for my beating heart to calm, but once it does, I'm able to take in my surroundings. I'm in awe of Pierce's family ranch. The property stretches far past where I can see, with trees and shrubbery surrounding the area. A gorgeous, modern, red barn is situated in the center, and the ground is covered with a thin layer of snow, making everything look picture-perfect.

We ride for a few minutes in silence, staying behind the girls, and I find myself relaxing against Pierce and enjoying the ride.

"What are you thinking about?" Pierce asks after a little while, breaking the silence.

I don't know how he knows I'm lost in my own head, but I answer honestly without thought. "I can't remember the last time I felt this relaxed."

"Good," he says. "That's how you should always feel when you're with me."

Because I have no idea what to say to that or how to feel about it, I don't say anything at all. Instead, I pull out my phone and snap a few photos of the girls on their horse, wanting to capture Jordan's first time riding. After going around the fenced-in area a few times, the girls get bored and ask if they can go play in Tilly's tree house.

"I can take them," Jackson says. "You guys finish your ride."

I let Jordan know we'll be up to the main house soon and

to behave, then Pierce takes off in the opposite direction. Unlike the way he was taking it easy while we followed the girls, he now picks up speed. With the cold air whipping around us, I get lost in the beauty of the ride and the scenery around us.

"That's Jackson's place," Pierce says, snapping me out of the moment. The house he's pointing to is a barn-style home, similar to their parents', but a bit smaller and gray.

"It's pretty."

He makes a clicking sound, and the horse takes off again. We ride for a few minutes before we come across a single-story ranch-style home. It's white with black shutters and a black door.

"This is Beckett's place," he says.

"Both your brothers live on the ranch?"

"We all do," he says, making the noise that has the horse running forward once again.

We ride for a little while longer, around a large pond that Pierce tells me everyone swims in during the summer and past another barn that Pierce says holds a bunch of equipment.

"And this is my place," he says, when we stop in front of the most beautiful two-story log cabin home, complete with a hunter-green roof, a large chimney stemming up the side of the home, and a wraparound wooden porch. It looks like the cabins you see online that advertise those expensive ski resorts. The ones I could never afford to visit, let alone purchase.

"It's gorgeous," I breathe. "Like beyond gorgeous."

"Thank you," he says. "Want to see the inside?"

"Sure." If it's this breathtakingly beautiful on the outside, I can't even imagine what it's like on the inside.

Pierce stops at the porch and climbs off the horse. He helps me off and then ties the reins to a hook that must've been put there for this reason.

Taking my hand in his, he guides us up the porch and through the front door. "You don't lock your door?"

"Nah," he says with a chuckle. "Nobody would dare come onto this property, and even if they did, we're miles off the main road."

We stop in the foyer, and the interior of the home blows me away. The walls and ceiling are made of wood. There's a circular staircase, also wood, and wooden beams run along the vaulted ceilings that lead to the second story, which is open. I can't see the rooms, but a wrought iron railing runs horizontally from one end to the other. A gorgeous brick fireplace is erected on the far-right wall, and minimalist country chic furniture fills the open area.

"You live here alone?" I ask because this looks like a family home, not something a thirty-year-old bachelor would live in.

"For now," he says. "One day, I hope to share this home with my wife and, if it's in the cards, our children."

"So, you built this house in hope that one day you'd get married and have kids?"

"Honestly," he says, "I built it to stay busy."

I chuckle. "You built this super big, expensive house because you were bored? When I'm bored, I read a book."

He glances at me but doesn't laugh. "As I'm sure you can

tell, my parents have a bit of money. This ranch has been in my mom's family for years. My dad loves living here, but his dream was to be a firefighter. My grandfather ran it until my brother Jackson took over. From a young age, he loved working on the ranch, so it made sense that he would run the place.

"Beckett and I followed in our dad's footsteps and became firefighters. Now that Dad's retired, he helps out around the ranch more often. Beckett and I help out occasionally, but Jackson's the one who handles the majority of the work. My parents having money doesn't mean we do," he says. "I'm a firefighter who makes a firefighter salary."

The tone in his voice causes me to go on the defense. "I don't care about your money, and your financial situation is none of my business. I was only joking because you said you built it to keep busy."

I turn, ready to leave, and Pierce gently grabs my hand, spinning me back around. "I'm sorry. I didn't mean for it to come out like that." He pulls me over to the couch. "I was in a serious relationship for a while. She would brag to her friends that she was dating a firefighter. Social media and the sexualization of jobs like mine make it seem like being a firefighter is sexy." He glances at me sheepishly, and I can't help but smile because he's not wrong—he's the definition of a sexy firefighter.

"I could totally see you on a calendar," I half-joke, making him bark out a laugh.

"I actually did one for charity recently. I'm holding Cinder." He shrugs, and I wonder if I can nonchalantly ask where I can buy this calendar.

As if he can read my mind, he says, "It's available at several stores in town." He winks, and my cheeks heat up.

"I mean, I am in the market for a new calendar," I flirt, wondering who this woman is and what she did with the shy, nervous woman who couldn't flirt to save her life.

"I'll get you one," he replies. "Only if you promise to hang me on your fridge so I can have breakfast with you."

I crack up laughing. "Deal."

We're both quiet for a minute, and I almost forget the point of this conversation until Pierce speaks, his tone serious once again.

"I told her I wasn't rich, that my parents were, but she didn't listen to me. And I guess I didn't listen to her in many ways. She kept making comments about wanting more. She expected lavish trips and expensive gifts. Every time I tried to make her happy, it was never enough." He sighs. "I knew we were wrong for each other, but when you spend so many years together, the idea of fixing what's wrong seems easier than starting over.

"Her attitude made it hard for my family to like her, especially when they felt she was only staying with me in hopes that I was lying, and I was really rich." He shakes his head. "She got bored living in Christmas Valley and wanted to start a family, but the idea of having a baby with her had me panicking. So when she asked to move to the city for a job opportunity she was given, working as a paralegal for an attorney her dad was friends with, I agreed. I applied to the stations in Boston and was hired.

"We rented an apartment in the city, and we both worked a lot of hours. She mentioned she had to work late at the office one night, so I thought I'd surprise her with dinner. Joke was on me, though, because she was already having dinner." He chuckles humorlessly. "Caught her with her married boss's dick in her mouth, and I officially became a cliché."

"I'm sorry," I tell him, placing my hand on his. "But you're not the cliché. She is."

He smiles softly and nods. "I ended things between us and moved back home. Thankfully, I was able to get my job back here, and I've spent the past three years focusing on work and building this place."

"It really is a beautiful home."

"My brothers and I were each given the money to build our own place since our parents knew we couldn't do that on our salaries. It was important to them, especially my mom, that we live on the property near each other. My brothers were given the money as a wedding gift, but when my mom saw me struggling after the breakup, refusing to date, she gave it to me early."

He laughs softly. "I'm almost positive she did it based on that famous quote from *Field of Dreams*: 'If you build it, they will come.'" He chuckles. "I think she was hoping once I built the home, I would fill it with a family." His eyes lock with mine, his gaze turning heated. "I didn't get it until now."

"Pierce," I whisper. "I... I can't be that person," I tell him, despite wishing I could be.

"Why?"

"Because..." I swallow hard, unsure if I should tell him the truth or go with a lie. The look in his eyes, begging me to tell him why we could never work, has me going with the truth. "I lost Jordan's dad in a fire." I close my eyes, not wanting to cry but knowing it will happen regardless. "One minute, Trent was alive, and the next, I was attending his funeral."

"Shit, Kels."

Before I can open my eyes, strong arms envelop me. He holds me tightly, rubbing his hands up and down my arms while I cry against his chest. It's not that I'm still pining after Trent. I know he's gone. One day when I meet the right guy and I'm in the right place in my life, I'll move on, but it won't be with Pierce.

"I'm sorry," I whisper against his chest. "I appreciate everything you've done for Jordan and me, but I just can't do it. The thought of letting you in and..."

"Shh, I get it," he says. "I don't like it and wish I could convince you otherwise, but I get it."

When we pull away from each other, he reaches out and wipes the tears that have settled on the tops of my cheeks. "Thank you for telling me. You ready to head back up to the main house?"

"Yeah, Jordan and I should probably get going."

"What? Why? I thought you guys were going to eat over. Jordan was excited about roasting the marshmallows."

"I know, but now that you know..."

"Changes nothing," he says. "We're friends, like you insisted before."

"Yeah, I did, but I know a part of you hoped I would change my mind. And now that you know it won't happen..."

"Still changes nothing. We're friends. Now, let's go eat dinner and then roast some marshmallows *as friends*."

Eight

PIERCE

It would be my luck that the first woman I'm interested in would be against dating a firefighter. Not that I can blame her—she and Jordan lost someone close to them in a fire, so it makes sense that she'd be afraid to give her heart to someone who fights fires for a living.

What she doesn't realize is that the risk isn't as high as she thinks. I looked it up out of curiosity, and only about seventy firefighters, on average, die a year in a fire. That's a small number in the grand scheme of things, especially since Christmas Valley hasn't had any firefighter deaths, ever. I have more of a chance of dying in a car accident or crossing the street than in a fire.

But knowing that her fear isn't based on numbers, and that it comes from her heart, means I need to handle the situation carefully. If I didn't think she felt the chemistry between us, didn't want to get to know me on a deeper level... If she didn't look at me like she wants me but wishes she didn't, I'd give up, throw in the towel, and chalk it up to having one-sided feelings. But I can see it in her eyes. She feels the chemistry between us and wants me on a deeper level, and if I wasn't a firefighter, I know damn well she would be letting me take her out.

So, I'm not giving up.

"Can someone pass me the chicken?" Beckett asks from across the table, pointing at the perfectly roasted chicken.

"Can I have another roll, please?" Tilly adds.

We're all sitting around the picnic-style table in my parents' house, eating dinner. Both of my brothers, their wives, and their kids are here, as well as my parents. Kelsie looked a bit overwhelmed when we got back to my parents' place and saw that everyone had arrived.

Like every week, when we have a family dinner, the women were cooking and gossiping while the guys were watching and talking about whatever sports were on. To some, it might seem odd how close of a family we are, but I don't know what I would do without the love and support of my family.

I don't know anything about Kelsie's family, but based on her reaction, I guess she's not used to big family get-togethers. On the other hand, Jordan is more than comfortable running around with Tilly and soaking up all the attention from everyone.

My hope is that regardless of what happens—or doesn't happen—between Kelsie and me, she'll let down the wall she's erected and let my family in. The idea of her going at everything alone doesn't sit well with me, not when she's got so many people in this town who already care about her.

"Kelsie," Mom says with a smile. "Dorothy said you're planning to go to college in the spring. What is your major?"

The question is only meant to make conversation, since Kelsie hasn't said a word since we sat down, but Kelsie glances around the room nervously, as if she's being put on the spot.

"Oh, umm..." Kelsie chews on the corner of her lip for a moment, clearly uncomfortable with being the center of attention. "Yeah," she finally says. "I'd like to be a nurse one day, maybe even a nurse practitioner." Pink tinges her cheeks, and she shrugs. "I don't know. It's just a thought. We'll see."

"I think it's a wonderful thought," Mom says, refusing to let Kelsie discredit her own dreams. "I was a nurse for twenty years. If you need anything, please let me know."

"Thank you," Kelsie says.

"What made you want to become a nurse?" I ask her once everyone goes back to talking and eating.

"When I gave birth to Jordan, Trent and I were so young and scared," she confesses, glancing up at me through her lashes. Her bright emerald eyes meet mine, and if it wasn't creepy, I'd snap a picture of her to look at later when she's back home and I'm thinking about her. "But the labor and delivery nurse on duty was so sweet and compassionate," she continues, "keeping us updated and not treating us like the teenagers we were. And then, after she was born and I was moved to recovery, the nurse was so helpful to Trent and me, going above and beyond to explain everything.

"Their kindness stuck with me, and when I thought about what I'd like to do, nursing kept popping into my head." She shrugs nonchalantly. "A lot would have to go right in order for it to happen, though. So, for now, I'm just taking it one day at a time."

"Jordan's mommy," Tilly exclaims, getting Kelsie's attention. "Can Jordan come to the station for turkey? Uncle Jackson's making a big turkey"—her arms fly outward to show just how big, and the adults laugh at her exaggeration—"and he always lets me help cut it. And Daddy and Uncle Pierce let us go down the super big pole. And Cinderella will be there!"

"I want a big turkey and to go down a super big pole!" Jordan replies, eyes wide in excitement. "Can we go, Mommy? Please."

"Oh, umm…" Kelsie smiles nervously. "I don't know."

"You should come," I add. "Unless you have other plans."

"No, it's just Jordan and me this year, but I wouldn't want to intrude."

"Nonsense, dear," Mom says. "We would love to have you."

Everyone voices their agreement and then goes back to their side conversations.

"You guys should come," I insist, so only she can hear me. "There are a bunch of us. Everyone cooks and brings something. It'll be fun. If you ask nicely, I'll let you go down the super big pole too." I wink playfully, and her eyes go wide, her cheeks turning pink. I have no idea why, until I replay what I just said in my head and realize what it sounded like.

I let out a quick laugh and then lean in, making sure only she hears what I say next. "I meant the pole at the station, but if you want to slide down my pole, I won't be opposed."

She makes a choking sound, her face getting even redder, and I chuckle at how adorable she is.

"Friends, Pierce," she says, glaring my way. "We can only be friends."

"Who are you trying to convince, Kels?" I eye her pink-tinted flesh, and she flushes harder. "Me...or you?"

Without giving her a chance to answer, I stand and take our plates to the sink. Kelsie can keep telling herself all she wants that we can only be friends, but we both know that deep down she wants more than that. Now, I just have to convince her that it's okay to give in to what we both want.

Nine

KELSIE

PIERCE

Colored or white lights?

I GLANCE AT MY PHONE, CONFUSED BY HIS QUESTION. It's been a little over a week since we hung out at his family's ranch, and every day since then, he's been sending me random questions. Usually, they're about me—what's my favorite color? Favorite food? Am I a lefty or a righty? What kind of music do I listen to?

At first, I simply responded, but when he started typing his answers without me asking him any back, I felt terrible and started to participate, shooting back a few questions of my own. I thought the game would be over quickly, but it's still going strong. And—not that I would admit this to him since I have a feeling that he was full of it when he said he's fine as just friends—I'm rather enjoying it. Oftentimes, the questions and answers lead to a conversation, and it's been nice having an adult conversation.

Except at this moment, because I'm not sure what the heck he's talking about.

KELSIE

What does that mean?

He's at the station, so I pocket my phone, since it can take him a while to respond, returning to wiping down the tables in preparation for closing. It was crazy busy this morning, but it's died down, and Dorothy said we're closing early for the holiday weekend—which is a good and bad thing. I'll get the next four days with Jordan, but it means I won't be making any money either. I've considered picking up a second job, but I'm not sure how that will work if I try to start school in the spring—something that is necessary if I ever want a job that won't leave me living paycheck to paycheck.

My phone buzzes in my pocket, so I pull it out to check it and find two GIFs from Pierce: one is of a Christmas tree with multicolored lights, and the other is of one with white lights.

KELSIE

White is so elegant, but there's something about colorful lights that makes the tree feel magical.

PIERCE

I agree. Themed tree or random?

KELSIE

You skipped right past me asking a question, but to answer your question: Before the house caught fire, I had ornaments I collected growing up and a couple from when Jordan was born. Unfortunately, when we lost everything in the fire, we lost them as well. So, Jordan and I have started a new ornament collection. Every year, we buy a new one to add to the tree. It's not themed, but not random, either. You?

PIERCE

This is my first Christmas in my house, but I think I'll use the tree at the station as my own. You get a tree yet?

My heart sinks at his question. I was hoping that finally living on my own would mean having a real tree again, but real trees are expensive. As much as Jordan and I want one, I can't justify spending that kind of money.

But I'm not about to tell Pierce that, so instead I type back:

KELSIE

Going this weekend.

It's not a lie since I'm planning to get one this weekend—only it will be fake and small enough to sit on our table. I had wanted to get it before Thanksgiving—since that's always been the tradition—but I kept putting it off, hoping to squeeze enough money from somewhere to get a full-size tree. Unfortunately, that won't be happening—and I know Jordan will be sad.

I push my phone back into my pocket so I can finish closing the café. Dorothy shows up as I'm putting the last of the bakery items into the freezer to lock up. She wishes me a

Happy early Thanksgiving and says she'll see me Monday.

Then I head out to pick up Jordan from school. I'm not even a block from work when Pierce pulls up next to me in his massive truck, his passenger window rolled down.

"I was hoping to catch you before you got off," he calls through the window with a boyish grin.

I can't help but notice that his hair is longer than the last time I saw him and a bit tousled, giving off *I just woke up* vibes—even though I know he didn't. His face is scruffy, so when he smiles, that adorable dimple is hidden. When he's clean-shaven, he's handsome, but with his hair like this, he looks ruggedly sexy.

His smirk widens into a full-blown smile, and I realize I've been caught checking him out.

"Aren't you supposed to be working?" I ask, making him chuckle.

"Took the afternoon off. You going to get Jordan?"

"Yep, and then heading to the store."

"Not for Thanksgiving stuff, right?" he asks, quirking a brow.

"Umm... I never said we were going."

"We'll discuss that later," he says. "Hop in, there's somewhere we need to be."

I glance at him skeptically, unsure what the heck he's up to, but after a moment, I get in anyway.

After we've picked up Jordan, Pierce brings us back to our place. "Grab a coat and put on some boots," he says.

I look at him, waiting for him to explain why, but when he stays tightlipped, I sigh and do as he says.

"Are you going to tell us where we're going?" I ask after we've been driving for about thirty minutes.

"Nope, it's a surprise."

"Oh, I love surprises!" Jordan yells from the back seat, where she's practicing reading a book her teacher gave her to bring home.

"I don't," I grumble, making Pierce laugh.

Fifteen minutes later, I spot a sign that reads: **Mistletoe Christmas Tree Farm** and my head whips around to look at Pierce, who refuses to make eye contact with me. The only indication he knows that I know is the small smirk on his lips.

We pull up to an adorable red barn and Pierce parks. Without waiting for anyone to help her out, Jordan unbuckles and opens the door, jumping out.

"Oh my God!" She squeals. "There are a million Christmas trees." She rushes toward the tree closest and sighs in awe, having never seen a real tree in person like this before. When Trent was alive, we had a fake tree we reused to save money.

"Pierce." My eyes fill with tears, knowing I'm going to have to admit that I can't afford one and pop Jordan's happy bubble. "You shouldn't have done this. I can't..."

He gently presses two fingers to my lips. "Consider this my gift to you."

I should probably argue, tell him this is too much. But as my eyes return to Jordan, who's smiling bigger than I've ever seen, my heart swells, and before I can think about what I'm doing, I wrap my arms around Pierce's waist. "Thank you," I whisper into his chest, ignoring the deliciously masculine scent emanating from him. "This means so much to her...and me."

His entire body relaxes as if he was worried I wouldn't accept his gift. "You're welcome," he says, pressing his lips to the top of my head. Butterflies attack my belly, and I immediately shoo them away. My heart might want to overlook the fact that Pierce is a firefighter right now, but it will *definitely* remember what he does for a living if I let him in and something happens to him. My only chance at keeping him at a distance, at protecting my heart, is to think with my head.

"I want this tree!" Jordan yells, pointing at a tree so tall it wouldn't be able to stand upright in our living room.

"Not happening," I tell her. "That tree is way too tall."

We spend the next hour looking at dozens of trees, until we find the perfect one. It's tall, but not too tall, thick and beautiful, and the perfect size for our place. The tree farm worker gets it wrapped up and puts it in the back of Pierce's truck while we go into the barn for him to check out.

"Hot chocolate or coffee?" he asks, stopping at the warm beverages counter.

"Hot chocolate, please!" Jordan answers first.

"Same," I agree. "I try not to drink coffee after three o'clock, or I'll have trouble sleeping."

"Three hot chocolates with marshmallows," he tells the cashier.

While we're waiting for our drinks, we check out the place. There are wreaths and decorations—both indoor and out—and...

"Mommy, look! A baby tree." Jordan grins. "It's so cute."

"We're already getting a tree," I remind her.

"I know," she says. "When I'm bigger, I'm gonna get two trees. One for Santa and one for my room so I can put all of Daddy's ornaments on the tree. It'll be like he's with me in my room."

I choke up at her words, hating that her dad is gone and wishing I could bring him back. Life can be so cruel sometimes. At least his mom was decent enough to give Jordan Trent's ornaments after he passed away. I also found a few online that we previously bought together to replace the ones we lost in the fire.

"It is the perfect tree to put your dad's ornaments on," Pierce says with a warm smile, handing each of us our cups of hot chocolate. "I'm going to pay. Why don't you guys go get in the truck where it's warm?" He hands me his keys, and Jordan and I head outside.

Jordan stops at the back of the truck to admire the tree. "It's going to be the best tree ever," she says. "Thank you, Mommy." She throws her arms around my waist and hugs me tightly before we climb into Pierce's truck to wait for him.

"Can we set up the tree when we get home?" Jordan asks.

"We'll set it up tonight, and tomorrow we can decorate it after dinner."

She nods happily at my answer.

Pierce jumps into his truck a few minutes later, and we take off toward home. I should remind him I still need to go to the store, but he's already done so much getting us this tree that I don't. We can go later, after he drops us off.

He must remember, though, because instead of going

toward our house, he turns off Main Street and pulls into the grocery store parking lot. When he parks, he grabs my hand before I can exit. "I'd really love it if you would join us for Thanksgiving tomorrow. I don't want to force you into it, though. If you change your mind, the invitation is open. We'll be at the station all day. We hand out meals to those in need, and then we all eat in the afternoon."

"Thank you," I tell him. "But I think it's best if Jordan and I eat at home."

I don't tell him my reasoning is because I'm starting to feel too much toward him and that's not good. Spending more time with him won't help the matter. I need space.

He sighs, clearly unhappy with my response, but nods, respecting it. He walks around with us while I buy a small turkey and sides to cook tomorrow, as well as some groceries for the next few days since we'll be home.

When we return to the house, Jordan and I bring in the groceries while Pierce insists on handling the tree. I clear out an area in the living room and, thanks to the tree farm worker who put the tree stand on while we were there, Pierce sets the tree up easily. When he cuts the wrapping off, the branches fall, and Jordan and I both gasp at how beautiful it is. Tears prick my eyes, feeling like, for the first time since Trent died, Jordan and I have found a real home.

"I love it," she breathes, running her fingers along the branches. "It smells like"—she inhales dramatically— "Christmas."

"It does," I agree. "The best smell ever."

"Oh no," she says, glancing my way with big eyes. "We

forgot lights."

Shoot, she's right, and I doubt the grocery store carries any. "I think we have some from our tree last year," I mention. Although, I doubt it will be enough to cover the entire tree.

"I've got you covered." Pierce winks and takes off outside.

When he returns a few minutes later, he's not only holding several boxes of lights in one hand, but the small tree Jordan loved is in the other.

"The baby tree!" Jordan shrieks. "Is it for me?"

"It is," he says, setting the boxes down and walking into her room. "Where do you want it?"

Jordan points to an empty spot in the corner of her room, and Pierce sets it down.

"Thank you!" she cries, hugging him. "I love it so much."

We spend the next couple of hours making the trees look perfect and putting the lights on Jordan's tree. When Jordan complains she's hungry, Pierce insists on ordering pizza. We end up eating in the living room while we watch our go-to pre-Christmas movie: *Miracle on 34th Street*. It's been a tradition for years because the film begins on Thanksgiving with the Macy's parade.

When the movie ends, and it's time for Jordan to go to bed, she thanks Pierce and me again for the best day ever. As I put her to bed, I can't help but wonder what I've gotten myself into. I had literally told Pierce we couldn't join them for Thanksgiving because I wanted—no, *needed*—some space, yet I turned around and spent the entire afternoon and evening with him.

It's more than that, though. I thoroughly enjoyed it.

Hanging out with Pierce is as effortless as breathing. He's sweet and funny, and not only does he treat me with respect, but he's good to Jordan. He's patient and kind. While most guys would probably prefer to spend the night watching sports or having a drink with friends, he seemed perfectly content with eating pizza and watching a Christmas movie.

I kiss my daughter good night and walk out to find Pierce has cleaned up.

"You didn't have to do that, but thank you."

"It's no problem." He glances at the door. "I should probably get going…"

"Or you can stay and hang out," I blurt out, shocking the hell out of myself.

My words must also surprise Pierce because his eyes go wide. "You sure?"

"Yeah," I breathe. "I'm sure."

"Okay." He nods. "Do you want to watch a movie or something?"

"Ever play Rummy?" I ask, taking myself by surprise again.

Growing up, my grandma taught me how to play, and when Trent and I started dating, we'd play. On nights when Jordan couldn't sleep, we'd play for hours. I haven't played since he passed away, and I have no idea what made me suggest Pierce and I play.

Actually, I do know. I want to spend more time with him to get to know him. In spite of knowing I shouldn't, I still want to.

"The card game? Sure."

I rummage through my junk drawer, remembering I left

a deck in there, and then we sit at the table across from each other. I shuffle, and he deals, and then we play...

"How long were you and Trent together?" Pierce asks, picking up a card and discarding it. We've been playing for hours, moving from subject to subject effortlessly, as if we've known each other for years.

"He was my first and only boyfriend," I admit, picking up a card. "We started dating at the beginning of our senior year and fell hard. We were both planning to go away to school, but then I found out I was pregnant. It was hard, but we made it work. We were together for almost four years before he passed away."

I place down three sevens. "What about you?" I ask, discarding a card I don't need. "Any other serious relationships besides the one with the cheating idiot?"

He chuckles at my refusal to call her by name, but I can't help it. Anyone who would cheat on Pierce is an idiot.

"Before her, I dated a few women casually, but since her, I haven't dated...haven't wanted to date, until now." His eyes meet mine and butterflies fill my belly at his admission. He hasn't wanted to date in three years, but now he wants me.

"Why me?" I blurt out.

It's not that I'm fishing for compliments, but I honestly don't get it. I've seen the single women in this town and have heard several of them mention him and how they would give their right arm to snag his attention. Yet, he's interested in me.

He doesn't miss a beat when he says, "Why not you?"

He picks up a card and glances at it, but instead of making a play, he holds on to it, giving me his attention. "You're beautiful, sweet. You're a damn good mother. I enjoy talking to you and being around you. When I'm not with you, I can't stop thinking about you, and when I am, I can't get enough. And if that's not enough, there's Jordan. The kid is your mini. I want nothing more than to spend more time with both of you."

He lays his cards down and grins.

"I'm out," he says as if he didn't just metaphorically knock me on my ass with his response.

"Damn it," I groan, showing the cards left in my hand. "You won for sure."

I shove the cards his way and yawn, and he smiles softly.

"It's getting late, and as much as I'd love to keep playing, I'd bet a certain little girl will be up at the crack of dawn begging to decorate her tree."

I laugh because he's not wrong, then stand so I can walk him to the door.

"Thank you," I tell him once we're outside near his truck. "You made our Christmas so special. If there's any way that I can repay you..."

"Seeing both of you happy is all the payment I need," he murmurs, bridging the gap between us, his eyes locking with mine. "I need to be honest with you, Kels. I know I told you that I'm okay with being friends, and I am, but only because you've friend-zoned me."

He smirks playfully, and I groan, shaking my head. "It's not that..."

"I get it," he says. "You're scared. The last thing I'd ever want is for you to be scared. The only thing I want is for you and that little girl to smile and be happy. And as much as I believe I could make you happy, you have to be on board, but you're not."

He reaches out and tucks a wayward strand of hair that fell out of my messy bun behind my ear, and I visibly shiver at his touch, wishing he'd keep touching me.

"You already know that I like you and want to spend more time with you," he continues. "If you ever change your mind, I'm here."

"Pierce," I whisper, wishing I could change my mind.

It's been three years since Trent died, and the truth is, I'm lonely. I crave adult interaction. I miss being intimate with someone. Pierce and I obviously aren't intimate, but hanging out with him, texting, playing cards, talking... It has all lit a fire within me that had been snuffed out the day I lost Trent. I'd be lying through my teeth if I tried to say I'm not attracted to Pierce.

"I know," Pierce says, stroking my cheek with his knuckles. "Just know I'm here in whatever capacity you want me to be." He leans in and presses a soft kiss to my cheek, and my eyes close as my body warms at his touch. "I hope to see you tomorrow, but if I don't, have a good Thanksgiving, Kels."

When I open my eyes, Pierce is getting into his truck, and I immediately notice that he took all the warmth with him, leaving me shivering in the cold.

He's barely pulled out of the driveway, and I'm already missing the warmth he emits. The problem is...that warmth leads to fire, and fire leads to nothing but destruction.

Ten

PIERCE

"Here you go." I hand the last meal we're giving out to the gentleman. "Have a good Thanksgiving."

He smiles warmly and lifts the bag in appreciation. "Thank you. This means the world to my family."

I watch him leave and stay standing outside, hoping to see a certain auburn-haired beauty and her mini walking this way, but the streets are pretty much dead. It's three o'clock, and since most of the businesses are closed for the holiday, there's no reason for anyone to be out. People are home with their loved ones, enjoying the holiday.

"Hoping to spot a certain green-eyed woman?" my mom asks, sliding her arm around my back and hugging me from the side.

"Yeah." I sigh. "I don't know what it is about her, Mom, but I can't get her off my mind."

"Oh, you know what it is." She smirks up at me. "For one,

she's beautiful."

"Yeah, she is," I agree, picturing how she twirls her curly auburn hair when she's nervous or how her emerald eyes shine when she smiles at me. Most of the time, she's sporting a neutral expression, like she's almost afraid to smile. So when she does, it makes it that much more special, like I did something to earn it, and I want to figure out how to keep getting her to do it.

"She's had a rough go at it. She lost Jordan's dad in a fire." I don't want to put her business out there, but my mom and I are close, and I know she'd never repeat anything I tell her.

"Oh, dear. I can't even imagine. What about her family? It seems like they're all alone."

"I don't know where their family's at, but yeah, it doesn't look like she has any support at all." I turn to face her. "She's such a good mom, though. Would do anything for her daughter...including run herself into the ground to support her."

Mom nods in understanding.

"When I was with Tanya, she'd beg for materialistic shit. Nothing I bought her was ever enough. But yesterday, when I took Kelsie and Jordan to buy a Christmas tree, they acted as if I bought them a damn mansion. There were actual tears in Kelsie's eyes. I want them to be mine. I know I've only known them for a short time, but I want to give them the world, despite how crazy that sounds."

"It doesn't sound crazy," Mom says. "When you know, you know. Your dad and I knew we were going to spend our lives together after the first date."

"Yeah, well, unfortunately, Kelsie isn't on the same page as me."

"Are you sure?" Mom asks. "I saw the way she looked at you at dinner, and it wasn't the look of someone who wasn't interested."

"Oh, she's totally interested." I chuckle humorlessly. "Only she's gotten it into her head that because she lost someone in a fire, she can't date a firefighter." I shake my head. "I mean, I get it. I don't know all the details, and I've never lost someone close to me, so I won't try to fully understand where she's coming from, but I understand her fear. It's just..."

I blow out a harsh breath. "It sucks that the woman I'm interested in is against dating a firefighter. If I had any other career, she'd give me a chance. But she can't risk letting me in and losing me in a fire as well, so instead, she keeps me at arm's length. Maybe I need to face the fact that we'll never be anything more than friends."

"Well, I wouldn't throw in the towel yet," Mom says, nodding over my shoulder.

I turn around and blink several times to make sure I'm not seeing shit, but every time my eyes open, I still see them: Kelsie and Jordan, walking our way.

"Is the invitation still open?" Kelsie asks when they reach us.

She's donning an adorable black beanie on her head with her auburn curls hanging in loose pigtails. Her cheeks are slightly flushed from the cold, and her heart-shaped lips are pink and plump and so fucking kissable. Jesus, I wish I could kiss her...

A throat clears, snapping me from my thoughts, and I realize I never answered her question.

"Of course," I choke out, stunned that they're here.

"We made brownies." Kelsie smiles softly and hands me the container she's holding.

"They're so yummy," Jordan adds. "Mommy let me lick the batter. Is Tilly here?" she asks, changing the subject quickly.

"She is," Mom says, taking the container from me. "Probably sliding down the pole for the millionth time. Why don't we go find her?"

"Yes! I wanna go down the pole!" Jordan takes off up the sidewalk, and my mom follows her inside, leaving us alone.

"I didn't think I was going to see you today," I say, tugging on a curl playfully.

"I didn't plan on coming," she admits honestly, averting her gaze to somewhere off in the distance.

Gently pinching her chin with my thumb and forefinger, I turn her face so she'll look my way. "What made you change your mind?" I ask, our eyes locking.

"It just... It felt like...it wasn't where we were supposed to be."

Her admission has my heart sputtering in my chest at the possibility of what that means.

"And how does it feel now that you're here?" I ask, needing her to say the words out loud.

"Like, maybe, this is where we should be."

It's not an actual confession of feelings, but fuck if it's not a step in the right direction.

"I'm glad you guys are here," I tell her, sliding my arm

across the top of her shoulders. "Let's go eat some turkey."

"MY GOODNESS, I CAN'T REMEMBER THE LAST TIME I ATE that much." Kelsie sits back on the couch, rubbing her fake food belly. "You're going to have to roll me out of here." She looks my way with a playful grin, and I smile back, happy that she and Jordan showed up.

While Jordan spent the afternoon playing with Tilly, Cinder, and the other kids, Kelsie bounced around, talking to the adults. It's no secret that I have feelings for her, but because she's new to town and keeps to herself—and because my ex was a selfish, stuck-up snob that nobody liked—my family, friends, and coworkers have been trying to get to know her. They want to make sure my taste in women this time around is better than the last time. Based on the looks they've given me, she's more than passed the test.

"I'm a strong guy. It'd probably be easier to carry you out." I smirk, and she chuckles, shaking her head.

"Ehh, after all the food I just ate, it'll be good for me to walk home."

"Or I can drive you."

"I can't ask you to do that."

"You're not asking." I lean in so our faces are close. "Any chance I can spend time with you, I'll take."

"Pierce..." She groans. "You agreed to just being friends."

"And I told you I want more."

She swallows thickly before she whispers, "I'm scared."

Her confession has me wanting to wrap her up in my arms. Instead, I nod in understanding, refusing to ignore her feelings. "How about you keep an open mind? We can spend some time together and get to know one another. See where things go."

"Okay," she agrees after several seconds, shocking the hell out of me. "I'll keep an open mind... See where things go. But no promises."

"Mommy, can we go home and decorate the trees?" Jordan runs over and asks.

"We sure can," Kelsie says.

After the girls thank everyone and say goodbye, and I insist on taking them home, we jump into my truck with Cinder sitting in the back with Jordan.

"Whoa! Look at those lights!" Jordan screeches as we drive down Main Street past the Rodgerses' house. "They're so pretty."

I stop the truck in front of their house so Jordan can get a better look. "They're participating in the Battle of the Christmas Decorations," I explain, pointing to the sign on their lawn. Bill and Dawn Rodgers always put their lights up before Thanksgiving. "Soon, many houses will be decorated. It's a Christmas Valley tradition."

"What's a battle?" Jordan asks.

"A competition," I tell her. "They decorate their houses and lawns. Then everyone goes to all the houses so they can vote on whose lights are the best. Whoever gets the most votes, wins."

I look back and see Jordan's eyes widen.

"What do they win?" she asks.

"Twenty-five hundred dollars."

"Wow!" she gasps. "Mommy, we should do the battle. Then we'll have money to pay the lady that you need to give money to."

Kelsie sighs and closes her eyes, obviously embarrassed by Jordan's admission. When she opens them, I notice they're watery, but she won't look at me. "Not this year, Ladybug," she chokes out.

"But, Mommy, if we win—"

"Lights cost money, and putting them up takes a lot of time. And with how many houses will participate, the chances of winning are slim. Maybe next year."

Jordan's face falls. "Maybe means no," she grumbles, sitting back in her seat.

I take off again, but the mood is somber now. Both girls are quiet, and I want to ask Kelsie if she needs any help, but I don't think she'd take kindly to that. From my minimal time with her, I can tell she's prideful. The last thing I want is to make her feel like I view her as a charity case.

When I pull into their driveway, Jordan perks up again, remembering that she gets to decorate the trees.

"Thank you for today," Kelsie says. "We had a wonderful time."

"Anytime." I lean in and kiss her cheek. Normally, I'd walk them to the door, but I don't want her to feel obligated to invite me in when I know decorating the trees is something personal for them.

Instead, a few hours later, when I'm in bed, I shoot her a text:

PIERCE

How'd the tree decorating go?

KELSIE

<insert pictures of both trees>

PIERCE

They look great.

KELSIE

Thank you again for the trees.

PIERCE

You're welcome. Any plans for tomorrow night?

KELSIE

What's going on tomorrow night?

PIERCE

Tree lighting ceremony. There's food and drinks, fun stuff for the kids to do. I was thinking the three of us could go together.

KELSIE

Sure. It sounds like a good time.

PIERCE

It is. Pick you up at 5? We can get dinner first.

KELSIE

Sounds good.

I consider ending the conversation there, but instead I push for a little more.

PIERCE

Did you mean what you said about keeping an open mind?

KELSIE

I did, but I also meant it when I said I was scared. I like you, Pierce, but I'm afraid of getting hurt.

PIERCE

I'm not going to hurt you. Not if I can help it.

KELSIE

That's what I'm afraid of. That you won't be able to help it.

I type:

PIERCE

I understand.

Except before I hit send, I delete it and go with what I really want to say. She might not like it, but it's the truth.

PIERCE

I could get into a car accident or get hit crossing the street. The same goes for you. I understand that because you lost Trent in a fire, the idea of me being a firefighter scares you, but you could date a doctor and he could still get cancer and die. Nothing in life is guaranteed.

I wait for her to respond, praying that my words don't push her away. Bubbles appear, indicating that she's typing, and then disappear. When a text doesn't come through, I panic, thinking I've fucked up, and hit call.

"Hello?" she says softly.

"I shouldn't have texted—"

"You're right."

"I am?" I mean, I know I am, but I wasn't expecting her to say that.

"You are," she agrees. "It's just hard. I like you, and I feel the chemistry between us. I want to see where things go between us, but please be patient with me. I haven't been with anyone since Trent, and knowing you're a firefighter scares the shit out of me. Fires and me—we don't get along."

"We'll take things at your pace," I promise. "And, Kels... Fires and me—we don't get along either."

"There's a mountain of snow! Can I go play?" Jordan's bouncing on the balls of her feet, dying to make a run for it but waiting anxiously for the okay from her mom.

Kelsie glances behind her and frowns. "No, Bug. It's not free."

Jordan's face falls, and Kelsie sighs.

"Actually, I have a bracelet for her... for all of us." I knew this would be an issue, so when I told my mom I was bringing the girls, I asked for three bracelets ahead of time.

Kelsie eyes the bracelets warily, so I explain, "Perks of being the son of the town's entertainment committee's chair." I shrug nonchalantly and grab her wrist. I put a bracelet on it and then place another one on Jordan's.

"C'mon, let's go tubing."

"Yay! Thank you!" Jordan squeals before she takes off ahead of us toward the mountain.

"You do too much for us," Kelsie says as we walk over to where the tubes are. "At this rate, I feel like I'll never be able to repay you. It all just keeps tallying higher."

"Hey," I say, stopping her in place. "This isn't a tit-for-tat sort of thing. There are no tally marks, and I'm not keeping track or score or whatever, and you sure as hell don't owe me anything."

I step toward her and palm her cheek. "I care about you and your daughter, and if I can do something to make you guys happy or make your life easier, I will do it. I'm not paying your rent. I'm spending time with you. Even if you were rich, I still would've bought the bracelets because I'm a gentleman taking the woman he likes and her daughter out."

A small smile spreads across her face, and she nods.

"No more keeping track, Kels. Please."

"Okay. No more keeping track."

"Good. Now grab a tube so I can race you down the mountain."

"Oh, no, I hate heights." Kelsie shakes her head and steps back. "I'm good. You guys go. I'll be waiting down here for you."

"What? It's not even that high."

"Nope, I'm good. Go, have a blast."

"All right." I shrug, grabbing a tube and following Jordan.

We get to the top with our tubes, and Jordan glances at me nervously. "Umm, this is kind of high." Her gaze darts between me and the downslope of the mountain. "I think I'm a little scared."

"Would you feel better if you went down with someone?"

I ask. "I could go down with you if you want, and if you don't like it, you don't have to go down again."

Jordan thinks for a moment, considering it, then peers up at me anxiously, reminding me so much of her mother. "I don't know," she admits. "I want to, but I'm really scared."

"If you don't want to, you don't have to," I tell her, kneeling in front of her. "But I promise, I'll keep you safe."

"Pinky promise?"

She extends her pinky, and I take it, locking it with mine. "I pinky promise."

"Okay, I'll go."

"Hey, Greg," I yell to the kid who's running the mountain. "Can you grab me a two-person tube?"

He exchanges our individual tubes for a two-person tube, and then, after I climb on, I help Jordan get on in front of me.

"You ready?" Greg asks.

"Jordan?"

"I'm ready!" she yells, excitement and worry mixed in her tone.

"Let's do this!" I say, making sure my legs are caging her in securely.

Greg gives us a shove, and we slide down the mountain, the wind whipping around our faces. Jordan screams the entire way down. When we get to the bottom, I have no clue if she was scared shitless or loved it.

But then she climbs out of the tube, and I spot the biggest grin on her face. "That was awesome!"

"What took you so long?" Kelsie asks.

"I was scared," Jordan admits, her eyes as wide as saucers.

"But Pierce pinky-promised to keep me safe, and it was so much fun. We went so fast!" She mimics our speed with her hand, making me chuckle at her dramatics. "Did you see us?"

"I did," Kelsie says. She glances my way, and mouths *thank you*, and I nod once in acknowledgment.

"Can we go again?" Jordan asks.

"Sure," I tell her. "You wanna go with me or by yourself?"

"By myself. You can go with Pierce, Mommy!" Jordan exclaims. "Pierce, pinky promise my mom 'cause she's afraid like I was."

Kelsie looks my way, horror mixed with embarrassment etched in her features, knowing she can't say no to her daughter or she'll be setting a bad example.

I extend my pinky and look at her, waiting to see what she'll do. She eyes it for several seconds before she hooks her pinky around mine and glances up at me with fear in her eyes.

With our pinkies linked, I gently tug her toward me, so our bodies are almost flush. "I pinky promise to keep you safe, Kels," I swear, tightening my hold on her finger. "Always."

She swallows thickly and looks up at me, nodding in understanding that I'm not just referring to the mountain. I'll always keep her and her daughter safe, no matter what it takes.

When we get to the top of the mountain, Jordan insists on going down first. We cheer her on, and once she's cleared the way, Kelsie and I get into our tube. With my thighs clenched around her, my front is pressed against her back, which is stiff as a board.

"Breathe, Kels," I whisper into her ear, causing a tremor to visibly course through her.

She does as I say, her body relaxing against mine, and I can't help but note how her body fits perfectly with mine.

Greg gives us a shove, and we take off down the mountain. Kelsie immediately latches on to my legs, and I wrap an arm around her waist. She screams the entire way down, and when we get to the bottom, she turns around, her bright green eyes locking with mine.

"That was so much fun! Thank you!"

With her body tucked against mine, our faces are only inches apart. All I would have to do is lean in slightly and our mouths would connect. I'm thinking about how I wouldn't dare do it when her mouth connects with mine, her soft lips brushing against my own.

I don't kiss her back at first, shocked that her mouth is on mine, but the second it settles in that she's kissing me, I take full advantage of the moment and kiss her back.

It's not a long kiss, but it's damn good, filled with chemistry, want, and the promises of more. When she pulls back, her gaze is a mixture of lust and shock, her lips are slightly puffy and pink, and all I want to do is kiss her again and again.

"I... I didn't mean to do that," she admits, her cheeks tinting the most beautiful shade of pink.

"It's all good," I say, trying like hell to sound nonchalant. "Feel free to kiss me anytime."

I shoot her a wink, and she opens her mouth to say something, but before the words can make their way out, Jordan runs over.

"Mommy, you did so good! Wanna go again?"

Kelsie's gaze leaves me so she can look at her daughter. "Sure. Wanna ride with me this time?"

"Yes!" Jordan squeals.

We spend the next hour tubing and chatting while we're in line. Kelsie doesn't bring up the kiss, but she doesn't have to for me to know that I'm slowly getting to her, burrowing under her skin, and soon, she'll be mine.

Eleven

KELSIE

I kissed Pierce. In a moment of madness, high on the adrenaline from going down the mountain, I kissed him. And he kissed me back... And holy shit, was it a good kiss.

No, *good* doesn't even cut it. It was mind-blowing, world-altering. Metaphorical sparks flew between us, and if we weren't outside with my daughter—and most of the town—nearby, I would've kept going because the second our mouths touched, I felt the connection I'd been trying to fight between us. When I said I'd be open-minded and give us a chance, I didn't plan for us to kiss the next time we saw each other, but I don't regret it in the slightest. As a matter of fact, I wouldn't be against doing it again.

"The tree lighting is going to happen soon. Want to get some warm drinks and find a seat?" Pierce asks, shaking me from my thoughts.

"Sure," I choke out, wondering if he's still thinking about

the kiss the way I am… the way I've been thinking about it for the last damn hour.

Pierce buys us each a hot chocolate and then we make our way over to where his family is all standing and chatting.

"Kelsie!" Marta smiles. "So nice to see you." She kisses my cheek. "Are you having a good time?"

"We're having a great time. Your son even got me onto that mountain despite my fear of heights."

"It was so much fun," Jordan adds.

"Are you excited about the tree lighting?" Marta asks Jordan.

"Yep. It's the biggest tree I've ever seen in my life." She looks around. "Is Tilly here?"

"She's around here some—"

"Jordan!" Tilly shrieks. "You're here!" She runs over and stops in front of Jordan. "I have hot chocolate too!" The girls bump their cups playfully and are still giggling when the mayor—according to Pierce—begins to speak.

He talks about the tradition of the tree lighting ceremony and then everyone begins the countdown. When we hit one, thousands of twinkling, multi-colored lights appear, bringing the beautiful tree to life as fake snow is blown into the air, making the event even more magical. The crowd cheers, and Christmas music begins to play.

Everyone around me, including Tilly and Jordan, starts dancing, and when I glance up at Pierce, he's smiling down at me.

"What?" I breathe, my eyes landing on his lips, wishing I could taste him again.

"Dance with me."

He extends his hand, and without thought, I take it, letting him pull me flush against him. The music is fast-paced and upbeat, and Pierce has no problem dancing like nobody is watching. At one point, when the girls are shaking their butts to the music, Pierce joins in, making me push him away and crack up laughing.

"You look gorgeous like this," he murmurs, pulling me into his arms when a slower song comes on. He wraps his arms around my waist as mine go to his neck.

"Like what?" I ask, confused because I'm wearing a simple winter coat, jeans, and boots. Nothing special...

"Happy," he says, shocking me with his admission. "You have the most beautiful smile, and your laughter is so addicting. I could listen to it for hours."

"You're acting like this is the first time you've seen me smile or heard me laugh." I roll my eyes, playing off his words.

"It's not, but I don't see it enough. If it were up to me, you would smile and laugh as often as possible every day. I think tonight is the first time since I've met you that you let loose, left all the outside bullshit out, and just had fun."

I want to argue with him and tell him that's not true, but he's not wrong. Most days, I'm just trying to survive. Take care of my daughter. Provide a roof over her head and keep her belly fed. And because of that, sometimes I forget to actually enjoy life.

"It's because of you," I admit. "You make me smile and laugh. And it's not just me... Jordan too."

He opens his mouth to respond, but before he can,

someone shouts, "Mistletoe!"

"What?" I look over Pierce's shoulder and find Marta grinning from ear to ear.

"Mistletoe," she repeats, pointing up.

I glance up and see we're standing under a mistletoe hanging from the decorations.

"You know what that means," Pierce says with a glimmer of mischief in his eyes. "You have to kiss me."

"I have to kiss you?" I scoff, suddenly nervous. Kissing him in the heat of the moment without any eyes on us was one thing, but here, with everyone watching. No way. "Why can't you kiss—"

My question is cut off when Pierce frames my face between his hands and brushes his lips against mine. The moment our mouths touch, it's as if the entire world ceases to exist, and it's just Pierce and me. One second our mouths are moving against one another, and the next, his tongue is caressing my own. His hands glide down my neck, over my arms, and land on the curves of my hips, pulling me closer to him. It's cold outside, yet in Pierce's arms, I feel nothing except warmth.

All too soon, he pulls back, ending the kiss, and I find myself once again wanting to be back in his embrace, craving the warmth he emits.

He presses his forehead against mine and sighs. "So damn sweet. Two kisses, and you already got me addicted like a kid in a candy store."

"Sugar's bad for you," I half-joke, trying to make light of his words because I have no idea what the hell I'm doing. With Trent, it was easy. I was young and carefree. He was cute and fun, and we fell fast and hard like most teenagers do. It's different with Pierce, though. I can't quite put my finger on it—and maybe that's because I've only ever loved and been with one guy in my life—but when he looks at me, touches me, kisses me...it feels more intense.

"Maybe," Pierce says, his lust-filled eyes meeting mine, "but it's still damn good."

We spend a little while longer with Pierce's family—thankfully, nobody comments on the kiss—before we say good night and Pierce drives us home.

He walks us to the door, and I debate whether to invite him in. On one hand, we just spent hours together. On the other, it was with a bunch of other people, and I'd really love to spend some time with him alone.

"Would you like to come in?" I ask once Jordan's disappeared into her room to get ready for bed. I should bathe her, but it's late, and she's exhausted.

"I'd love to," he says, stepping inside.

I go about putting Jordan to bed, and I'm shocked when Pierce joins me to say good night as I perform our nightly routine, where I kiss her and her stuffed ladybug, Dots. As her eyes flutter closed, I know she'll be asleep before I even close her door.

Now that it's quiet and just the two of us, I'm unsure of what to do or say. Pierce must realize that because he smiles softly and takes my hand in his, guiding us down the hallway. I assume he's taking me to my bedroom and I'm about to tell him I'm nowhere near ready for that, when he passes my room and goes to the back door that leads out to the screened-in patio. He clicks on the heating lamp and sits us on the bench-swing Gertrude left, grabbing the throw blanket I left out here and sliding it across our laps.

It's a chilly night, but it feels like summertime between the heating lamp, the blanket, and Pierce holding me in his arms.

We sway in silence for a few minutes, enjoying the quiet. He snuggles me closer, and my head goes to his shoulder as I sigh into his side, soaking in his warmth and comfort. I've never felt like this before, so safe and protected. His job scares the hell out of me, but I believe him when he says he'll never hurt me, and he'll always keep us safe. For so long, it felt like my life was filled with chaos, and many days it still does, but when I'm with Pierce, it's as if everything calms, and I'm able to breathe.

"What's going through your head?" Pierce asks, breaking through my thoughts. I glance up at him, our eyes locking, but instead of answering him, I do what I really want to do. Lifting my head, I lean in and brush my lips against his. They're warm and strong, and when he kisses me back, they mold to mine like two pieces of a puzzle that fit perfectly together.

The kiss quickly intensifies, our tongues stroking each other's. I moan into his mouth, desperate for more, and he lifts me into his lap, somehow managing to keep the blanket wrapped around us.

With my legs on either side of him, he tugs me closer. One hand wraps around my waist, and the other delves into my hair, holding my face to his. We kiss for God knows how long, making out like a couple of horny teenagers, and I love it. The simplicity of it, the connection I feel with him. When we break apart, I pout, not wanting it to end. Pierce must be on the same page as me because his lips trail down my jawline and neck, peppering kisses along my flesh that go straight through my body, ending at the apex of my legs.

"Pierce," I gasp when my hips rock against his groin, and pleasure—enough to feel good but not enough to get me off—courses through me.

"I've got you, sweetheart," he murmurs, pulling my face down to his so our lips connect once again, his tongue delving into my mouth. He tastes like the perfect combination of lust, want, and need, and when he grips the curve of my hip, grinding me back and forth against his hardness, my body convulses as pleasure rushes through me. I've never come this hard in my life, and he hasn't even taken my clothes off. I can't imagine how intense it would be without our clothes on, neither of us holding back.

As I come down from my orgasm, our kissing slows down and then comes to a stop. When our eyes meet, embarrassment starts to creep up as the reality of what we just did—what *I* just did—hits.

But just before the feeling can settle in, a small smile spreads across Pierce's face. "That was the most beautiful thing I've ever felt. I can't wait to make you come over and over again in my bed." He tightens his hold on my hair, locking eyes with me. "Tell me you felt it, Kels, the way your body responded to mine. It's like you were made for me."

"I felt it," I admit, getting aroused by his dirty talk. "I feel it."

"Good," he says, leaning in and kissing me again. "Because you're mine, sweetheart, and now that I've gotten you in my arms, I have no intention of ever letting you go."

He presses his lips to mine for one more quick kiss before he lifts me in his arms and carries me inside as my head wraps around his declaration.

You're mine...

I'm his.

And crazily enough, I'm okay with that.

We stop at the bathroom, and he sets me down. When I look at him in confusion, he says, "So you can clean up. As much as I'd love to take you to bed, I don't want our first time to be with your daughter across the hall."

"You know parents do have sex with their kids in the house," I say with a laugh. "That's how siblings are born."

"I know." He smirks. "But when I'm inside you for the first time, I plan to make you scream my name all night long."

Twelve

PIERCE

PIERCE

Any fun weekend plans?

I'M SITTING IN MY LIVING ROOM, STARING AT THE phone, waiting for Kelsie to text me back. It's been less than twelve hours since I last saw her—since she kissed me, then straddled me, and came on my lap. Since I declared that she's mine and she didn't deny it—and I'm already missing her like crazy.

It's Saturday and I'm bored. I could probably find something to do, but what I really want is to spend more time with her and Jordan. Get to know them better.

KELSIE

If you include cleaning the house as fun then we're having a blast.

PIERCE

How about you take a break from cleaning and go ice skating with me?

KELSIE

What time are you picking us up?

Yes! Now that's what I'm talking about.

PIERCE

Thirty minutes?

KELSIE

See you soon!

I let Cinder out to do her business, grab my skates since I have my own, and head out to pick up the girls. They're sitting outside on the front porch when I arrive, Jordan practically bouncing in place.

I help the girls into my truck then we take off to the city. We have an indoor rink in town, but the one I'm taking them to is outdoors. I think the girls will appreciate the vibe. They love all things Christmas, and the rink we're going to is decked out for the holidays.

It's about an hour drive, so we stop to grab a couple of coffees and hot chocolate for Jordan. Once we arrive at the rink, I rent them skates and then we head onto the ice.

"Do you need any help?" I ask them, extending my hand like a gentleman. My brothers and I grew up playing hockey, so I'm a damn good skater.

"Nope," both girls say in unison, gliding onto the ice.

"Mommy used to skate when she was little," Jordan says, "and me too."

"You're still little," Kelsie says with a laugh.

"I'm five. I'm not little," Jordan argues.

"Okay," Kelsie concedes.

Jordan takes off around the rink, and I extend my hand for Kelsie, hoping she'll take it. She stares at it for several seconds, and I wait patiently for her to decide. Last night, we were caught up in the moment. We kissed at the light ceremony and allowed the sizzling chemistry between us to guide our actions at her place. I'd be lying if I said I wasn't worried she might be having second thoughts now that she's come down from her orgasm.

When she threads her fingers through mine, I pull her toward me for a kiss, but she shakes her head. "Jordan might see."

I nod in understanding. I don't have a kid, so I don't know how it works. Though, if I were in her position, I'd want to make sure whatever's going on between us was serious before I involved my child.

We spend the morning skating then have lunch at a nearby burger place. When we're walking back to the truck, Jordan spots a park, so we end up spending the afternoon playing on the equipment.

When I drop the girls off and go back to my place, it's quiet, and I don't like it. I play fetch with Cinder for a bit, then throw a load of laundry into the washer. I go through each room, picking up even though the place is spotless—because it's not lived in. The opposite of Kelsie's place. It might be small, and they may not have any money, but she's made sure to fill that place with love.

I'm sitting on my couch, staring at the fireplace and

wondering if it'd make me look desperate if I invited myself over for dinner, when a text from Kelsie comes through:

KELSIE

**Jordan and I are doing a pizza and movie night.
If you don't have plans, you're welcome to join.**

I'm out of my seat and into my truck so fast I forget to text her back until I'm almost out of the ranch and onto the main road. Once I let her know I'm on my way, I text my nephew to offer him twenty bucks to let Cinder out later. He's a teenager who can always use the money, so of course he says it's no problem.

"I THINK SHE'S OUT." KELSEY GLANCES DOWN AT A snoring Jordan and giggles softly. "Let me put her to bed." She gathers her up and disappears down the hall, returning a few minutes later. "Out like a light."

"Kid can sleep, huh?" On the way home from ice skating, Jordan passed out and didn't wake up until we got home.

"Play hard, sleep harder," she says with a laugh. She glances at the paused Disney movie and then back at me. "If you don't have anywhere to be, we can...umm...watch a more adult movie." She shrugs shyly, and I reach out and grab her hand, tugging her to me.

"There's absolutely nowhere else I want or need to be." I frame her face and look into her beautiful emerald eyes. "I want to kiss you, Kels. Can I kiss you?"

"I think we passed your need to ask if you can kiss me around the time I orgasmed in your lap," she says off-handedly. Realizing what she just said, her eyes widen, and she flushes a dark shade of pink.

"Last night, the chemistry was flowing, and the hormones were high. I don't want you to do anything you'll regret."

"I don't regret anything we did last night," she says, shaking her head. "And I won't regret kissing you now."

The second her words stop, her mouth attacks mine, her tongue penetrating past my parted lips. We kiss like this for several minutes, until I feel her grind against my groin. And I know if I don't stop things now, I might not ever...

So, with every ounce of restraint I have, I end the kiss and pull her off me, setting her down next to me. When she pouts, not thrilled about me ending our make-out session, I run my finger across the seam of her lips then lean in and give her a soft kiss.

"As much as I want things to escalate, I meant what I told you before: when we're together for the first time, I want to be able to take my time with you, make you scream my name. And that can't happen with Jordan sleeping in the other room."

She rolls her eyes, but the pout is replaced with a small smile. "Fine. Pick a movie." She hands me the remote then lies on the opposite end of the couch.

I swipe through several movies, then stop on one she says she loves and click play. I honestly don't care what we watch—just hanging out with Kelsie is good enough for me.

We watch the movie briefly before I start craving her

touch. It's crazy how much of an addiction she's become in such a short amount of time. Since she looks comfortable the way she is, with her head on the pillow, I lift her feet onto my lap and start massaging her sock-clad feet.

"That feels good," she moans quietly.

"How does this feel?" I ask, moving my fingers to her calves.

"Like heaven."

I chuckle and keep massaging until she shifts slightly and says, "Higher."

I pause what I'm doing and stare at her, finding her now on her back with her legs open enough for me to see up the tiny cotton shorts she's wearing.

I can see what she's doing, and a part of me wants to stop it from happening, but the look of unadulterated lust in her eyes has me obeying her request.

Grabbing the blanket off the back of the couch, I drop it on top of us, just in case Jordan were to walk out. I shift closer to Kelsie so her feet are dangling on the other side of my body and the backs of her knees are resting on my lap. Then I go back to massaging her creamy flesh for several minutes before she spreads her thighs even more and says once again, "Higher."

Fuck, this woman is going to be the death of me. With my eyes still on the screen, since hers are, I slide my fingers along the inside of her thighs and up one of the gaps in her shorts. When my fingers reach her underwear, it's damp.

Pushing the material to the side, I run my fingers up her pussy lips. There's a tiny bit of hair there, and even though I can't see it, I imagine it's trimmed neatly, just the way I like it.

With my fingertips, I part her lips and push two fingers into her warmth, making her moan loudly. When I pull back, she swings her gaze to me.

"Be quiet so we don't wake up Jordan."

"She won't wake up."

"I'm not risking it." I push my fingers back inside her hole. "You make a noise, I stop. You want to come, be quiet." Despite her glare, her walls clench around my digits, telling me she likes this game.

I go back to fucking her slowly and deeply, and she stays quiet, until I find her G-spot. And then she groans. It's not loud, but I can hear it, so I retreat my fingers.

"Pierce!" she whisper-yells.

"Are you going to be quiet?"

I trace the outline of her pussy with the pads of my fingers, and she stifles a moan.

"Yes, please, I'll be quiet," she whispers.

"Good girl."

My fingers penetrate her once again, and she covers her mouth with the pillow to silence her moans.

"Nuh-uh," I taunt. "I want to see you come all over my fingers."

She lifts her face and glares, but it quickly morphs into a look of pleasure when my thumb lands on her clit. "Yes, right there," she begs.

Even though that counts as making a noise, I love that she's telling me what she likes, so I let it go, continuing to massage her clit. When her orgasm hits, it's hard, and her entire body tightens. I'm watching her, so I see her mouth open as her pussy grips my fingers, and she comes silently, making me wish I could hear her scream.

When she's come down from her high, I assume she's standing to get cleaned up, so I'm taken aback when she grabs the blanket and throws it over us with one hand, finding my dick with the other.

"What are you doing?" I whisper dumbly.

"About to make you come...quietly."

With a flirty wink, she goes about giving me the best damn hand job of my life. I'm close to blowing my load when she dives under the blanket and shocks the hell out of me by taking me into her mouth. Her wet lips have just wrapped around the head of my cock when I explode into her mouth, a low growl crawling its way up my throat and threatening to come out.

When she lifts her head back up, she smiles sweetly then licks her now-plump lips.

"That was...unexpected," I rasp, making her laugh.

"Didn't want to get the blanket dirty." She shrugs, and I chuckle at her playfulness, loving this side of her.

"Get up here and kiss me." I pull her into my lap and wrap the blanket around us, as if that will make a difference, and kiss the hell out of her for several minutes before I pull back gently, hating what I need to say next. "I have to get going."

"It's late. You could stay..."

"As much as I love the idea of that, you didn't even want to kiss me in front of Jordan, so I don't think you'll be okay with her waking up and finding me here."

She nods in agreement, her lips curving down into a frown. I hate that she's sad about me leaving, but I also love it because it means my feelings aren't one-sided.

"I work for the next two days, but you can text or call me anytime."

"Okay," she concedes, climbing off me.

I grab my keys and give her a kiss goodbye.

When I go to pull back, she holds on for a moment longer. "Be careful," she says, and I know she isn't talking about driving home. She's worried about me going to work.

Because I'm a firefighter.

And my woman is terrified of fires.

"Always," I murmur against her lips.

Thirteen

KELSIE

"Hey, Kelsie, the elementary school is on the phone for you."

Since the school only calls for one reason during the day—when something has happened to your child—I rush over to the phone. "Hello, this is Kelsie Albright."

"Hello, Ms. Albright. This is Joan in the front office. Sorry to call you at work, but we sent a message and haven't heard back."

I pull my phone out of my pocket and check the screen. Sure enough, there's a missed call, a voicemail, a text message, and an email stating that the school must close due to a broken heater and that parents need to pick up their kids.

"I'm sorry," I tell her. "The café was busy, and I didn't feel it vibrate."

"No worries, dear. There are still a few kids whose parents we haven't gotten ahold of, either. How soon can you be here to pick up Jordan?"

I glance around at the bustling café, the morning rush still in full swing, and sigh. "I'll be there as soon as I can."

We hang up, and I try to find Dorothy. Aside from leaving her during the busiest time, I'm about to lose a ton of money between my hourly wage and tips, but that's just the way life goes sometimes.

"Everything okay?" Dorothy asks when I find her talking to a couple of customers at the table in the corner.

"No." I smile nervously, having no doubt that despite Dorothy being nice, one day, she's going to have enough of the shit that comes with me being a single mom and fire me. I just have to hope today isn't that day. "The elementary school's heater broke, so the kids were all sent home. I'm sorry... I need to go get Jordan. I don't have anyone else—"

"Kelsie, breathe," she coos, guiding us away from the table so we're alone. "It's okay. Family comes first. Go get your little girl. I can stay and cover your tables."

"Okay, thanks," I mutter, already trying to figure out my bills without an entire day of wages.

When I arrive at the school, Jordan is the last one left, and I feel like the worst mom in the world for not checking my phone earlier. The second she sees me, she smiles wide and runs over, wrapping her arms around me.

"It's a no-school day! Can we have a movie day?"

"Sure," I tell her.

After thanking the secretary for watching her until I could get there and signing her out, we head home.

Despite my money situation looming in the back of my

mind, Jordan and I have a great mother-daughter day. After we watch a movie, we eat lunch and then play spa, giving each other manis and pedis. Afterward, Jordan insists on doing my hair and makeup, which takes us to dinner and bath time.

As I'm tucking her into bed, my phone goes off. When I check it, my heart sinks because it's the school letting us know that due to the cold weather and the heater still being out, school is canceled for another day.

After a therapeutic cry in the shower, I grab my phone to call Dorothy to let her know that I'll be missing work again, when Pierce's number flashes across my screen.

"Hey," I say, trying to sound upbeat despite my sour mood. The last thing I want is for him to know about my money situation. Technically, he already knows since he's the one who bailed me out at the grocery store and my daughter loves to unintentionally spill our business to him every chance she gets, but he doesn't need to know just how bad it is. I'm not sure I could handle the sound of pity in his voice. He would try to help me out, but there's nothing he can do without giving me money that I would never take.

"Hey," he says back. "How was your day?"

"Good," I tell him, wondering how the hell the man manages to sound as sexy over the phone as he does in person. I mean, seriously, does he have a single flaw?

He's a firefighter, my brain reminds me. Which is the biggest flaw he could have. Yet, it didn't stop me from letting him make me come twice, declare me as his, or from me giving him a hand job that ended with him shooting his load down my throat.

Despite my trying to push him away, I've caught feelings for Pierce. I thought maybe once he wasn't around, the fog would clear from my brain, and I would chalk it all up to not being touched in years and being horny. Then we spent the past two days texting and video chatting while he was working, and I've only fallen harder, telling me these feelings I have for him are real and aren't going anywhere—and that's scary as hell.

"I heard the elementary school is shut down because the heater isn't working," he says, steering me back to the now.

"Yeah." I clear my throat. "Jordan and I made it a girls' day."

"Nice. I'm actually watching Tilly tomorrow. My brother took Sara on a trip to celebrate their anniversary. My mom was supposed to watch her, but my dad twisted his ankle and is acting like a big baby, so she's playing nurse."

"You're watching Tilly tomorrow? You don't have to work?"

"I got off this morning. We work forty-eight hours on and ninety-six hours off."

"Wow, you get four days off?" What I wouldn't give to only have to work two days a week.

"Yeah." He chuckles. "It's nice having four days off, but sometimes I get bored. I'll usually end up back at the station, hanging out with the guys or helping my brother on the ranch."

"I think I need to become a firefighter," I joke. "Those hours are awesome."

"Does that mean you're not *completely* anti-firefighter?"

"I'm not anti-firefighter," I confess. "I'm just scared. The night Jordan and I lost Trent was terrifying. I thought we were all going to die, and I felt so helpless. Jordan and I almost did die, and Trent lost his life. I don't know what I would do if something happened to you."

"I get it," he says, "and I'm not trying to downplay what happened because you're right, fires are scary as hell. But I don't go into them without my team of men, and we're always dressed in our bunker gear. I'm a trained professional. You don't have to worry about me."

"Only I will," I tell him. "You're already too far under my skin for me not to worry about you."

"I like the sound of that," he says. "Me under your skin. But before that can happen, you'll have to let me take you out on an actual date."

"As nice as that sounds, right now isn't the best time. Jordan's home and—"

"You got me off track," he says with a chuckle. "Jordan is the reason for my call."

"Oh?" I say curiously.

"I imagine you have to go to work tomorrow, so I'm calling to offer my babysitting services."

"You're offering to watch Jordan for me tomorrow?" I ask in shock at the turn of events. I went from thinking he was calling to ask me out on a date to him offering to watch my daughter so I could go to work.

"You'd actually be doing me a favor," he says. "My niece said I'm boring, and she'd be thrilled to spend the day with Jordan."

Well, when he puts it like that... "That would actually be great. Thank you."

"Wow, did you just agree without argument?"

"I did," I reply with a laugh. "The truth is, I was dreading calling out from work, and I was just thinking about what I would do when you called, so you're saving my butt."

"Anytime, Kels," he says. "Are you okay with us hanging at your place? I planned to take them to the ranch in the morning to see the animals but figured we could go back to your place in the afternoon. That way, the girls can play in Jordan's room."

"Of course. I'll give you my key in the morning."

My lack of concern over allowing him to be in my home and watch my daughter makes me realize how much I already trust Pierce—which is both comforting and frightening.

After we go over what time he'll pick her up, we say good night since we both have to get up early tomorrow.

When Jordan wakes up, and I tell her she'll be spending the day with Tilly and Pierce, you'd think I told her she's going to Disney she gets so excited.

Once Pierce arrives, I remind Jordan to behave and take off to work. The day flies by. Aside from the few pictures Pierce sent me of the girls with the horses and then one more text letting me know they're at my house and will see me when I get home, I haven't heard from him.

As I'm about to clock out from my shift, I overhear Dorothy mention that Nancy, who works the afternoon shift, caught a bug. I hate to take advantage of Pierce watching Jordan, but if I can snag this shift, it would compensate for the one I missed yesterday. I send a text to Pierce asking if it'd be okay. When he texts back, telling me they're all good and he's got everything under control at my house, I sigh in relief.

"THANK YOU SO MUCH FOR COVERING FOR NANCY," Dorothy says when I clock out several hours later, beyond thankful to Pierce for watching Jordan. Not only did I make back what I lost yesterday, but apparently, the afternoons are busier than the mornings, so I made double what I usually make.

"You're welcome. See you tomorrow."

The walk home is quick, but when I arrive at my house, I do a double take, wondering if I'm at the right place. When I left this morning, there were no lights on my house or my yard, but now, the entire place is covered in Christmas lights and decorations.

And not just any decorations—it looks like Disney threw up all over the yard. Several of the Disney princesses are on one side, with the characters from *Frozen* on the other. Mickey and Minnie are on the roof, sitting in a sled with Pluto pulling them. My door is decorated like a giant present, and there are more princesses with snowflakes in the windows. Even the sidewalk has lit-up candy canes trailing up both sides.

I'm still staring at it all in shock and awe when the front door opens, and the girls run out, followed by Pierce.

"Mommy! Mommy! Did you see all the decorations?"

Jordan exclaims.

"They're kind of hard to miss, Bug," I say with a small laugh. "You guys were busy."

"Pierce let us help, and it was so much fun! I got to pick out all the stuff, and he said tomorrow he's gonna enter us in the battle."

The battle of lights. I completely forgot about that. The chances of us winning are small, but he spent the day decorating our house so Jordan could enter the battle. Because she's hoping to win the money for me to pay our bills.

My eyes meet his, and he looks nervous, as if he's unsure how I'll react to what he did without telling me. Honestly, until this moment, I wasn't sure myself, but as I watch my daughter smiling because she's so happy and proud and excited, the only thing I can feel is gratefulness toward the man who goes out of his way to make my daughter and me happy every chance he gets.

"Thank you," I tell him when I reach him. "This is amazing."

I give him a quick kiss on his cheek, and when I step back, he asks, "You're not mad?"

"No. If you had asked, I would've said no. Which is exactly why you didn't." I shrug, and he smiles, knowing I'm not wrong. "And while I don't even want to know how much you spent on all this"—probably as much if not more than the amount of the prize—"I know you did this for my daughter and me. You're a wonderful guy, Pierce, and we're so lucky to have you in our lives."

Fourteen

KELSIE

"Good morning, what can I get—" I glance up from my notepad where I take my orders and am met with hazel eyes that I've recently come to know all too well.

"Hi," I say dumbly when Pierce smiles at me. Today, he's freshly shaved, and when that sexy dimple pops out—not for the first time begging me to lick it—I giggle to myself at the face Pierce would make if I actually acted on it.

"What's so funny?" he asks, tilting his head to the side.

"Huh?"

"You laughed."

Oh, shit! Did I laugh out loud? Jesus, I need to get a grip.

"It was nothing," I mutter. "So, to what do I owe the pleasure of you showing up here?" I ask, changing the subject. "Was babysitting, putting up a house full of lights, and then spending the evening watching Disney movies not enough for you?" I joke, remembering the way he fell asleep on my couch last night halfway through Cinderella. I felt bad waking him up, even though he had to get Tilly home. She needed to get some sleep and get ready for school this morning, since the heating system has been fixed and they're returning to school.

Pierce's features turn smoldering as he leans in and cups the side of my face. "If you're implying that it's even remotely possible that I could be sick of you, you need to get that shit out of your head right now." His lips brush my own, and my stomach knots at the small yet intimate gesture.

He presses his forehead against mine and sighs. "Who needs coffee when I get to taste you?"

For a brief moment, I forget we're in a public place, surrounded by people who know Pierce and will no doubt be talking—until I open my eyes and find Dorothy knowingly smirking at me.

"Oh God," I moan, closing my eyes. "Everyone just saw you kiss me."

"Good," Pierce says. "Now they know you're mine. So, all those guys who've been eyeing you will know they don't stand a chance."

I lift my head and shake it, having no clue what the hell he's going on about.

"Are you here for coffee or just to make a public display of affection?" I try to glare at him, but I know it doesn't hit its mark when he simply smiles at me in amusement.

"Both," he says with a nonchalant shrug. "I'll have the breakfast special, coffee with a hint of milk and sugar, and you on the side." He rakes his gaze down me, and I playfully push away from him.

"One breakfast special coming up... minus the side of me." When he pouts, I laugh. "In case you didn't notice, I'm at work."

Without giving him a chance to argue, I walk away, putting a little more sway in my hips to mess with him. When I hear him groan, I know it worked.

"Have dinner with me."

"Tonight?" It's day two of Pierce visiting me at the café, and as much as I want to be annoyed, I can't help but feel a little special.

According to Dorothy, Pierce never hangs out at the café—which is something I figured since I've never seen him during any of my shifts, until now. Also, from what several patrons have told me, Pierce never seeks out or talks to any women either...until now.

I don't know what about me has him suddenly wanting more, but I won't question it. The more I get to know him, the harder I fall. I'm still scared shitless, but I'm starting to think Pierce is worth the risk.

"Yes, tonight," he says. "I was thinking you and Jordan could come over to my place, and I could cook. Afterward, we can hop on my golf cart and ride around, looking at lights. The battle has started, so everyone's lights are up."

The way he includes Jordan instead of asking me to find a sitter has me falling that much harder for this man. He's single without any kids and doesn't have to be bogged down by a child, yet he offers to babysit and includes her in our plans without thought.

"That sounds like fun," I tell him. "Jordan will love checking out all the lights."

"Good," he says, standing since he's finished his breakfast and coffee. "I'll pick you up around four o'clock." He leans down and kisses me. "Have a good day, sweetheart."

"Wow! Those lights are so cool!" Jordan points at the lights on a house, her eyes wide in awe. There are hundreds of homes on the map, and I'm almost positive Pierce has taken us to most of them. It's chilly outside, but he had the foresight to grab warm blankets that we're currently snuggled up in while Pierce drives us around from house to house on his fancy golf cart that has all the bells and whistles, including windows to keep the wind out.

It's been a wonderful night. Dinner was delicious—he cooked us spaghetti and meatballs, which is Jordan's favorite—and afterward, he took us to see the horses Jordan loves before heading out to look at the lights.

"Not as cool as ours," Pierce says back to Jordan with a scoff, "but they're decent."

I laugh at his go-to response and shake my head, knowing there's no way we're going to win the battle of the lights contest. Our lights are beautiful, and Jordan loves them so much, which is all that really matters. But these people go all out, clearly taking this contest seriously. I can't even tell you who will win, though it definitely won't be us.

We ride around for a bit longer and eventually return to our place. I should probably call it a night since we have school and work in the morning, but I'm craving some alone time with Pierce, and it's Jordan's bedtime.

"Want to come in?" I ask when he parks in our driveway.

"You couldn't keep me away," he murmurs with a grin.

Jordan's bedtime routine is done quickly, thanks to her being exhausted. Then it's just Pierce and me.

"Want some coffee or—"

Before I finish my question, Pierce spins me around and pushes me up against the fridge—where I was looking to see what I have to offer him. The door slams shut as my body presses against the cold steel. Pierce gathers my hands in his and brings them over my head, using the freezer door to hold them.

Our eyes briefly meet, and then he fuses his mouth to mine, his tongue sliding inside and tangling with my own. With his body flush against mine, his hardness presses up against me. Without breaking our kiss, I lift my leg slightly and run my knee along his length, causing Pierce to moan into my mouth.

"Fuck, Kels," he says breathlessly as if he were running a marathon instead of kissing me. "Do you have any idea how goddamn sexy you are? How hard it is to be around you and not be able to touch you?"

Without waiting for me to answer, he drags his fingers

along the outside curve of my breast and down my side, not stopping until he gets to the bend of my knee. He trails fiery kisses down my neck as he hitches my leg around his waist. Between his kisses and touches, my brain is mush. I have no idea what he's doing or what his goal is, until the top of his thigh strokes my center through the thin material of the pajama pants I changed into when we got home.

"Oh God," I groan when he strokes me harder, taking me higher and higher, as he hits my clit with the perfect amount of pressure.

"That's it, sweetheart," he murmurs, sucking and licking my overheated flesh as he continues to stroke me back and forth, working me up to the point where I'm dangling off the edge. "Come for me."

He caresses me once more, and that's all I need to fall off the precipice. His mouth descends on mine, swallowing down my moans as I come, hard. He doesn't stop his assault on my clit and mouth until I'm forced to push him away because the physical sensations he's eliciting are too much. In typical Pierce fashion, he doesn't move far, continuing to hold me as I come down from my orgasm.

"I could watch you do that every day for the rest of my life," he croons, peppering soft kisses to my jawline, cheeks, and lastly my lips.

"Every day?" I choke out. "I'm not sure my body could handle that."

He grins devilishly. "I'm okay with us finding out."

Fifteen

PIERCE

SARA

Just thought I'd let you know that Jordan is spending the night with Tilly tonight...

PIERCE

I owe you forever.

SARA

I know.

I SEND HER A ROLLING EYE EMOJI, THEN PULL UP KELSIE'S name and hit call, already planning our date in my head. When I mentioned to my mom that I wanted to take Kelsie out on a real date, but Kelsie wasn't keen on relying on others, Mom told me she'd handle it. And based on Sara's text, she came through in the best way.

"Let me guess," Kelsie says when she answers, "you want

NIKKI ASH

to know if I'll go out with you."

"Uh," I splutter, unsure what to say since I wasn't anticipating that response from her.

Kelsie laughs through the phone, and I sigh in relief. "You're lucky you're so cute," she says, "or I might be upset that you manipulated your way into making sure I was kid-free so you could take me out."

"In my defense, I only told my mom I wanted to take you out. The rest was her and Sara."

"Yeah, yeah," she says, her tone filled with mirth. "Jordan is packing for her sleepover as we speak. What time are you picking me up?"

I glance at the time. I'll need to let Cinder out, take a shower, and make reservations. "Six good?"

"Yep, see you then."

At six o'clock on the dot, I pull up to Kelsie's house with a bouquet of flowers. I went with pink roses since they're pretty and feminine like her, and I don't know what her favorite flowers are—something I need to ask her.

When she opens the door, dressed in a gray sweater dress that molds to every one of her sexy curves and knee-high boots that show off her creamy thighs, I halt in my place, needing to take her in. Her auburn hair has been straightened, and she's wearing a bit of makeup, making her lips look extra plump and kissable and her beautiful green eyes pop. I love every version of Kelsie I've had the pleasure of seeing, whether she's in mom-mode or working at the café, but this version of her just might be my favorite.

"You look gorgeous," I tell her, leaning in and kissing her

170

cheek, not wanting to fuck up her lipstick *yet*.

"Thank you. It's been a long time since I had the time to actually do my hair and makeup." She shrugs a shoulder. "I feel like a grown woman."

"And you definitely look like one," I agree, doing one more sweep over her face and body. When my gaze meets hers, her cheeks are an adorable shade of pink.

"For you." I hand her the bouquet, and her eyes widen in excitement.

"Wow!" She takes them from me. "They're so pretty." She brings the roses up to her nose and inhales. "And they smell so good. Thank you."

We walk inside, and she sets them in the center of the table. "Good thing you got a vase because I don't own one." She admires them for a few seconds, spreads them out, then snaps a picture with her phone. "Sorry," she says, hitting me with a shy smile over her shoulder. "I just love flowers so much."

Her words crack at the end, and I reach out to turn her around, finding her eyes glassy with emotion. "What's wrong?"

"Nothing." She shakes her head and laughs. "I just always read about guys buying women flowers in my romance books, and I realized this is the first time someone has bought me flowers. I don't know why that's making me so emotional. I swear I'm not crazy," she mutters, making us laugh.

"Hey," I tell her, gripping the curves of her hips and pulling her toward me. "You were in a serious relationship that ended under awful conditions. I'd be more concerned if you didn't have any emotions or hesitations about moving forward."

"Thank you," she says, circling her arms around my neck. "You have no idea what your patience and understanding mean to me."

She lifts slightly and brushes her soft lips against mine. The sweet taste of her has me wanting to say, 'fuck the date,' and take her straight to bed. Instead, I pull back and take her hand in mine to get us out of this house—and away from the temptation.

"So, what's on the agenda?" Kelsie asks once we're in the truck and driving down her street.

"I was thinking Italian for dinner and pool at the billiards afterward."

It's nothing fancy—though the restaurant is on the more upscale end—but it will allow us plenty of time to talk and get to know one another. Since she's been busy being a mom, I figured taking her somewhere she wouldn't go with her daughter would be fun.

"That sounds great," she says with a smile. "Are you good at pool?"

"I'm decent."

"Decent, my ass!" Kelsie shouts over the music playing on the jukebox. "You're a damn shark!"

She glares at me playfully and downs a shot, and I throw

my head back with a laugh, completely enthralled by the woman in front of me.

Dinner was perfect. The food was delicious, and the conversation flowed naturally. Afterward, I took her to Eightball, the billiards bar my brothers and I frequent when we have boys' nights. At first, she was a bit hesitant, clearly out of her element, but once the alcohol was flowing through her veins, she started to let loose.

"Admit it," she says, tugging on the front of my shirt so our bodies collide with one another. "Admit you're a pool shark."

I chuckle at her dramatics and palm her cheek. "I don't know what you're talking about," I joke.

Before she can argue, my mouth descends on hers and my tongue delves between her parted lips. When her body leans against mine and she moans into my mouth, I know I've successfully distracted her.

"I might've played a time or two," I murmur against her lips.

"Is there anything you're not good at?" she whispers, pecking my lips. "You're like the perfect man, Pierce."

"I'm not perfect," I mutter, shaking my head and kissing her again. "Nobody's perfect."

"Maybe not." She sighs. "But I'm starting to think you're perfect for me."

"Adler!"

"What?" I glance up from where I'm lifting weights.

"I called your name three times. You didn't hear me?" Wade asks, quirking a brow.

"Sorry, man. Guess I have a lot on my mind."

"More like you have *someone* on your mind." Wade smirks. "How's it going with Kelsie, anyway?"

"Good."

I can't help but grin as I remember our date. I don't recall the last time I enjoyed myself the way I did last night. We laughed, ate, drank, and flirted. It was one of the best dates I've been on, and at the end of the night, I hated having to kiss her good night and walk away. She'd let loose and had a good amount to drink, so the last thing I wanted was for her to regret spending the night with me. I also knew I had to get up early this morning to go to work.

My phone dings with a text from Kelsie. I smile at the beginning of her message, then sigh at the second half:

KELSIE

> Morning! Last night was so much fun. I can't remember the last time I enjoyed myself like that. Dorothy asked if I could come in to cover a shift for someone who called out sick, so if you text and I don't answer, that's why.

I consider telling her that she already worked five days this week and she deserves a break, but I know she'll hit me with, 'I need the money.' Instead, I text back:

PIERCE

> I had a great time too. Have a good day at work. Dinner Monday? I can come over and we can order in.

KELSIE

Sure! Sounds good.

"Look at you, all doe-eyed and shit," Wade says, grinning wide. "Let me guess, you're texting with—"

His words are cut off as the tone sounds through the station. I grab the receiver, take down the information from dispatch, then relay it to my team. Because of my position, I don't always go out on runs, but since we're a small unit in a small town, and I have a guy out unexpectedly, I head out with my team.

By the time we arrive, the fire is out of control. The Inn at Christmas Valley is a two-story bed-and-breakfast that's been around for several generations. As we assess the situation, we quickly realize that it's worse than expected. Unfortunately, older homes often mean the fire spreads quicker and causes more damage. I grab the radio and rattle off commands. When I learn just how many people are there and that several are elderly, I put a call in to our neighboring station and start gearing up, preparing to help my team once they arrive.

Sixteen

KELSIE

SARA

> The girls are having a blast and begging for Jordan to spend the night again. They want to do a Disney Princess movie night and play dress-up. I told them I had to ask you first. I'm okay with it if you are.

I stare at my screen, unsure how to respond. Sure, I'd love to have another night to myself—any single mom, or mom in general, who tells you otherwise is full of shit—but I'm also missing my little girl.

Rather than texting Sara back, I call her.

"Hey," she says. "Did you see my text?"

"I did. Are you sure it's not too much?"

"Your daughter is an angel. It's definitely not too much."

I smile at the compliment. "Could I talk to her to make sure she's okay with it?"

"Of course!"

A few seconds later, Jordan comes onto the phone. "Hey, Mommy! Can I sleep at Tilly's again, please?"

"Well, hello to you, too."

"Sorry." She giggles. "Hello, I love you. Can I spend the night, pleeeeasssse?"

I chuckle softly. "I love you too. And yes, if you want to, you can. But tomorrow you have to come home. I miss you, Ladybug."

"I miss you too! Thank you!"

Without so much as a goodbye, Jordan's gone and Sara's back on the phone. "I think they're having a good time," she says with a laugh.

"It sounds like it."

"Beckett had to go out of town for a firefighter conference, so it's just me and the girls. If you want, you can come over for coffee after your shift. Maybe stay for dinner."

Her sweet invite warms my heart. Even though the thought kind of makes me nervous because it's been a while since I've let anyone in—aside from Pierce, which hasn't been the easiest—I say okay. Sara is one of the good ones, and I'd genuinely like to get to know her.

Since I don't have a vehicle yet, we agree that after my shift, I'll go home and shower. Then, she and the girls will pick me up once I'm ready. I hate being such an inconvenience, but she insists it's not a big deal.

We've only just hung up, and I'm walking over to greet a couple who sat down, when I hear someone mention Pierce's name. "...not sure what happened. Only that he was transported to the hospital."

"The Inn is—"

"Pierce is in the hospital?" I gasp, cutting into their conversation.

The gentleman nods. "A few people were brought in. Bad fire. Destroyed the entire Inn. Poor Mary-Beth..."

He continues speaking about the devastation, but my only thought is that Pierce is in the hospital. He's been injured. *Was he burned? Is he alive?*

Memories from three years ago hit me hard...

The heat.

The smoke.

The choking.

The fear—and acceptance—of death.

Waking up in the hospital room, thinking Jordan and Trent were gone.

Finding out Trent was gone.

Oh, God. Pierce can't be gone.

Before I know what I'm doing, I'm running out of the café and onto the sidewalk, needing to get to Pierce. Only when I'm several blocks from the café, do I realize I can't get to him because I have no car. And the town doesn't have a hospital, which means he was brought to one in the city.

I pull my phone out and dial his number, but he doesn't answer. I hang up and call back again, and this time when his voice comes over the phone, letting everyone know that he's not available and to leave a message, I do.

"Pierce," I choke out. "I need to know you're okay. Someone said you were in an accident and brought to the hospital. Please call me." I hang up and Google the closest hospital.

"I'm looking for a possible patient: Pierce Adler."

"Sorry, ma'am. We can't give out patient information over the phone."

"Can you at least tell me if he's there?" I beg, needing to know something, anything.

"He was brought in. However, no information regarding his condition has been put into the system."

I thank her and hang up, then look around, realizing that I'm standing on the sidewalk, crying. I can't go to the hospital since I don't have the money to pay for the ride, so I do the only thing I can do—walk home.

I text Dorothy to apologize and let her know I left. And then I call Sara, hoping maybe she'll know something. When she doesn't answer, I drop onto the couch, raise my knees to my chin, and cry more.

I knew there was a chance this could happen. I knew I could lose Pierce like I lost Trent. Only I took the risk, anyway. Because I've fallen in love with Pierce. I can't pinpoint the moment it happened, or when my feelings shifted, but what I do know is that I am in love with him. With his smile, his laugh, the way he cares about my daughter and me. If he is okay, instead of pushing him away, I won't waste another moment without telling him how I feel.

I'm in love with Pierce Adler.

And there's a chance I'll never get to say those words to him.

There's a chance I'll never get to kiss him again.

180

Make love to him...

Thinking about everything we might never get to have causes my body to wrack with sobs. I'm so lost in my thoughts and fears, I don't hear the door open or him walk in. One second I'm in a ball on the couch, mourning over what could've been, and the next I'm in Pierce's arms.

My legs wrap around his waist, and my arms encircle his neck, holding on to him like there's a chance he might disappear as he walks us to my room and lays us on the bed.

"Sweetheart," he coos, wiping my tears, and for a moment, I wonder if I'm dreaming or hallucinating.

I reach out and touch his face: his cheeks, his nose... I run my fingertip along his bottom lip and then the top.

He smiles softly and presses a kiss to the pad of my finger. "I'm real. I'm here," he says, as if he can hear my silent question. "I'm okay."

I'm then reminded that he was injured and had been in the hospital. Frantically, I sit up and push him down, running my eyes and hands over his body to ensure he is okay.

"Kels," he says, sitting up as well. "I'm okay, baby. I heard your voicemail on my drive over to you, but you didn't answer the phone. I called Dorothy, and she said you left upset."

"I didn't hear you call," I mumble, searching for my phone. It must be in the living room. "I was so scared. I thought..."

"I know," he says, cupping my face. "I know. I heard the fear in your voice, but I'm okay. A beam landed on my shoulder, and they insisted on bringing me in to make sure nothing was broken."

"Let me see," I demand, gripping the bottom of his shirt

and lifting, needing to see with my own eyes that he's okay.

He carefully removes his shirt and I spot a bruise on the left shoulder already forming. It looks painful, although it could have been worse in the grand scheme of things. He could be dead.

But he's not. He's alive and okay.

Climbing into his lap, I press my lips to the injured spot. "Pierce," I choke out, emotion clogging my throat. "I was so scared. I called the hospital, and they couldn't tell me anything. I tried Sara, but she didn't answer. I called you." I lift my gaze to meet his. "The entire time, I kept praying that you were alive and okay because..." I suck in a sharp breath and release it, needing to tell him how I feel. "I've fallen in love with you."

His eyes widen then soften, with his lips splitting into the most breathtakingly beautiful smile. "You love me, sweetheart?"

"I do," I admit. "When I found out about the fire, my only thoughts were that I never got a chance to tell you. I know it happened quickly and unexpectedly, but it doesn't change the fact that I've fallen for you, and I don't want to waste a single second not being with you. Life's too short." I press another kiss to his shoulder. "It can be taken from us at any moment." I kiss each of his cheeks. "I don't want to be scared anymore."

I lean down and press my lips to his heart, so thankful that unlike Trent's, Pierce's is still beating. "I don't want to live in fear anymore," I tell him, meeting his hazel eyes that are so full of life. "I just want to live and love and do it all with you."

"Jesus, Kels," he says, gripping the side of my neck. "You're so damn brave, sweetheart. Pouring your heart out to me like this after everything you've been through, after thinking something happened to me. You're amazing."

He slants his mouth over mine and kisses the breath right out of me, a reminder that we're both alive. We break apart long enough for us to pull my shirt over my head and toss it to the side and then undo my bra. When I remove the straps and drop it onto the floor, Pierce backs up slightly, drinking in the sight of my breasts. His tongue runs slowly along his bottom lip, and he shakes his head.

"So beautiful." He lifts my breasts, feeling the weight of them in his palms. "So perfect." He takes one into his mouth and sucks on my nipple, eliciting a moan from me. "So goddamn lovable."

I freeze at his words, and our eyes meet.

"I love you, Kels. I think I might've loved you since the moment I saw you in the grocery store. You and your mini. You're both mine." He leans in and nips my bottom lip then soothes away the pain. "Tell me, baby. Tell me you're mine."

"I'm yours," I breathe, the words spilling out far too easily.

"Damn right, you are."

His mouth is back on mine, and we kiss for several minutes, getting lost in each other, making silent promises that should be too soon for either of us to make, but knowing neither of us cares about anything other than the way we feel.

While we kiss, Pierce tweaks my nipples and massages my breasts, working me up higher and higher until I'm squirming in his lap, begging him to take me over the edge.

"Not yet," he murmurs, changing our positions so I'm lying on the mattress with him hovering over me. "I've dreamed... Hell, I've *fantasized* about the day I get you...*all of you.* I'm going to take my time and memorize every damn inch of you." His hands land on either side of my head as he trails fiery kisses along my neck and chest. "Then, when I'm done, I'll do it all over again."

He stops abruptly, his brows creasing. "Wait, where's Jordan?"

He glances around as if she's going to pop out of the closet, and laughter bubbles out of me. At the same time, my heart soars, knowing that even in a moment of lust, he cares about more than sex. Pierce Adler truly cares about my daughter and me.

He loves us.

"She's spending the night with Tilly." And then it hits me... "I was supposed to go over there for coffee and dinner since you were working tonight."

"You're not going anywhere," he growls, pulling his phone out and typing something. A second later, it dings, and he responds, then chucks it to the side. "Done. It's just you and me."

The thought has my sex clenching in anticipation.

"What about Sara?"

"I told her we'll come over for lunch...tomorrow."

He bends down and kisses me passionately for several seconds before breaking the kiss and working his way down my body.

With every love bite, every lick, and every kiss, my body

tightens in anticipation of what's to come. When Pierce reaches my belly, he undoes the button of my jeans and trails kisses downward as he pulls the zipper down. Once my pants are off, he presses a soft kiss to my panty-clad mound then sucks in a sharp breath.

"Fuck, baby. You smell so good. I bet you taste just as good."

I groan at his dirty talk and squirm, loving the way he says whatever's on his mind. "Feel free to find out," I say, lifting my lower body slightly.

His head pops up, his molten gaze meeting mine. "You want me to taste your pussy, sweetheart?" he asks, wetting his lips and then sucking the bottom lip into his mouth.

"Yes," I choke out, desperate for his mouth to be on me.

"Yes, what?" he goads.

"I want you to eat my pussy."

His eyes light up, and a sexy smirk quirks at the corner of his mouth, causing the left dimple that I love to make an appearance. "Your wish is my command."

Swiftly tugging my panties down my legs, he spreads my thighs and licks up my center. "Fuck, yes," he murmurs before licking me again, this time making sure to hit my clit.

I don't realize how intently I'm staring until he looks up at me, licks his lips, and says, "That's right, baby. Watch me make you come."

He slides a couple of fingers slowly inside me. Then, without his gaze leaving mine, he reaches up and pinches my nipple, sending shocks of pleasure through my body. He does it again, this time harder, and my back arches off the bed as I cry out in a mixture of pleasure and pain.

"Holy shit," he purrs. "You're soaking my fingers, and I haven't even gotten started yet."

He hasn't even gotten started yet?

Before I can ask him what the hell he's talking about, he pushes his fingers deeper into me in tandem with his tongue as it hits my pussy. The pleasure is so unexpected and intense that I damn near see stars. With strong, intentional strokes to my clit, it's clear he's hell-bent on doing just as I asked of him—making me come.

He adds another finger, and while he might only be getting started, I'm about to end this right—

"Not yet," he demands, lifting me up like I weigh nothing and flipping me onto my hands and knees. He gives my ass a smack that has me groaning. Then he grips my cheeks, lifting my bottom half into the air and spreading me so he can continue devouring me from behind. I've never had a guy so intimately close to *that* area, but the way his wet tongue hits my clit as he plunges several fingers into me, forces me to focus solely on my pleasure.

It only takes a few more strokes of his tongue and fingers before I shatter around him, coming harder than I've ever come in my life. I know I've said that before, but holy shit, it's like every time I'm with him is better than the last. More intimate, more intense.

I'm still riding the waves of my orgasm when I feel the head of his cock push into me. I haven't seen it—aside from under the covers when I gave him head where it was too dark to get a good look—though from the way it's stretching me, I know it's long and thick, and the way it's rubbing my insides has my body begging for a release all over again.

"Oh God," I pant as he bottoms out in me. "Fuck me, Pierce. Please, fuck me." I don't know what's come over me, but I need him to move, to make me feel good.

He reaches around and massages my breasts, and I assume he's going to fuck me in this position. But then he tightens his hold on my body and pulls up, so my back is flush against his chest, with his cock hitting me even deeper at this angle.

"I'm never going to last," he confesses into my ear. "So, you'll need to come soon because I'm not coming until you do."

Oh, shit. "Pierce, I can't." I shake my head, having never had more than one orgasm at a time.

"Yes, you can, sweetheart," he croons, tweaking my nipple while his other hand sweeps my hair to the side to press his lips to my heated flesh, trailing kisses along my neck and shoulder.

"Pierce," I moan when his hand glides around my front and finds my already sensitive clit.

"That's it... I can feel it. You're so close. Come, baby. Come and choke the fuck out of my cock," he says as he slides in and out of me, stroking places I didn't even know existed.

I don't know if it's his cock hitting me just right, his fingers stimulating my nipple, the sensual kisses he's trailing along my flesh, or the way his thumb is rubbing my swollen clit—or maybe it's a combination of all of the above—but all too quickly, the overwhelming pleasure is sending me over the edge and into the abyss, as bright colors followed by darkness fill my vision.

Everything goes quiet, and when I finally open my lids, I'm in Pierce's arms, his warm hazel eyes looking down at me.

"You came so fucking hard." He smirks, clearly proud of the fact that he made me orgasm so hard I'm almost positive I blacked out. "Let's take a shower. We both need to get cleaned up."

Seventeen

KELSIE

WITH MY ARMS WRAPPED AROUND HIS NECK, HE CARRIES me to the bathroom and sets me on the counter. Lost in the fog of my orgasm, I watch as he turns the water on and finds two towels under the sink. It isn't until he spreads my legs and pushes a single finger into me that I snap out of it.

"What are you doing?"

I try to close my legs because there's no way I can handle another orgasm after the two he just gave me.

"Feeling my cum mixed with yours." He grins mischievously. "I've never been a possessive guy, yet the thought of you being filled with my cum does crazy shit to me, sweetheart. If I have it my way, I'm going to make you come every chance we get."

Thanks to my post-orgasm brain, it takes me a second to piece together what he's just said, but when I do, I gasp, realizing an important detail we forgot.

"I'm not on birth control."

Pierce blinks several times while I hold my breath, preparing for the freak-out. But then he simply shrugs... *Shrugs!*

"Pierce, did you hear me? I'm not on birth control. I could get pregnant."

"I bet you looked beautiful when you were pregnant."

"Pierce-I don't know your middle name-Adler, be serious for a moment, please. We just started this. I already got pregnant once by accident. I don't want to make the same mistake twice."

"It's Joshua..."

"Huh?"

"My middle name is Joshua, and Jordan wasn't a mistake," he says, his tone suddenly serious. "I know you would never consider her one, and if you were to get pregnant, this baby wouldn't be a mistake either. They would have been conceived out of love."

He steps toward me and presses his palm to my face. "I love you, Kels. If you're not ready to have a baby, I'll use protection from now on, but anything created between us wouldn't be a mistake. I might not have known Trent, but I know you, and I know that when Jordan was created, it was out of love. So, you want to tell me who the fuck told you that she was a mistake?"

Tears fill my eyes as I admit, "My parents and Trent's. We were young, and she was an accident. We used protection, but I still got pregnant, and my parents told me to abort my baby, or they would cut me off."

192

"And you chose your baby," he says, a soft smile on his face.

"She was a surprise. Still, you're right, she's not a mistake."

"Our baby wouldn't be one, either," he says. "But as I said, if you're not ready to have a baby, I'm okay with that."

"You are?"

"I sure as hell wouldn't be opposed." He shrugs. "The thought of you swelling with my baby inside you turns me on." He smirks. "But until you're ready, we can practice...a lot."

The thought of being with Pierce regularly excites me. It's been years since I've been with a man sexually, and even when I was with Trent, it wasn't like it is with Pierce. The man knows what he's doing, that's for sure. Which makes me wonder...

"How did you go so long without sex?" I blurt out.

He told me that after he and his ex broke up, he wasn't interested in being with other women. He confided that she was the last woman he was with, and that was three years ago. Yet, when he's around me, it seems like he's far too sexual to have gone years without sex.

Pierce backs up slightly and looks into my eyes. "The truth is, I didn't even think about sex the past few years. After Tanya and I broke up, I was bitter as fuck. Not because I was in love with her, but because I gave up so much for her and she turned around and cheated. I told myself I needed time to get my life back on track, which led to me working a shit ton of hours and building my house."

"And you didn't meet anyone who could satiate the

craving?"

I've seen the way women look at Pierce and talk about him. Any single—and most likely married—woman would gladly help him scratch that itch.

He wraps his arms around me, picks me up, and carries me into the shower. It's not a large shower, but it's spacious enough to fit both of us comfortably. After closing the curtain, he pushes my back against the wall. Despite the hot water, the wall is cool, and I gasp when I touch the cold tiles.

"I wasn't looking," he admits. "But then I saw you." He tightens his hold on me, so our bodies are flush against each other. "And it was like the fire that had been dimmed was instantly stoked. My world was cold for so long. Then when I met you, I could suddenly feel the warmth whenever I was around you."

At his words, butterflies swarm my chest. "It's never felt like this," I whisper, nuzzling my face into his neck to hide my shame.

"What do you mean?"

"With Trent, I never felt this want...this *need*. I loved him. I swear I did, but—"

"Hey," he says, lifting my face and cupping my cheek. "What you feel for me doesn't lessen or diminish what you felt for him. It's just different. You guys were young and, from what you said, had many stressors... between him going to school and you having a baby."

"Does it feel different for you? Different than the way you felt about Tanya?"

"So fucking different," he says, stroking his knuckles down

my cheek. "With her, it felt forced, but with you, it feels so damn easy. I want to be with you all the time. When I'm not with you, I think about you. It's not just you, though. I think about Jordan too. I want to take care of you both."

"Pierce," I huff. "I don't want you to feel bad—"

"Don't even think about finishing that statement," he says. "There's a difference between wanting to help out of pity and caring about someone so much you want to be the reason they're happy." He frames my face in his hands. "I just want you guys to be happy, baby."

"I am happy," I admit, realizing I'm telling the truth for the first time in a long time. For so long, I was faking it, just trying to get through each day. Maybe my money situation hasn't improved. But I'm living my life again...*feeling* again, because of Pierce. I don't know what the future holds, but I know one thing: I want Pierce in our lives.

"Good," he says, dipping his head and peppering kisses along my jaw and then across my shoulder. "Now, enough talking. I'm about to make sure you stay happy."

"And how are you going to do that?" I ask coyly, knowing damn well how he plans to do it if the way he's sucking on my neck is any indication.

"Orgasms, baby," he demands. "I'm going to give you lots and lots of orgasms."

"WHY AREN'T YOU ASLEEP?" PIERCE'S RASPY VOICE FILLS

the otherwise quiet house.

We've spent the evening bouncing between making love and talking, with some food thrown into the mix. After the third—or maybe it was the fourth—time we made love, we showered and climbed into bed, both of us spent. Pierce pulled me into his arms, and I laid my head on his chest.

We talked until he fell asleep, but instead of doing the same, I've been lying awake thinking about everything that's happened today: Thinking I'd lost Pierce, him confessing his love for me, me admitting that I love him as well. And the most significant admission—Pierce saying he'd love it if I happened to get pregnant.

The crazy part is that the idea doesn't scare me the way it probably should. I have no doubt he'd be a wonderful dad. However, what has my brain in overdrive is what comes with getting pregnant—or what is supposed to come with getting pregnant.

"I want to get married," I blurt out, cringing when I realize I only voiced half of my thoughts. "What I mean is... I want to get married before I get pregnant again."

Pierce rolls to his side, his fist resting under his temple, giving me his undivided attention as if he wasn't just asleep a few minutes ago.

"When Trent died, Jordan and I were left with nothing. No car, no home, no money. We were young and never thought anything would happen, so we didn't consider the future. The next time I get pregnant, I want it to be once I'm married and we're financially stable.

"I know you mentioned being okay with me getting

pregnant, but I don't feel like either of us was thinking clearly. We were caught up in the moment. A baby is a lot of work, and I've already missed out on so much time with Jordan because of having to work. Plus, I still need to get through college." I sigh at the thought of adding years of schooling to my plate, knowing it's necessary but dreading it all the same.

"Hey," Pierce says, reaching out and tucking a strand of hair behind my ear. "I get it. You have dreams. You want to become a nurse."

"No, I don't," I admit. When he raises a questioning brow, I elaborate. "Many feminists would hate me for saying this, but I have no desire to go to school or work. When I was a teenager, I had always planned to go to college but never had any idea what I wanted to do. It was just that in the house I was raised in, it wasn't about *if* you were going to college but *where*, so there wasn't exactly a choice.

"Then I got pregnant and became a stay-at-home mom, and I loved it so much," I say, choking up as I remember how precious my time with Jordan was—still is. "After Trent died, leaving us with nothing, I knew I had to go to college if I wanted any chance of taking care of my daughter. Since nursing sounded like something I'd enjoy, and it pays well, I chose that."

"But you don't want to be a nurse," Pierce clarifies.

"I want to be a mom... a stay-at-home mom. If I can't do that, I don't want to have another baby until my husband and I are financially stable so that I can stay home. I know some women love working outside of the home, and I think that's awesome. Everyone should do what they want to do in life.

As for me, I loved being home. I loved cooking, cleaning, and taking care of Jordan and Trent. And I hate that I've missed out on years of being with her because I had to work after Trent passed away.

"She's in school now, so I make sure my hours match hers. Even then, I still miss out on so much, like class parties and field trips. And I have to worry about paying the bills instead of being there for my daughter. If I had another baby, I wouldn't want to work. I'd want to be home." I shrug and chuckle softly. "Sorry, I didn't mean to get so deep in the middle of the night."

"I like when you get deep," Pierce says, gripping the curve of my hip and pulling me toward him. "I love that you feel comfortable enough to talk to me. Kels, I love you. Every day I fall more in love with you. I know to some it might seem crazy, but I want a future with you and Jordan, and lots of damn babies. I want to marry you and for you guys to move into my house with me."

"It's only been such a short time, though," I point out, despite being able to imagine everything he just said vividly. The lazy mornings in bed, family dinners, spending holidays together...

"I know," he agrees. "But if it were up to me, I'd marry you tomorrow." He shrugs. "But I know it's not just about me. We have Jordan to think about as well. And you're right. You deserve to feel secure when we decide to grow our family. If, by some miracle, you got pregnant tonight, I'm okay with that, but we'll use protection moving forward. So when the time comes to take that step, we'll make sure it's done properly."

He cups the side of my face. "And, sweetheart, I'd like nothing more than for you to stay home with our kids. So if you don't want to go to school, don't. Fuck feminism. Life's too short to spend it doing what you think society deems appropriate."

"Thank you," I breathe, my heart swelling with so much love for this man. "So, where do we go from here?"

"We take it one day at a time. Just know that I'm ready whenever you are... marriage, moving in, all the fucking babies. I'm on board."

He leans in and kisses me tenderly, and I hitch my leg around him, grinding myself against his warmth. Since we're both naked, his hard length slides between my pussy lips, and I lift my leg higher, giving him easy access to slide right in.

"Sorry, sweetheart," he groans, backing up slightly. "As much as I'd love to sink into you, the stores are closed, and I don't have any condoms with me."

I frown, not liking what he's saying. I'm turned on and want him inside me. Now that he's shown me how good sex can be, I'm addicted.

"We've already done it several times tonight," I whisper, sliding my hand to his shaft so I can guide it into me. "What's once more?"

"That's your pussy talking," he says with a chuckle. "As much as I want to listen to it, I'm going to be the voice of reason and say no." He kisses my lips, then murmurs against my mouth, "But don't worry, I can make you feel damn good without ever entering you."

"Nothing feels as good as you inside me." I pout, then groan when his thumb lands on my clit.

"Challenge accepted."

Eighteen
PIERCE

"Pierce!"

Jordan, dressed in a fluffy pink princess-looking dress with her makeup done and a crown on the top of her head, runs over and throws her arms around my legs, shocking the hell out of me. Sure, we've gotten close the past several weeks, but I didn't know we'd reached the *hug you when I see you* stage yet. "Tilly's mommy said you were in a fire, and I was so scared. I thought you went to heaven like my daddy." She glances up at me with a mixture of fear and relief in her features, and without thought, I pull her up into my arms.

"I'm good, Princess."

"You pinky swear?" She lifts her tiny pinky, and I hook it with my own.

"I pinky swear. Being a firefighter is my job. I was trained to go into fires and save people. Nothing's going to happen to me."

She nods solemnly. "My daddy died in a fire. I wish you were there. Then you could've saved him, right?"

"I would've tried," I choke out, the lump in my throat making it hard to speak or swallow.

"Can we go ride the horses?" she asks, switching topics with a quickness that could give someone whiplash.

"Sure, but let's first have lunch. I heard you guys made some delicious food."

"We're having a tea party!" Tilly exclaims, running out of the kitchen and straight for me. I set Jordan down and give my niece a hug.

"A princess tea party," Jordan adds. "One day, when Mommy has lots of money, we're gonna go to Disney and have tea with the princesses. Right, Mommy?" Jordan looks at her mom for confirmation.

When I glance at her, I notice her eyes are wet, and for a second, I wonder why. Until I remember the conversation Jordan and I just had.

"Hey," I say, pulling her into my arms. "I'm okay."

"I know," she rasps. "But I didn't even think about Jordan. I was so wrapped up in you, I forgot to call her. I had no idea that she knew you were hurt or that she was worried. We could've lost you, Pierce." She sniffles back a sob, and I hug her tighter.

"You're not going to lose me." I kiss her gently, relishing in her pillow-soft lips that I can't get enough of. "I'm not going anywhere."

"Look, Tilly, Pierce is kissing my mommy!" Jordan giggles.

"That means they're gonna get married, and we're gonna be sisters!" Tilly yells.

"Really?" Jordan questions.

"No," Kelsie says, bursting their bubble. "If we were to get married, it would make you cousins."

"I wanna be cousins!" both girls exclaim, jumping up and down excitedly.

"Mommy, marry Pierce!" Jordan adds. "Then I'll have a baby brother like Tilly!"

"Baby brother?" I question.

"Mommy and Daddy are having a baby!" Tilly yells.

"Sara!" I shout.

A second later, my sister-in-law walks out of the kitchen, holding a three-tier tray filled with dozens of tiny sandwiches and desserts. "Hey," she says, out of breath. "Sorry, I was finishing up in the kitchen and—" She stops in her place when she sees us all staring at her and sighs. "The girls spilled the beans, didn't they?"

"That depends. Are you pregnant with my nephew?"

"I am," she says, a huge smile spreading across her face. "The girls overheard me talking to Beckett and promised not to tell anyone." She glares playfully at the girls, who have the decency to look guilty.

"I'm sorry," Jordan says with a frown. "I was just telling my mommy and Pierce that if they get married, then I'll get a brother too, 'cause mommies and daddies have babies, and I want a baby brother like Tilly."

Sara glances from me to Kelsie and lets out a laugh. "Did I miss something?"

"Jordan saw us kiss," I say with a shrug. "And it all spiraled from there."

"Oh, so you're not getting married?"

"Oh, we are," I say, flinching when Kelsie playfully—or maybe not so playfully—smacks my chest, silently telling me to shut up. "What? We are...as soon as you're ready. You heard your daughter. She wants a baby brother."

"Pierce," Kelsie hisses. "One, we don't even know if the baby will be a boy, and—"

"We're having a baby?" Jordan shrieks. "Yay!"

"No, Lovebug," Kelsie says, glaring my way before she kneels in front of her daughter, who's looking at her in confusion. "Pierce and I are dating. That means we're boyfriend and girlfriend. One day, we hope to get married and have another baby."

"When?" she asks, making me chuckle.

"We're not sure," Kelsie says. "If we got married, that would mean we would move in with Pierce and—"

"Where does Pierce live?" Jordan questions.

"With me!" Tilly exclaims.

Jordan's eyes widen. "You live here with Tilly? I thought you lived in your house with Cinderella."

"No, Princess," I say, trying to contain my laughter. But fuck, this kid is adorable and totally helping my case. "I do live in my house with Cinder, but I live on the property. Tilly, my parents, my brothers, and I all live here on this ranch."

"With the horses?" she asks, with hope laced in her tone.

"Yeah." I nod. "We all live here with the horses."

"I wanna move here, please," she begs, folding her hands

together and giving her mom the most adorable puppy dog eyes. "Please, Mommy."

"That would mean leaving your room," Kelsie explains.

"Yeah, but she'd get another room in her new house," I say nonchalantly. "And we can paint it and decorate it however she wants," I add, not above emotional bribery.

"Pierce, you're not helping," Kelsie groans.

"Do you actually think I'll steer her away from wanting to move in with me? If it were up to me, you guys would move in today, and we'd be married by Christmas."

"Please, Mommy!" Jordan continues to beg.

"We'll see," Kelsie says, standing.

"We'll see and maybes always mean no." Jordan pouts.

"Not if I can help it," I say with a smirk aimed at Kelsie.

"How about we discuss this later?" Kelsie suggests. "Right now, I'd like to have a princess tea party with the most beautiful princesses in all the land."

Her words cause the little girls to change pace, remembering they're dressed like princesses.

"I helped make the sandwiches," Jordan announces, climbing onto her chair.

"And I poured the tea," Tilly adds, sitting next to Jordan.

"So, you're pregnant, huh?" I say to Sara, pulling her into a side hug.

"We're three months along. We're going to tell everyone tonight at dinner since you're off today."

"Congratulations." I kiss her temple, then sit down.

"Nobody else knows yet," she says. "So, keep a lid on it until tonight. Yeah?"

"I don't think I'm the one you have to worry about." I chuckle and nod toward the little girls filling their plates with food.

"Yeah, we should probably announce it the second we get there," Sarah says with a laugh.

"If you want to be the one to tell everyone, that's probably a good idea," I agree. "Is Beckett coming to dinner?"

"Yep, he's on his way home now. He said he'll meet us at your parents'."

When I glance over at Kelsie, I find her sitting across the table, her face devoid of all emotion. I squeeze Sara's hand, then walk over to Kelsie, sitting down next to her.

"You okay?" I whisper, so nobody can hear.

"I wasn't expecting her to be so okay with moving in with you," she whispers.

"She's only five, Kels. Kids trust their parents, and she saw us kiss, which tells her you care about me. Then, add in the fact that we have horses on the property, and it would mean living next to Tilly. You never stood a chance."

Kelsie playfully rolls her eyes. "So, you're saying that I should just give in now, since moving in with you is inevitable."

When our eyes meet, I'm hoping she's being serious. If she is, I'll gladly grab the guys and have the girls' stuff moved into my place before nightfall. Then she bursts out laughing and shakes her head. "We're not moving in with you tonight!" she whisper-yells. "You're crazy."

"What will it take?" I ask, needing to know what I'm working with.

"I want to do things right," she murmurs, her cheeks

turning that beautiful shade of pink I've quickly come to love. "Date, engagement, marriage, move in, babies…in that order."

Noticing that she didn't give a timeframe, only that she specified an order, I lean in and kiss her cheek, already making plans to go to the jeweler tomorrow. "You got it, sweetheart."

"Cinderella loves me so much," Jordan coos as the puppy licks her face in excitement. "When Mommy and I live with you, can Cinderella sleep with me?"

"Cinder sleeps in her crate for now, but once she's trained, she can sleep anywhere, including with you."

"Wow," Kelsie gasps, "pulling out all the stops, huh? What's next? You going to offer to take her to Disney to see the princesses?"

I want to tell her that's already in the works, but it's a surprise for both of my girls. Instead, I simply shrug, opening the door so Cinder can run outside and do her business. I haven't seen her since yesterday. My brother Jackson was nice enough to pick her up from the station and take care of her for me last night, so I asked if we could grab her before dinner. Of course, Jordan was on board since she loves Cinder.

"So…" I slide my arm across the backs of Kelsie's shoulders as we walk down the path, following Jordan and Cinder as they run toward the pond up ahead. "Next Saturday is the Christmas festival. I'd love it if you and Jordan went with me."

Now that I know the order Kelsie wants things to go in,

I've concocted a plan of sorts. It all starts with surprising her with a date this week—I just need to get Sara on board to watch the girls—proposing to her at the festival, getting married on Christmas, and ending with the two of them moving into my place before New Year's.

"I thought you had to work," she says.

"I switched shifts with Kurt. He doesn't give a shit about the Christmas festival. He got tickets to see some rock band he's obsessed with. They're playing during his shift, so we switched. I'm working Wednesday and Thursday this week."

"Well, in that case, we'd love to go to the festival with you." Kelsie leans into my side, and I dip my head, inhaling her sweet scent. "Jordan is excited to see Santa."

"Perfect." I kiss the side of her temple. "It's a date." And hopefully an engagement...

"You're going to what?" My mom shrieks—in excitement or disbelief, I'm not sure.

"You don't think it's too soon?" Sara questions.

After Sara and Beckett announced they were expecting a little boy, we sat down and enjoyed a delicious dinner—complete with my mom's famous homemade stuffed shells and garlic bread. Once we were all stuffed, the girls asked if they could take Cinder outside to play, and I offered to do the dishes, so I could talk to my mom and Sara alone. If I have any chance of this all happening like I want, I'll need them on board.

"Mom and Dad got engaged pretty quick," I note, nodding toward my mom. "And even if they didn't, I know Kelsie's the one. I can feel it. Since the moment I laid eyes on her and Jordan, I knew one day they'd be mine to love and care for. I wasted so many years with the wrong woman, then allowed my stupidity in staying with her to make me bitter. I just want to be with Kelsie, and I don't see why we need to wait."

"Okay," Sara says. "What do you need from us?"

I look at my mom, praying she's on board. It won't change anything for me if she's not, but our family is close, so I'd prefer to have the support of my family.

"I've got your back," Mom says. "Always."

Nineteen

KELSIE

"Good evening. This call is to inform you that school will be closed tomorrow…"

I sigh in frustration as I listen to the rest of the voicemail. Apparently, there's a snowstorm that's expected to come through late tonight. Jordan's school will be closed, which means the café will also be closed. I knew it was a possibility since it's been talked about all week on the local news, but I was hoping the weather people were wrong—it wouldn't be the first time.

"What's wrong?" Pierce asks, making me jump. He grips the curves of my hips and tugs me gently toward him, framing the side of my face. "Who was that?" He nods toward the phone in my hand.

I pocket it and shake my head. "No school tomorrow due to the storm."

"Snow day," Pierce says. "Makes sense with the amount of

snow expected to come in tonight. So, why do you look like someone ruined your favorite book?"

I chuckle at his analogy. He finds it amusing and intriguing how much I enjoy reading romance novels. On a few occasions, he's even had me read him a few scenes, jokingly saying he was taking notes. Pierce doesn't need to take notes, though, since he's got the whole book boyfriend thing on lock. The guy puts half of the heroes I read to shame.

"Snow day means no work." I shrug, trying to sound nonchalant since I hate the topic of money. Pierce has plenty, and I have none, but I don't ever want him to feel like he needs to take care of me—despite his obvious want and need to do so.

"You know," he says, pulling me even closer and dipping his face so his lips are near my ear. "There are perks to snow days." He tugs gently on my earlobe then kisses the sensitive spot just under my ear.

"Like what?" I groan as a shiver races through my body, making Pierce chuckle.

"Like spending the morning in bed."

"With a five-year-old? Not happ—"

"Mommy!" Jordan yells, cutting me off.

I turn around, expecting Pierce to let go of me. Instead, he pulls me toward him, so my back is flush against his chest, his chin resting on my shoulder.

"Mommy, Pierce, guess what?" Jordan asks, stopping in front of us, a massive grin splayed across her face.

"You ate so many s'mores you turned into a marshmallow," Pierce deadpans.

After dinner, we went outside to sit around the bonfire and roast marshmallows. I was inside using the restroom when my phone rang with the call from the school.

"What? No, silly!" Jordan cackles. "Do I look like a marshmallow?" She spreads her arms to the side, and in her thick, white jacket, she kind of does.

"You look like a fluffy, white marshmallow," Pierce taunts, letting go of me. He grabs Jordan by the waist and lifts her, carrying her over to the couch. Dropping her down gently, he starts tickling her. "I think we need to roast this marshmallow. What do you think, Kels?"

"I bet she would taste so sweet," I say, joining in to tickle her. "We can stick her on a graham cracker with some chocolate."

"No way!" She shrieks. "I'm not a marshmallow!" She giggles as Pierce and I tickle her some more. "Stop it!" She laughs, her arms and legs flailing around. "I'm not a marshmallow. I'm a person!"

"Oh," Pierce says in mock confusion. "Are you sure?"

"Yes," she tells him, her tone exasperated. "That's not what I wanted you to guess."

"Oh," he says again. "Okay, so what's up?"

"Tilly's grandma..."

"Marta," I correct.

"Yeah, her! She said Tilly and I can have a snow party at her house tonight 'cause there's no school tomorrow. Can I go, please?" Jordan begs, laying it on thick by popping her bottom lip out and batting her lashes.

"What's a snow party?" I ask.

"A party for snow!" Jordan says, like it's obvious.

"Okay..." I start, a bit confused, but Jordan hears the word and shrieks in excitement, mistaking my okay for yes.

"Thank you, Mommy!" She leaps into my arms and hugs me. Then she takes off outside before I can even get a word in edgewise.

"What the heck just happened?" I ask.

"You agreed for Jordan to spend the night with my mom." Pierce smirks, and something tells me this was a setup. And then my thoughts are confirmed when he adds, "Which means we get to have a snow party as well...in my bed."

After learning a snow party is a pajama party that includes the movie *Frozen*, snacks, and building a fort in the living room, followed by waking up in the morning and playing in the snow—AKA Marta's sweet way of giving both her sons a night alone with their women—we say good night to everyone and head back to Pierce's house.

As we step inside, Cinder runs past us straight to her food and water. I remove my jacket, hang it on the coat rack, then sit on the bench so I can take off my boots.

When I stand, I take a moment to look around Pierce's home with new eyes. Now that he's made it clear he wants Jordan and me to move in with him, I try to imagine this as our home, and surprisingly, it comes quite easily. The living room is all brown leather and wood, giving it a cozy look. The walls are a bit bare. I can picture family portraits lining the walls: Jordan's school pictures, family vacations, wedding photos, if we have a baby...

The kitchen is beautiful with state-of-the-art appliances

that would make cooking meals and feeding my family easy, even pleasant.

The dining room table seats six people, and it makes me wonder how many kids Pierce wants. Does he want to fill the house with babies, or is he more of a "family of four" type of guy? I can see us sitting at the table with our kids, eating dinner and discussing our day.

My thoughts go back to the last time I saw Trent—at the table, talking about our day—and a wave of guilt washes over me for a second because he's gone, and I'm alive. I get a future while his life has ended. He'll never have his career, a family, or a chance to live, love, and be happy.

As if Pierce can feel the shift in my energy, he wraps his arms around me from behind, nuzzling his face into my hair. "What's going through that head of yours?" he murmurs. "I can practically hear the cogs turning."

"Trent," I admit with a humorless chuckle.

I expect Pierce to make a sarcastic comment about the fact that I'm thinking about another man in his home, but I should know better since that's not the type of person Pierce is. He's kind, gentle, and patient.

And he proves that once again, when he turns me around and, still holding me, swipes a tear away. "What about him?" he asks, his tone tender.

"He never got a chance to be happy." I sniffle, more tears sliding down my cheeks.

"I don't believe that," he says with conviction. "I might not have known him, but with you and Jordan by his side, it would've been impossible for him not to be happy."

"He had school and work. He was doing his best to take care of us, but it was a lot. My parents cut me off when I refused to have an abortion, and his parents wouldn't help with anything other than his school. We were young and raising a baby. We were both tired and stressed a lot of the time. I kept telling him that it would pass. He would graduate, and we would start our life together. Except he never graduated."

The tears fall harder, and I release a choked sob. "He's gone, his life is over, and I'm still here. For so long, I was going through the motions, only focused on Jordan and trying to stay afloat. I think a part of me didn't want to date because I felt guilty. How could I possibly move forward when Trent didn't get to? Then you showed up. I'm feeling so much, and for the first time, I can imagine it: the family, the love, the happiness... And I want it," I whisper. "But I'm afraid."

"I already told you I'm not going anywhere," he says, tucking my hair behind my ear before cupping my face.

"I know. You're good at your job, and you'll be okay. That's not what I mean." I take a deep breath and then admit an insecurity that's been running through my mind since the first time Pierce made it clear he likes me. "You have a beautiful home, a career. You're financially stable, you have a close, supportive family, and you're so sweet and patient and loving. You're like every woman's perfect man..."

"But..." he prompts.

"I have nothing to bring to the table. I'm a broke, single mom with no family or friends. I have no assets or education or—"

"That's enough," he says forcibly, shaking his head.

I'm momentarily taken aback because I've never heard Pierce use that kind of tone with me. I must make some kind of face because his features soften instantly.

"I'm sorry," he says. "It's just that I don't give a fuck about any of that. My family can be your family, this home can be your home. My money can be yours. Who gives a shit about whether you went to school? You said it yourself: you want to be a wife and a mom, and I'm completely okay with that."

He reaches up, framing my other cheek. "All I want is you, sweetheart. I want your mind, your heart. I want that adorable little girl that comes with you. I want to fill you with more babies, if that's what's in the cards for us. I want you in this home, sharing a bed with me. I want mornings and days and nights with you."

He bends slightly and presses his mouth to mine. The kiss is soft and sweet but ends too quickly. "I just want to be happy with you," he whispers against my lips. "Trent is gone, but you're still alive, and you deserve to find *your* happiness. Now, the question is, do you think you can find that happiness with me?"

"Yes," I blurt out without needing to think about it. I know I can because I'm already happy. Every time I'm around Pierce, it's as if everything else fades away. It's just me, him, and Jordan. The bills I'm behind on don't matter, the mostly empty fridge is pushed to the side. My stress over having to go to school when I'm dreading it is out of my mind.

When I'm with Pierce, I'm only focused on the now, on being with him. I laugh and smile and enjoy myself. Could I be happy without him? Yes. But do I want to be? The answer is no. I want Pierce in our lives.

"I want everything you said," I admit. "The babies, the home, and sharing a bed with you. I want the mornings and days and nights. I want the dinners, the vacations, and the family. I want it all, and I want it with you."

"Then marry me," he says.

"What?" I gasp.

"Marry me." He gets down on one knee and looks up at me while my heart flutters rapidly. "I planned to ask you this weekend at the festival, with a ring and a romantic proposal, but I can't wait. I wasted years of my life with the wrong woman, on the wrong path, and you know firsthand how delicate life can be. It can be taken from us in the blink of an eye."

I nod profusely in agreement, because despite the craziness of him down on one knee proposing marriage, he's not wrong. We've both learned the hard way that life can change at any moment.

"I don't want to waste another day," he continues. "I've fallen in love with you and your daughter, and it'd make me the happiest man on earth if you'd marry me and share your life with me. I want you, Kelsie, for however long I can have you."

"Yes," I breathe. "Yes, I'll marry you."

A huge smile spreads across his face. Then he's on his feet, lifting me into his arms, his firm lips curling around mine. My legs wrap around his waist, and we kiss as he walks us to his bedroom. When he lays me in the center of the bed, he breaks the kiss, and I pout, wanting his mouth on mine.

"Tell me again," he requests, his mouth against my lips.

It takes a second for me to understand what he's talking about, but once the fog clears from my brain, I give him the words he wants to hear.

"I want to marry you, Pierce. I want forever with you."

His eyes light up with a mixture of love and desire as his fingers wrap around the hem of my shirt, pulling it over my head. Then, with a quick flick of the clasp, he removes my bra. He slides down the bed so he can unbutton and unzip my jeans. With his fingers hooked into my panties and jeans, he tugs the material down my legs, leaving me completely naked and ready for him.

"I can't wait to make you my wife," he says as he climbs over me and softly kisses my lips. He peppers more kisses along my neck, stopping at my breasts to give each of them attention. He continues to move downward, planting kiss after kiss along my torso. "One day, this belly will be carrying my baby," he murmurs, pressing a lingering kiss to the area just below my belly button.

His words cause my body to go haywire: my heart picks up speed, butterflies fill my belly, and my lady parts clench in need.

As if he can tell that he's affecting me, he glances up and smirks before he spreads my legs and starts eating me out with the eagerness of a starved man.

His tongue flicks across my clit and my head drops back onto the pillow as I moan his name, begging for more. Another flick, then another... More moans... More begging... Then his fingers slide into me, curling up and working in tandem with his tongue. My orgasm hits me so hard I see stars. My legs shake, and my heart feels as if it's pounding out of my chest. I try to push Pierce away, but he holds my hips down, licking and fingering me straight into another orgasm.

"Pierce!" I moan, almost positive I just gushed all over the bed—my orgasm was *that* strong. I want to beg him to stop, yet at the same time, it feels so damn good, I kind of want it to last forever.

"Fuck yes," he murmurs once I've come down from my orgasm. "I could eat this sweet pussy every damn day."

My legs tighten at the thought, and he chuckles. "You like that idea, don't you?"

"Yes," I whisper. "Though right now, I want you to fuck me."

I sit up and reach around him, fisting his shirt and pulling it over his head. Then I lie back down so I can enjoy the view. Pierce is a man who enjoys working out, and his hard body is proof of his dedication. Reaching out, I run the tips of my fingers along each ridge of his abs, until I get to the top of his jeans. I give him a look that says I want them off, and he obeys, unbuttoning his jeans and exposing his delicious happy trail that disappears into the band of his boxer briefs. One day, I'm going to lick my way down that happy trail, but right now, I need him inside me.

When he tugs the material down, tossing his jeans and boxer briefs to the side, his hard length springs up, hitting his stomach. It's thick with a single vein running down its side. The head is plump with a bead of precum peeking out, and my mouth waters, wanting to taste it.

"Come here," I rasp.

He looks at me in confusion, but when I wrap my fingers around his shaft, I don't think he cares what I'm doing, as long as I'm touching him.

"All the way up here," I say when he stops moving.

His eyes widen in understanding, and then he moves forward, straddling my chest. One hand clasps the headboard for support, and the other cups the side of my face as I lift my head slightly and lick the precum off his head.

"Jesus," he mutters. "You're going to have me coming like a teenage boy if you keep that up."

"What if I do this?"

Without giving him a chance to answer my rhetorical question, I take his entire length into my mouth and down my throat.

When the tip of his cock hits the back of my throat, and I moan around him, he pulls out and shakes his head. "No way, sweetheart. I'm not blowing my load down your throat, not tonight. Not before I've fucked you."

He slides back down my body and spreads my legs. Gripping his hard length, he teases it between my slick lips while I wait with bated breath for him to enter me so I can feel him inside me.

"Pierce," I groan, lifting my hips in an effort to get him to move this along. I'm all for foreplay, but right now, I just want him.

When I press my legs and feet against his back, he slides in, and we both sigh in unison at how good we feel together.

"God, Kels," he mutters, dropping his palms to either side

of my head. "I could live inside you forever."

"Good, because that's the plan," I half-joke. "Now, please fuck me."

He chuckles at my straightforwardness but does as I say. With one hand holding himself off me so he doesn't crush me, he delves his fingers through my hair, tugging just hard enough to lift my face to his. Our lips meet at the same time as he pushes into me, and I moan into his mouth, never wanting this to end.

Every swipe of his tongue and nip of his teeth, every curl of his lips and thrust of his hips is his way of telling me how much he loves and wants and needs me. I'm enough just as I am. And if his actions weren't enough, he murmurs the words against my lips as we both find our release.

When our hearts have slowed and we've had a moment to catch our breaths, he pulls back slightly, taking his warmth with him. His gaze meets mine, but instead of seeing a man in love, all I see is remorse. "I'm sorry," he murmurs, shaking his head. "I'm so sorry..."

"For wh—" But before I can finish my question, I feel it... his cum leaking out of me.

We had sex again without protection, and he's blaming himself.

I wait for the worry to creep into my thoughts, but the only thing that pops into my head is the idea of Pierce and me having a baby together. And I know in this moment that he's the one for me. I already knew, but the fact that I'm not freaking out over the possibility of getting pregnant just reconfirms it.

"Stop," I tell him, locking eyes with him. "We were caught up in the moment, and I practically begged you to do it." I sit up and wrap my arms around him, climbing into his lap, not caring that we're both sweaty and sticky. He turns us so he's sitting against the headboard and holds me close. "Besides," I continue, "we agreed not to waste any more time, right?"

His face lights up with hope, and my heart swells in my chest. *Yep, he's the one.*

"What are you saying?" he asks, needing the words from me.

"I want to marry you, Pierce, and I don't want to wait. Name the time and place, and I'll be there."

"Christmas," he says, as if he's already thought this through.

"You want a Christmas wedding?" I ask, letting the idea sink in.

"It's fitting. You moved here because Jordan loves Christmas. Had she not, we never would've met, and I'd still be alone, wishing for you. It's like it was meant to be."

I run my fingers through his hair and nod in agreement. "Christmas."

"Fuck, yes," he growls, lifting me off him and throwing me onto the mattress. He climbs over me, grabbing my hands and pinning them above my head. "On Christmas, you'll be mine."

Twenty

PIERCE

Sweet scent, warm flesh, soft snoring, auburn hair splayed across my pillow. I lie in bed with Kelsie asleep next to me. She fell asleep with her head on my chest and her leg thrown over mine. But she moved off me at some point during the night, allowing me to wake up and watch her.

Fuck, I can't believe she's agreed to marry me. I also can't believe I asked without a damn ring. She deserves better than that, and despite her already saying yes, I'm going to do it right. The stores are closed today, but once they open, I'll find a ring that's worthy of her. Then, I'll properly ask her to marry me.

"If you take a picture, it lasts longer," she rasps, opening one eye and smiling lazily at me.

"If you insist." I grab my phone and snap a picture, then another.

"Pierce! I was joking," she whines, burrowing her face

into the pillow for several seconds before lifting her head and glaring my way. "I can't even imagine how rough my bedhead is right now."

"You look beautiful," I tell her, making her roll her eyes at me.

When I try to pull her toward me so I can kiss her good morning, she shakes her head. "Morning breath," she mutters, trying to escape my grip.

"Don't care." I fist the back of her head and bring her face to mine for a kiss. She gives in, swinging her leg over mine, and the morning kiss quickly turns into morning sex—and I could be biased, but I'm pretty sure that's the best damn way to wake up.

"MOMMY, IS PIERCE GONNA BE MY NEW DADDY?"

Jordan's question has Kelsie and me both stopping what we're doing to look over at her. After spending the morning in bed, we dressed and joined everyone at my parents' place for a snow day. We rode the ATVs, made snowmen until the girls yawned in exhaustion, and then I brought them home. I planned to drop them off, but Kelsie invited me over for dinner, and I'd be a fool to turn down any time with my girls.

After laying Jordan down for a nap, Kelsie and I cuddled on the couch to watch a movie. It's been nice spending the past few nights with her, and I'm dreading going home—or worse, to the station.

When the movie ended, Kelsie got up to start dinner, and I offered to help. She started cooking the chicken while I was chopping the veggies for the chicken noodle soup recipe.

Right now, we're both frozen in our spot, unsure how to answer the question Jordan just lobbed at us out of nowhere.

"What?" Kelsie asks, probably to buy herself time because I know she heard what her daughter asked.

"I heard Tilly's grandma tell her grandpa that you guys are gonna get married. Does that mean Pierce will be my new daddy?"

Jesus. I need to remember to make sure Jordan or Tilly aren't within earshot when I'm speaking. This is the second time Jordan's overheard an adult conversation that wasn't intended for her.

Kelsie moves the pot from the burner and turns the stove off. Then she calmly walks over to where Jordan is standing and kneels in front of her, while I stay where I am, having no clue what to do or say.

"How would you feel about Pierce and me getting married?" Kelsie asks.

"That means I get a brother, right?" Jordan questions, making me snort before I can hide it.

"Umm, maybe," Kelsie says. "We would like to have a baby, but we don't know if it will be a boy or a girl."

"I want a brother, but a sister would be fun too." Jordan shrugs. "But she can't play with my Barbies without asking."

"Okay." Kelsie chuckles. "Aside from us having a baby, if we get married, it would mean moving into Pierce's house with him—"

"And with Cinderella and the horses!" Jordan exclaims happily, remembering our conversation from the other day.

Damn, I love this kid.

"Yes," Kelsie agrees. "Are you okay with that?"

"Yes, can we move now? I wanna play with Cinderella, and Pierce left her at home." Jordan pouts, and I hide my smile. I've been around my niece and nephews as they've grown up, though I didn't pay attention to much of what they said. I don't know if all kids are like this, but Jordan is hilarious—although, based on the way Kelsie is chewing on her bottom lip, I don't think she finds her as amusing. Probably because she hasn't addressed Jordan's original question.

"No, we can't move now. Not until after we're married."

"When are you getting married?" Jordan asks.

"On Christmas," Kelsie tells her.

"Really?" Jordan's gaze volleys over to me. "Does that mean you'll be my new daddy?"

This time the question is aimed at me, and I feel like I need to say something. Even though Kelsie is her mom, I plan to be a part of Jordan's life, so that means answering her when she asks me something.

"You already have a daddy," I tell her, joining them on the floor. I kneel like Kelsie until I'm at eye level with Jordan. "Trent is your dad—"

"But he's gone," Jordan murmurs, her tone filled with so much sadness that I want to wrap her up in my arms and shield her from all of life's problems, so she'll never be sad again.

"He is," Kelsie says softly. "But even though he's in heaven, he'll always be your dad."

"Okay," Jordan mutters, her eyes falling to the floor.

"Hey," I say, tilting her chin up to look at me. "I can be your friend."

"I already got friends," she mumbles before walking away, leaving Kelsie and me in shock and kneeling on the tiled floor.

"I don't know what to say," Kelsie whispers once Jordan is gone.

"You? I'm pretty sure that little girl just stole a good chunk of my heart."

"She's so little. She doesn't understand. She sees kids with a mom and dad and siblings, and she wants what they have, but she'll get past it." Kelsie nods, as if trying to convince herself that what she's saying is true. Then she heads back to the kitchen and continues to make dinner. Since I have no idea how to make this better, I do the same thing.

Once dinner is ready, Kelsie calls Jordan to the table and, thankfully, she seems to be in a better mood. She rattles on about her upcoming Christmas show, how excited she is to meet Santa at the Christmas festival this weekend, and asks when she can see Cinder.

After dinner, Kelsie says she needs to get Jordan ready for bed, and since I've hung around enough and figure the girls can use some alone time, I tell her I'm going to head home.

"Or you can spend the night," she says softly, so Jordan can't hear. "She sleeps all night in her own bed, so as long as you're gone before she wakes up, we're good."

"Good afternoon, what can I get—" Kelsie's words fade when she looks up and finds me sitting at the counter, and a beautiful smile spreads across her face.

"What are you doing here?" she asks, leaning over and giving me a quick kiss. "Not that I'm complaining, but you didn't mention coming by when you were leaving this morning."

She says the last part softly so only I can hear. Her cheeks flush an adorable shade of pink, and I wonder if she's thinking about the way I woke her up this morning—with my tongue massaging her clit. After I made her come twice, I kissed her goodbye and snuck out before Jordan woke up.

I spent the morning looking at engagement rings and, with my mom's help, I purchased one. I told her I wanted the proposal to be romantic, something she'll remember forever, and I wasn't sure if the Christmas festival was the right place. After some brainstorming, we came up with the perfect place.

"I figured I'd surprise you." I shrug, trying to appear nonchalant so she doesn't think anything's up. "I know you get off soon, and I was thinking we could do something with Jordan this afternoon."

"Like what?" she asks curiously.

"It's a surprise."

"You and those damn surprises." She playfully side-eyes me. "I'll be off in twenty minutes. Want a coffee while you wait?"

"I'd prefer *you*, but a coffee will do." I smirk, and she rolls her eyes.

But as she turns to grab a mug, I catch the small smile on her lips.

When her shift ends, we drive to Jordan's school to grab her. Instead of running to her mom, she heads straight for me when she sees me. "Pierce! Guess what? Friday is my day for show-and-tell, and Mrs. Molly told me I could bring anything I wanted to show the class. I asked her if I could bring Cinderella, and she said I could as long as you bring her in. Can you bring her in, please?"

She clasps her hands together and hits me with the most adorable puppy eyes, and even if I couldn't do it, I'd find a way for it to happen. Because holy shit, how the hell could I ever say no to her?

"Jordan," Kelsie says, using the mom tone I've learned all moms have. "I'm sure Pierce—"

"—would love to bring Cinder to your school for show-and-tell," I finish. "I get off work Friday morning, so just let me know what time."

"Really?" Jordan shrieks. "Thank you!"

She throws her arms around my legs, and I glance at Kelsie, whose eyes are glassy.

"What's wrong?" I ask when we start to walk toward my truck.

"Nothing," she says. "Everything is perfect."

"Wow, what is this place?" Jordan gasps as she takes in the area.

I told the girls to dress warmly but wouldn't tell them why. After stopping for dinner, we drove about an hour north to a little town called Northwood. I purchased the tickets online, so once the woman scans them, we head into the exhibit.

"Mommy, look!" Jordan yells, pointing at the sculpted ice castles. "It's like a princess castle."

"Jordan!" Tilly runs toward us with Sara and Beckett on her heels, and Kelsie gives me a look of surprise.

"I didn't know they were coming," Kelsie says, walking over and giving Sara a hug. "What a great surprise."

"Pierce mentioned it, and we thought it'd be fun," Sara says casually.

"Kelsie," Beckett says. "Good to see you again."

We spend the next half hour exploring the ice castles, caves, and sliding down the ice slides, working our way toward the Chilly Alcove. By the time we make it there, the sun has gone down and the castles are now lit up. With them being so high and surrounding the area, it looks like we're in a winter wonderland.

Taking Kelsie's hand in mine, I guide her into the alcove I rented for tonight. Unlike the rest of the area that's open to the public, this area is private, the walls creating a bit of intimacy.

When Kelsie notices that my parents, as well as my other brother, Jackson, and his wife, Allison, and their two kids, Matthew and Anna, are standing to the side and smiling at us, her hand tightens around mine.

Before she can ask what's going on, I turn her around and drop to one knee—again.

Twenty-One

KELSIE

ONE MINUTE, WE WERE ENJOYING THE BEAUTIFUL ICE castles, the next, Pierce is on one knee, looking up at me with his family surrounding us. For a moment, I wonder if I imagined the last proposal, but I know I didn't. Which means he's proposing again—this time in front of his family and Jordan, in the middle of a magical wonderland.

"Kelsie," Pierce begins, his eyes filled with so much love and warmth, I want to burrow into his chest and hibernate all winter. "When I built my house, I tried to imagine what it would look like. I visited several model homes and made a checklist of everything I could want or need in my house. When the house was done, I looked around and inspected it. The kitchen had everything I wanted, the bedrooms were exactly how I envisioned them, and the fireplace was built to perfection. I designed every part of the house myself, and it all came out precisely how I imagined it, yet for some reason it felt incomplete.

"My family came over and told me it was beautiful and perfect, except every night, I'd look around and wonder what was missing. Then you stepped through the door, and I knew at that moment, it wasn't *something* that was missing, it was someone."

He glances over my shoulder and nods, and then Jordan is by my side. "*Someones*," he clarifies, and a ball of emotion clogs my throat as tears prick my lids.

The first proposal was for me. It was done the same way everything has happened between us: in the moment, filled with heart and without thought.

But *this* proposal isn't just for me—it's for Jordan, too, because we're a package deal. From the first day, Pierce has not only known it but welcomed it.

"Now," he continues, "when I look around my house, I see things differently. I see possibility. I see a kitchen filled with love, walls covered with family portraits, bedroom walls painted pink and filled with Barbies..."

He looks at Jordan, and she grins. "I love Barbies."

Pierce chuckles and turns back to me. "I can see nights spent by the fireplace, mornings in bed..." He shoots me a flirtatious wink, and my face heats up at the memories of our recent mornings in bed. "When I look around my house now, I see it in a whole new light because I know that once you and Jordan move in, it will feel like a home."

He reaches into his jacket pocket and pulls out a black box, opening it to expose the beautiful engagement ring that sparkles against the lights surrounding us.

"Kelsie Albright, will you help me fill the house with love and happiness and make it a home as my wife?"

"Yes," I whisper, wondering how the heck I ended up in this fairy tale when not too long ago it felt like a happily ever after wasn't anywhere near the path I was on. "Yes," I say again. "I would love nothing more than to fill our home with love and happiness."

He slides the ring onto my finger and stands. Cradling my face gently, he kisses me softly, then a bit more passionately. "Thank you," he murmurs against my lips before backing up slightly.

"Does this mean I get a brother like Tilly?" Jordan asks, making everyone laugh.

"We'll see," I tell her, not wanting to make promises we can't keep.

She opens her mouth to argue, but before the words are out, her eyes land on the box in Pierce's hand that wasn't there a moment ago. It's long and pink and nestled inside is a necklace.

"This is for you," Pierce tells her, kneeling in front of her.

"A princess crown," she whispers in awe. "For me?"

"Yep. Your mom is my queen"—he looks up at me and winks, and my heart races in my chest at his thoughtfulness—"which makes you my princess."

"Can I be Merida?" Jordan asks. "She has hair like me, and she's my favorite."

"Of course," Pierce says, holding in a chuckle. He unclasps the necklace and puts it on Jordan, who takes the charm between her tiny fingers, smiling down at it.

"Thank you," she says shyly, very unlike herself. "Can we move into your house now so Cinderella can sleep with me?"

"As soon as we're married," I tell her.

"Which will be on Christmas," Pierce adds.

His family takes his admission as a cue to come over and congratulate us.

"Congratulations," Marta says when she hugs me tightly. "Welcome to the family."

Family... Jordan and I are now part of a family. The thought causes the tears that were already threatening to spill over to fall. "Thank you," I murmur. "I've always wanted to be part of a real family."

"I LOVE SEEING MY RING ON YOUR FINGER." PIERCE AND I are lying in bed. It's just after midnight. Jordan's asleep in her room, and we're in mine, cuddling.

"I can't believe you went out and bought a ring today." I snuggle closer to Pierce, admiring the ring. I don't know much about rings, but it's simply beautiful. If I were to pick out one myself, I would go with something like this.

"Do you like it?" he asks, a hint of vulnerability in his tone, which is very un-Pierce-like.

"I love it." I shift so I'm looking up at him. "It's beautiful and perfect, but a ring isn't important to me. My mom has a huge ring on her finger. It's gaudy and flashy and screams wealth, but she and my dad have a miserable marriage.

WRAPPED UP IN YOU

"What's important to me is happiness, how you think about me and Jordan and want to take care of us. The way you look at me with a mixture of love and desire. You're patient and kind and smart and considerate. Pierce, you give us so much. I know I said it before, but I feel like you provide so much while I have nothing to offer. If there's anything I can bring to the table, please let me know. I don't care about the house or the cars or even the ring, as long as we're happy."

Pierce dips his face and kisses me passionately, sending a shiver racing through my body. "You and Jordan being in my life is all I need, sweetheart. I'm a simple man. All I want is to spend my days and nights with you. That's what will make me happy."

I nod, then lay my head on his chest. While we watch a show, Pierce runs his fingers through my hair and within minutes, I'm lost in my dreams.

I don't know how long I'm asleep, but when I wake up, Pierce is gone, and the side he was lying on is cold.

Since he took the warmth with him, I pull my blanket tighter around me and then grab my phone from the nightstand—1:00 a.m.

I unlock my phone and text Pierce:

KELSIE

You should've stayed. I woke up, and you were gone.

PIERCE

I thought we weren't doing the sleepover thing until you guys move in with me.

He's right. Despite Jordan saying she wanted to move in with him now, I told him I wanted to take things one step at a time.

KELSIE

I already miss you.

PIERCE

I miss you more. I'll see you tomorrow. Good night, sweetheart.

When I wake up again, it's from a knock on the door. Half asleep, I shuffle to the front door and open it. And standing on the other side is Pierce carrying two coffees, a container of milk, and a bag that most likely has breakfast inside.

"Good morning," he says, giving me a quick kiss as he passes by and goes straight to the table.

We enjoy breakfast, and once we're dressed and ready for school and work, Pierce insists on taking us, refusing to let us walk.

"A girl can get used to this," I tell him after he kisses me goodbye before I get out at the café. "Breakfast, a ride to work, and some morning love." I flutter my lashes playfully, and he shakes his head, cupping the back of my head to kiss me again.

"You better get used to it," he murmurs against my lips. "Get used to it and expect it. Have a good day."

KELSIE

I miss you. Wish you were here...

IT'S DAY TWO OF PIERCE LEAVING IN THE MIDDLE OF THE

night, and I hate it as much as I did the night before. He was at the café when I got off. We picked up Jordan and then spent the afternoon at home.

Today, he had Cinder with him, which made Jordan's entire afternoon. While Pierce and Jordan played with Cinder in our backyard, I did some laundry and made dinner. Afterward, we played a board game, then it was time for bed. She begged for Cinder to sleep in her bed but compromised with her sleeping in her portable crate in her room.

When I woke up to pee, Pierce and Cinder were already gone, and I couldn't help feeling like a piece of me was missing. After sharing a bed with him all those nights while Jordan slept at Sara's and then Marta's, I don't want to go back to sleeping alone.

PIERCE

> Same. Only a couple of weeks and we'll
> be able to sleep in the same bed.

Except for when he has to work, I think but don't voice. Him having five days a week off is well worth the one night he'll be sleeping away from the house, and it definitely beats our current situation.

PIERCE

> Speaking of which, my mom invited us to
> brunch on Sunday to discuss the wedding.
> You're sure you're okay with her and
> Sara helping you plan the wedding?

When he mentioned it to me, I felt so bad that not only would he be paying, but his mom and sister-in-law would have to take time out of their day to help me plan it, since I have no idea what I'm doing. He assured me they were both excited to do it. Thankfully, we agreed that it will be small. I have no family or friends, and since we're doing it on Christmas, only Pierce's family will be attending.

KELSIE

Of course!

PIERCE

Good.

KELSIE

Still wish you were here. I woke up horny.

The second I press send, I cover my eyes, shocked that I even wrote that to him. I mean, it's the truth, but it's not like me to send something so brazen to a man. Then again, I never really experienced dating as an adult.

I'm waiting for Pierce to respond when my phone rings, making me practically jump out of my skin. Unlike my standard ringtone, it's the one for video chatting.

"Hello," I say slowly as Pierce comes across the screen. It's dark where he is, but there's enough light shining through that I can make out his gorgeous face and see that he's not wearing a shirt.

"Hey, sweetheart," he says, his voice raspy from sleep.

He turns onto his side and props the phone against something, giving me the perfect view of his face, pecs, and a little bit of his torso.

"So, you're horny, huh?" He smirks devilishly, and my face heats up. With the bathroom light pouring into my room, he can make out my face, and based on the way his smirk morphs into a grin, I know he can tell I'm blushing.

"Tell me," he continues when I don't say anything, "if I

WRAPPED UP IN YOU

were there, what would we be doing?"

Holy shit, he wants to have phone sex.

I swallow thickly and clear my throat, mentally preparing myself to do this. "I would've woken up and rolled over, and you would've been here."

Pierce nods in understanding. "Then what?"

I close my eyes, trying to imagine what would happen next, but Pierce isn't having it. "Open those beautiful green eyes," he demands gently.

"I would lean over and kiss you so you'd wake up," I say, opening my eyes and meeting his.

"I love when you kiss me," he admits, making the butterflies in my stomach flutter. "Then what?" he prompts.

"Umm... I'd drag my hand down your stomach, until I got to your..." When Pierce doesn't say anything, I know he's waiting for me to finish my sentence. So I clear my throat again and then take a deep breath. "I'd drag my hand down your stomach," I say again to psych myself up, "until I got to your dick."

Pierce's gaze turns heated. "I love you touching my dick. It's so damn hard just thinking about you touching it."

My brows shoot up at his admission, and he grabs his phone, turns it, and shows me his hard length over the screen. It's still tucked into his boxer briefs, but I can make out the outline of it. "I wish you were here." I pout, wanting him something fierce.

"I know, baby, but pretend I am."

He pulls his dick out of its confines and my mouth waters at the visual. It's rock-hard, and there's a small bead of precum at the tip.

"If you were here, I'd lean over and lick the tip," I whisper.

With the pad of his finger, he rubs the precum around the head then strokes himself once before turning the camera so I'm looking at his face. "Your warm, wet mouth on my cock is the second-best feeling."

"What's the first?"

"In your pussy."

My insides tighten at his words, and I know if I stuck my hand down there, I'd be wet.

As if he can hear my thoughts, he murmurs, "Stick your fingers in your underwear and tell me how wet you are."

I do as he says and groan when my fingers reach my wetness. "I'm definitely wet."

"Good. If I were there, I'd finger you until you came while you sucked my dick. Stick your fingers inside your pussy, baby. Make yourself come."

I push two fingers inside, sighing at how good it feels. It's not nearly as good as Pierce's fingers, but I'm turned on and sensitive, so my touch is welcomed.

Pierce turns his camera back around, so I see him stroking himself, and I do the same. He can't see what I'm doing to myself, so I push my panties down and flip the camera again, showing him my fingers, stomach, and breasts.

"Jesus, Kels. You're so goddamn perfect. I can't believe you'll be all mine in a couple of weeks."

"I'm already yours," I moan.

"Damn right, you are," he growls, "but you'll have my name, and you'll be living with me. I'm going to fuck so many babies into you." His strokes get harder, and I know he's close. Wanting to come with him, I gather my juices and massage my swollen nub.

"I'm so close," I moan, my orgasm on the precipice.

"Come for me. Pretend my tongue is licking that clit and come, baby."

His words are my undoing. With a couple more strokes, I come hard and loud, unable to help myself. My legs tremble as waves of ecstasy flow through my body. When I open my eyes, Pierce is also coming, ribbons of cum hitting his stomach.

"Fuck, sweetheart." He turns the camera, giving me his face again. "Move in with me now. You're going to do it anyway. I want you in this bed with me, in my arms."

The desperation in his voice, mixed with the way I'm missing him and wanting to be with him every freaking second, has me nodding in agreement. "Okay. We'll move in with you."

His brows kiss his forehead in shock. "Are you serious?"

"Yes, you're right, we're going to move in with you anyway. Jordan loves you and Cinder. She's so excited to live on the property with you guys, and Tilly, and the horses. Let's do it."

"Hell yes," he says excitedly. "I have to work the next two days. But what about Sunday? We can pack your stuff Friday and Saturday before the festival and move you guys in on Sunday."

"Okay. That sounds perfect."

Needing to go pee, I tell him to hold on a second and put the phone down, so I can run to the bathroom. He does the same, returning at the same time as me.

I don't want to lose our connection, so I lie on my side and prop my phone up next to me, making it look like he's lying next to me.

"Thank you for that," I murmur, my eyes starting to droop. Between it being the middle of the night and having just climaxed, I'm suddenly exhausted.

"You never have to thank me, Kels." Pierce settles into bed and props his phone up as well. "I would do anything for you." After a few moments of silence, he says, "I love you, sweetheart. Get some sleep."

"I love you," I rasp, my eyes closing.

When I reopen them a few hours later, my phone is still propped up, but the screen is blank. I click on my messages and find one from Pierce:

PIERCE

**Sleeping next to you is my favorite thing to do.
Four more nights, and we'll be sleeping together for
the rest of our lives. Have a good day. I love you.**

Four days? And that's when it hits me... I agreed to move in with Pierce on Sunday. I wait to regret the decision, but when it doesn't happen, I allow myself to get excited. Because for the first time since Trent passed away, I've put myself first, and in doing so, I've fallen in love.

Twenty-Two

PIERCE

PIERCE

> **I think you should consider giving Dorothy your notice. Between planning the wedding and the holidays, we'll be busy.**

I'm staring down at my phone, watching the message bubbles appear and disappear. With every disappearance, I can feel Kelsie's anxiety rising. We've been texting and video chatting like crazy over the past two days since I've been at work. Tonight, while we were talking, she groaned at the mention of her having to go to work tomorrow. After we hung up, it got me thinking: why the hell is she still working when we're moving in together?

I stare at the bubbles for a few more seconds—ready to send another text—when the bubbles disappear again and my phone rings. "Hey, sweetheart."

"Pierce," she rasps, sounding half asleep. I probably should've waited to have this conversation in person, but when I heard the dread in her voice, I felt like it was something that needed to be said.

"Kels..."

"As much as I'd love to take off the next few weeks, that would mean no money coming in, which would mean paying my rent late—"

"I didn't say to *take off*. I said to give your notice, meaning to quit. You don't have to worry about money. I paid the rent for next month, and the realtor is putting it up for sale. Mrs. Jenson said she's happy for us and she's ready to sell the house. Aside from your cell phone, you have no other bills. So, you have no reason to work unless you want to. But you said you'd love to be home with Jordan."

"I know I said that," she says softly. "However, it's scary. What if something happens, and Jordan and I are left with nothing..." *again,* is what she's thinking but isn't voicing. Because when Trent died, they weren't prepared, and she was forced to rely on his parents, who treated her like shit. She told me all about them one night, and I swear to God, if I ever meet them, they'll be getting a piece of my mind.

"You're not alone anymore. In two weeks, when we get married, you both will be added to my insurance and life insurance policy, as well as my will and my bank accounts. God forbid something happens to me, not only will you be taken care of financially, but you'll have my entire family, who already considers both of you part of our family."

"Pierce..."

"And if the idea of divorce is running through your head, you better knock that thought away right fucking now," I continue. "You're it for me, Kels. You and Jordan are mine." I release a harsh breath then say the next words I don't want to say but need to. "With that being said, I don't want you to ever feel trapped. If at any point, you aren't happy and don't feel I'm the person you want to spend your life with..."

"No, Pierce. It's not that. It's just... I love you and appreciate everything you're saying, but I feel like I've never been able to stand on my own two feet. First, Trent took care of everything, and then I lived with his parents. When we moved here, I was finally independent, even if I was barely making ends meet."

"You're so damn strong, Kels. The day I saw you in the grocery store, despite the shitty situation, you held your head high and handled it gracefully. You go to work every day to provide a roof over your daughter's head and fill her belly with food. She's more than taken care of.

"You don't need me, and you're not depending on me. We're a team now. If you feel the need to work, I'll support you one hundred percent. But find a job you love instead of one you take out of desperation. We both know you don't want to work there, and you don't have to."

She sniffles through the line, and I wish I were there to hold her.

"Kels..."

"I love you, Pierce. I can't wait to be your wife. Thank you."

I release a sigh of relief at her words, thankful that in spite of her insecurities and fears, she trusts me and knows I've got her back.

"I love you, too, baby. Get some sleep and think about what I said. I have Jordan's show-and-tell in the morning with Cinder. After, I'll be by to pick you up from work, so we can grab our girl and start packing."

"EMILY SAID CINDERELLA WAS THE BEST SHOW-AND-tell ever!" Jordan says, running around the yard with Cinder. After we got back to their place, Kelsie said she had to do some laundry and make dinner. About ten minutes in, Jordan had asked her mom fifteen questions, and Cinder was yapping nonstop in the cage. When I suggested Jordan and I take Cinder out back so they could both burn off some energy, Kelsie looked at me like I was her savior. I don't know how single moms do all this shit on their own, but I'll tell you one thing: Kelsie is Superwoman.

"That's because she's the best dog ever," I agree, throwing the ball to Cinder, who bolts after it. "You excited to go to the Christmas festival tomorrow night?"

"Yep, I wrote my letter to Santa. Tilly said the Santa at the festival isn't the real one, that he's his helper, but that he'll give him the letter. You think that's true?"

Fuck. I don't know how parenting works regarding lying about mythical creatures and beings. I think for a moment about how my parents used to respond to me when I'd ask questions like this. "What do you think?"

"Hmm..." She taps her chin thoughtfully, and I hide my grin since she's being serious. "I think he might be Santa but maybe not. You think if he's not, he'll take my letter to him?"

"Yep. But just to be on the safe side, did you address it to him?"

"No! Do you know his address?"

"Of course. Why don't we go grab your letter and I'll help you?"

"Okay!"

I snag Cinder and clip her leash. We're walking back inside when I hear raised voices, telling me Kelsie isn't alone and whoever she's talking to isn't happy.

"Hey, Jordan, can you do me a favor? Go put Cinder in her cage in your room and wait in there for a few minutes, okay?"

She looks like she wants to ask questions, but the seriousness in my tone has her nodding in agreement.

Once I know she's safe, I continue down the short hall to the living room, where I find Kelsie and two other people. They're older, maybe late fifties. The woman's face is pinched, and the gentleman seems annoyed and upset.

"You've always been selfish," the woman says, not noticing me approaching. "If it weren't for your selfishness, Trent would still be alive. Instead, he's gone, and you're moving on like he didn't even exist. It should've been you—"

"That's enough," I bark, having enough of whoever this bitch is.

"Oh, you must be the fiancé," the woman hisses. "Did she

tell you she killed my son? That she's the reason he's dead? Huh? Do you even know the woman—"

"I said that's enough." I step over to Kelsie and pull her to my side. Her entire body is trembling and tears are streaming down her cheeks.

"It's only been three years," the woman wails.

"I'm very sorry for your loss." I tighten my hold on Kelsie, and her body sags against me. "But you will not walk into this home, or anywhere Kelsie and Jordan are, and make her feel bad for Trent's death. It was a tragic accident, but it wasn't her fault, and if you're going to spew that kind of shit around her, you won't be coming around. From what Kelsie's told me, Trent loved her and Jordan very much. I can't speak for him, but I know if something happened to me, the last thing I'd want is for my parents to blame the woman I love for my death, to make her life a living hell."

The woman sniffles, then rolls her shoulders back, as her nose rises toward the ceiling. "So, what? You're going to replace my son and play daddy to Jordan?" Her nostrils flare, and she glares at Kelsie and me. Since she couldn't get me on her side through her sob story, she's going on the attack.

"No," I tell her calmly. "I'm not here to replace Trent, and I'm not trying to be Jordan's dad. Trent will always be Kelsie's first love and Jordan's dad. But he's gone, and both girls deserve to be loved and cared for. And that's what I'm going to do every day that they'll allow me.

"And for the record..." I lean in slightly and lock eyes with the cold-hearted bitch, wondering how Kelsie lived with her for as long as she did. "Loving someone doesn't mean controlling them. It means supporting and helping them spread their wings and fly."

"I think maybe we got off on the wrong foot here," the husband finally says. "We came here to see Jordan. It's been months, and Kelsie hasn't been returning our calls."

"Because for the first time, I'm actually happy," Kelsie says. "And I knew if I let you in, you'd ruin it. And I was right. You took one look at my engagement ring and threatened to take me to court for custody of Jordan."

"The fuck?" I bark. "You both need to leave. Now." I remove my arm from around Kelsie and go to the door. "We're getting married in two weeks, then we'll be going on our honeymoon. Once we return after the New Year, we can sit down and discuss you both spending time with Jordan. Until then, you aren't going to ruin the girls' holidays. Think about what you want and the right way to go about getting it, then try again after the first of the year." I open the door, making it clear it's time for them to go. Thankfully, they leave without argument.

Once they're gone, I close and lock the door behind them and cut across the room, wrapping Kelsie up in my arms. She cries into my chest, and I hold her, letting her get it all out while I gently rub her back, so she knows I'm here.

"Thank you," she mumbles after several minutes.

"Baby, you never have to thank me."

"Yes, I do," she says, peering up at me with her glassy emerald eyes. "When Trent was alive, he'd let them walk all over me. He'd say it was because they paid for his schooling or that it's just the way they are and to ignore them. I didn't want to come between him and his family because mine had already disowned me, so I eventually shut my mouth and just took it.

"You're the first person to stand up to them, and it means so much to me." She lifts on her tiptoes and gives me a soft kiss. "Thank you for loving us."

"It's the easiest thing I've ever done." And that's the truth. These two girls make loving them as easy as breathing. Speaking of which... "Jordan's in her room with Cinder. I heard yelling and didn't know what was going on."

"Thank you. The last thing I want is for her to hear any of that."

When we get to Jordan's room, Kelsie takes a moment to compose herself before opening the door. "Hey, Lovebug..." Her words trail off, and when I peek in, I see why.

Sitting on the bed with her stuffed lovebug in her lap, Jordan's silently crying. She looks up, and the tears falling down her cheeks are like knives cutting open my heart.

"Hey, what's the matter?" Kelsie asks, sitting on the edge of the bed.

Jordan continues to cry, and Kelsie pulls her into her arms.

I notice several torn pieces of paper all over the floor, so I pick one up and see, 'Dear Santa,' written on it.

"Jordan, did you rip up your letter to Santa?" I ask, picking up the rest of the pieces.

"Yes," she whispers.

"Why?" Kelsie asks. "I thought you were going to give it to him tomorrow night."

"It's dumb." Jordan pouts.

"What? Why?" Kelsie asks.

When Jordan doesn't respond, I wonder if maybe she wants to talk to her mom alone. "Why don't Cinder and I go check on dinner and give you two girls a few minutes?"

Kelsie smiles sadly and nods in appreciation.

I open the cage for Cinder, but before I can grab her, she bolts straight for Jordan, jumping onto her bed and into her lap, licking the hell out of her face. Despite her being upset, she cracks a smile and pets Cinder.

"C'mon, Cinder," I call. "Outside."

Hearing the command word, she gives Jordan one more lick then runs off the bed and out the door.

As I shut the door, I hear Kelsie ask her again what's wrong, and when Jordan responds, my heart damn near breaks in my chest. "I asked Santa for a daddy. Jennifer said when her mom got married, she got a new daddy. But I heard you talking to Grandma and Grandpa, and Pierce said he'll never be my daddy." She chokes out a sob. "Everyone has a daddy but me."

I shouldn't be eavesdropping, but I'll be damned if that precious little girl thinks I don't want to be her dad. Kelsie and I will need to talk soon, because when I said they were mine, I meant both of them. And if Jordan wants a dad who's on this Earth to love her, that's exactly who I'll be.

Twenty-Three
KELSIE

"She's out."

Pierce nods and smiles, but it looks forced. The way every facial feature of his has looked all evening. After Silvia and Ron left, I had to deal with Jordan having a breakdown regarding her overhearing what Pierce said about not being her dad. He obviously didn't mean it the way her five-year-old mind took it, but it's a touchy subject for her, especially living in a small town where everyone knows everyone's business.

After I talked her down, she explained what upset her, and it all made sense. Unfortunately, I don't have a solution, and that's probably one of the most challenging parts of being a mom—knowing your child's needs and being unable to meet them.

Once she was okay enough to leave her room, we found Pierce in the kitchen, finishing up the dinner I started. We ate quietly, and then I bathed her. Instead of begging me to stay awake late, she shocked me when she said she was tired and wanted to go to bed. I think she had exhausted herself between school, playing outside, and her emotional outburst. With Cinder in her cage by her bed, and Dots tucked under her arm, she passed out before I could even turn off her light.

"I overheard," Pierce says.

I tilt my head slightly, unsure of what he's referring to since a lot happened tonight.

He grabs my hand and tugs me into his lap, where he's lounging on the couch. "She wants me to be her dad."

"Oh, that." I sigh and situate myself in his lap. My legs are thrown over the side and my head rests comfortably against his shoulder. "Apparently, eavesdropping is a trend tonight because she overheard you too, telling Trent's parents that you would never be her dad."

"That's not how I meant it," he murmurs.

"I know. I tried to explain that to her the best I could, but there was more to it than that. She showed me a flier in her backpack from school. There's a father/daughter dance in February before Valentine's Day, and she wants her dad to take her."

"Fuck." Pierce lifts my chin, and our eyes meet. "I meant what I said, Kels. I can't replace Trent, but I'd love to adopt her and make her mine if you let me. We can hyphenate her last name so she has his and mine. Of course, we don't have to do it now. Whenever you want, the offer is there. I would love nothing more than to officially make us a family."

His words make my heart squeeze inside my chest. Since the day I found out I was pregnant with Jordan, she and I were seen as a burden to everyone. My parents disowned me. Trent's parents looked at us like we ruined his life. Trent did the right thing and tried his hardest to be a good boyfriend and dad, and I have no doubt that he loved us, but I could see the stress in his features on a daily basis.

But when Pierce looks at us and spends time with us, he doesn't see us as a burden, as something he has to deal with. He looks at us with love and adoration. He isn't being forced to do the right thing. He genuinely wants us in his life. And I didn't know until this moment how much I needed that—for Jordan and me to be loved unconditionally.

"How did I get so lucky to meet a man like you?" I whisper, leaning up and kissing the corner of his mouth.

"It's not luck, sweetheart. You deserve to be loved and taken care of. Both of you do. And I feel so fucking blessed to get to be the man to do that."

"So do you." I trail kisses along his jaw as I reach out and rub his cock through the material of his pants. "You deserve to be loved and taken care of as well."

"Oh yeah?" he rasps.

"Yeah." I continue to rub my hand back and forth across his shaft, hardening it up. "You're always taking care of Jordan and me." I glance up and find him looking down at me, eyes heated with desire. "How about you let me take care of you tonight?"

The words are barely out of my mouth before Pierce is lifting me into his arms and stalking down the hall to my bedroom. He locks the door behind us then drops me onto the bed. And I can see it in his eyes, he has every intention of taking charge and taking care of me again, despite me telling him I want to take care of him.

So, before he can do that, I shuffle onto my knees and back up out of his reach. "Come lie down." I pat the mattress, not taking my eyes off him. "I want you to lie down and let *me* take care of *you*."

Clearly not used to being taken care of, he furrows his brow. But when I don't relent, he does as I said. Coming around to the other side of the bed, he lies down and crosses his arms behind his head.

I take a moment to admire how handsome he is. His eyes are so bright, they remind me of caramel apples: warm, sweet, and addicting. His hair is messy in that sexy way that only guys can pull off. His nose is broad and angular, and his jaw is sharp and masculine. He hasn't shaved in a few days, so his scruff is turning into a full beard. Even though I love him clean-shaven because it shows off his dimple, I equally love this look on him.

"What are you thinking about?" he murmurs. His heated gaze rakes down my body in a way that has me feeling naked and exposed, regardless of my being fully clothed.

"Your beard," I admit, crawling over to him and swinging my leg over to straddle his torso. "You remind me of a lumberjack. In the book I'm reading, the guy is a lumberjack. She was driving and got stranded, but he saved her. Now they're trapped in his cabin because of a snowstorm. He walks around with a beard and in flannel shirts, always chopping wood."

The corner of his mouth quirks into a sexy smirk. "You

want to roleplay, sweetheart?" He grips the curve of my hip with one hand, using his other to grab my ponytail and tug me closer. "I'm down for playing the lumberjack, and you can play the damsel in distress."

I chuckle and shake my head. "Maybe another time. Tonight, I'm in charge." I lean the rest of the way and press my mouth to his, giving him a slow and lingering kiss. His lips are smooth and plump, and when I suck on his bottom lip, a rumble erupts from his throat.

His lips part, giving my tongue access to deepen the kiss, and our tongues find one another, as I sigh into him, getting lost in his taste, in the way he kisses me every time as if it might be the last time.

When his hands glide down my body and land on my ass, squeezing my cheeks, I remember my plan: to take care of Pierce.

I break the kiss and lean back, lift his shirt over his head, exposing his sculpted body. I wish I could stare at him longer, but if I don't act soon, I'm afraid he'll grow impatient and try to take over.

I scoot down and run my tongue across his right pec then over his left, stopping for a moment to press a kiss to the area just above his heart.

The heart that loves as fiercely as it's currently beating.

The heart that's so big it allows him to love unconditionally and selflessly.

The same heart that he handed over to me and Jordan when he made us his and, in return, made him ours.

As if he can sense my thoughts, he runs his knuckles along

my cheek then gently pinches my chin, lifting it so our eyes lock.

"My heart, my body, my goddamned soul is yours. I hope you know that. You own me, baby. I'm yours."

I choke up at his admission, tears filling my lids and blurring my vision. When I close my eyes to get my emotions under control, I feel his lips press against one eyelid then the other, kissing my tears away.

"I'll never take it for granted," I tell him, needing him to know that I don't take him trusting me with his heart lightly.

I go back to giving his body the attention it deserves, kissing and licking each ridge until I get to the waistband of his pants. I give his happy trail a quick kiss and then move farther down, giving the outline of his hard cock an open-mouthed kiss.

I unbutton and unzip his pants, and he helps me remove them, leaving him in only his boxer briefs. He stares down at me hungrily, and I'm sure he's hoping my next move will be to take him in my mouth. But I meant what I said—tonight, it's my turn to take care of him.

"Roll onto your stomach, please."

His eyes widen at my request. But after a few moments, he obeys, stretching his arms above his head—the act causing his shoulder and back muscles to stretch in the most delicious way.

I grab my lotion from the dresser, squirt some into my palm, and rub my hands together to warm them up.

Climbing onto him so my legs are straddling his butt, I start with his broad shoulders, massaging the tension out of them. With every press of my fingers, his body relaxes more and more. At one point, he even groans in pleasure. I work my way down his back, massaging as deep as I can go.

"Jesus, Kels. You should become a masseuse," he mutters, sounding more relaxed than I've ever seen him.

I chuckle lightly and continue to knead my fingers into his muscles, working every kink and knot I can find. As his body loosens up, he feels like jelly beneath my fingers.

I tell him to roll back over, and when his eyes meet mine, they're calm and sleepy, but I know the perfect way to wake him up.

Pulling the front of his boxers down, I take his thick shaft in my hand, stroke it up and down, and then take it in my mouth. My gaze flits to his face just in time to see his eyes roll to the back of his head in pleasure.

I take him down my throat a few more times, getting him nice and hard and ready for me. When he's begging me to fuck him, I climb on top of him and, using his shoulder, I hold on with one hand while I guide him into me with the other.

"You know there's nothing between us," he warns, making sure I'm aware that if I keep going, there's a chance I might get pregnant since we're not using a condom.

The last time we had unprotected sex, we were caught up in the moment, but we both agreed we didn't want to waste any more time—if it happens, it happens. I haven't changed the way I feel about that, but I love that he's asking to make sure. That he cares enough to ask.

"I know," I tell him as I take him all the way into me until he's bottomed out, hitting all the most sensitive areas inside me.

With both hands on his shoulders, I start to move up and down, swiveling my hips so we're both feeling the effects of my movements. In the otherwise quiet room, our moans of pleasure softly fill the air, both of us holding back because we know a little pair of ears is in the other room.

"Fuck, Kels," Pierce groans, reaching up and massaging my breasts. "This is the best position. You on top, your perfect tits bouncing while your warm cunt chokes the fuck out of my cock."

He takes my nipples between his fingers and pulls on them, sending jolts of pleasure through my body and straight to my core.

My walls tighten, and Pierce moans. "I'm going to come soon, so if you don't want to chance me filling that sweet pussy with a baby, I suggest you get off me."

The thought of Pierce and me creating a baby out of love only turns me on more, and within seconds, I'm throwing my head back and coming hard all over his cock.

He reaches around me and fists my hair, then pulls my face to his for a hard, bruising kiss as he takes over from the bottom, thrusting in and out of me.

"Tell me you want me to come in you," he demands against my lips as another orgasm builds inside me. "Tell me, Kels. Tell me you want me to fill you with my babies."

His words are my undoing. "Yes," I whisper-yell as my orgasm rips through me, and I lose all control of my body. "Come in me, please," I practically beg. "Fill me with your babies."

"Fuck!" he growls as he thrusts into me so deep I have no idea where I end, and he begins. And as he comes inside me, coating my walls with his cum, telling me that he loves me over and over again, I can't help but hope that maybe we did make a baby.

Maybe we're both crazy.

Maybe we're moving too fast, and we'll regret this.

But as I open my eyes and see the way Pierce is looking at me—like he could love me forever, and it wouldn't be long enough—I know that even if we crash and burn, I'll never regret taking this ride with him.

Twenty-Four

PIERCE

"I'm so sorry I ruined the letter," Jordan says, looking at Santa—AKA Bobby Burns, the town pharmacist—with the saddest, most apologetic eyes. "Would it be okay if I mailed it? I was mad and I shouldn't have ripped it, but I'll write a new one, if that's okay."

Bobby—er, Santa—nods in understanding. "Of course. You know my address, right?"

"The North Pole?" Jordan asks.

"Yep," Bobby says. "That's me."

When we woke up this morning, we had breakfast and then spent the day packing up their boxes. By the time we finished, we needed to get ready to head to the Christmas festival. We all completely forgot about the letter Jordan ripped last night until we met up with my family and Tilly asked if they could go see Santa to give him the letter she wrote in class.

When Jordan remembered she didn't have a letter, the look on her face was sad as hell, and I hated that I couldn't fix it for her, but Kelsie and I assured her we would help her write a new one tomorrow.

Bobby pats the seat next to him and Jordan sits, her features filled with remorse. "I know you don't have your letter, but I can't wait to read it once it arrives. If you want, you can tell me something that you'd like for Christmas."

Jordan glances over at me sadly, her frown deepening. And my heart clenches, knowing she ripped the letter because she doesn't think she can have what she asked for—a dad.

"I don't know," she says solemnly. "I guess... I guess I want a new bike, please. Mine's at Grandma and Grandpa's house, so I don't get to ride it no more."

"Ahh, a bike," Santa says. "And what color would you like this bike to be?"

"Pink. It's my favorite color."

After taking a few pictures of her with Santa, we head over to the sidewalk to get our spots to watch the parade. In Christmas Valley, the parade is as big as the ones you see on TV. Float after float ride by—including our fire station's float that my brother and some of the other guys are on with their families. Usually, I'd be on it as well, but I wanted to be with Kelsie and Jordan when they experienced the parade for the first time.

With all the colorful lights and decorations, Jordan comes around, smiling and laughing, letting the whole letter situation go for a moment. We eat junk food and drink hot chocolate and have a blast. Jordan jumps up and down in excitement when we learn their house won third place in the 'Battle Of The Lights' competition.

We spend the next couple hours playing games and visiting the different booths that are set up. Once the girls are so tired that Tilly is passed out in her wagon, and Jordan is asleep in my arms, her head on my shoulder, we call it a night.

She doesn't wake up when we put her in my truck or when I take her out to lay her in her bed. Or when Kelsie and I both wish her a good night and turn off her light.

"Spend the night?" Kelsie asks once we're alone, cuddled on the couch.

"Didn't know not spending the night was even an option." I kiss her temple and she lays her head on my shoulder. "We should have my mom or Sara watch Jordan soon so we can go Christmas shopping," I mention, turning the TV on so we can find something to watch. "Can't risk them selling out of pink bikes."

I wait for her to argue that she doesn't have the money, but when she simply nods in agreement, I sigh in relief, feeling like we're finally getting somewhere.

"I spoke to Dorothy tonight," she comments. "Mentioned putting in my notice."

"And?"

"She said there's no need. She's got it covered, and if I ever change my mind, I always have a job at the café." She glances up at me with wide eyes. "I can't believe I'm jobless."

"You're not jobless, sweetheart. You just get to focus on the job you love—being a mom."

She smiles so wide, her entire face brightens up, and I know that despite being nervous about the changes, she's excited to focus on Jordan. Every woman should have a choice. If she wants to work, great. If she wants to stay home, awesome. But the day Trent died, Kelsie had her choices ripped from her, and I'm glad she finally has them back.

"WOW, MY ROOM IS PINK!" JORDAN RUNS INTO THE middle of the room that I had painted once Kelsie agreed to move in with me. "And my furniture is here, too, and my toys!"

Since moving is more manageable without a five-year-old running around, we asked Sara to watch Jordan for the day while we loaded their things into a moving truck I borrowed from a friend and hauled it across town to my place. There wasn't a lot to move, and with my brothers' help, we got it done in a few hours.

Kelsie and I spent the afternoon setting up Jordan's room and organizing our room to add in her stuff. I was shocked by how little she has, but it made sense once I thought about it. She's been living paycheck to paycheck and always puts Jordan first.

Well, that's going to change. I can't take her out on a shopping spree—she'd have a fit—so I'll have to get creative.

"Pierce, can Cinderella sleep with me now that I live here?" Jordan hits me with her adorable pleading eyes, and I hate that I have to say no.

"Once she's around six months old, she'll be able to start sleeping out of her crate, but I did put her crate in here so she can sleep in your room." I nod toward the crate in the corner, and Jordan grins happily.

Once Jordan has checked to ensure everything is where she wants it to be, we jump on my side-by-side and ride over to my parents' house for Sunday dinner. Along the way, we stop to see the horses, the pond, and the treehouse. To say Jordan is excited about living out here is an understatement.

"Kelsie," Mom coos, wrapping her in her arms. "Are you all moved in?"

"Yep," Kelsie says, hugging her back. "There wasn't much to move, since we left most of the furniture there, but we're all situated."

"Good." Mom sits on the couch with Kelsie.

"Hey." Sara joins them. "All moved in?"

"Yep," Kelsie repeats, looking a bit overwhelmed since everyone is here tonight. I imagine since it's just been her and Jordan for so long, it'll take some time for her to get used to all the attention.

"Now you can give that place a woman's touch," Allison adds, sitting across from her.

"Oh, well, I mean, the place is pretty perfect the way it is," Kelsie mumbles, her eyes searching for me.

"All right, all right, you guys can hog my fiancée when you go dress shopping tomorrow." I lift Kelsie off the couch and pull her into my arms on the love seat. She instantly melts into my touch, and I lean in and softly kiss her temple. "I got you, sweetheart," I murmur so only she can hear.

"Have you bought a dress for the Firemen's Ball yet?" Allison asks.

Kelsie looks at me in confusion, and I curse myself for completely forgetting about the upcoming charity function we host every year. Several other stations from surrounding areas come to participate. It's been an annual event since my grandfather was a firefighter, and my grandmother started the tradition.

"It completely slipped my mind," I admit. "I've been so wrapped up in Kelsie that I forgot about it."

"That's because you're in the honeymoon stage of your relationship," Sara says. "But we've got you covered. After we go wedding dress shopping, we'll find you something."

"Oh, that's okay," Kelsie argues. "I'm sure I can find something in my closet."

"Not happening, sweetheart." I wrap my arms around her tighter. "While you're at it, can you take her shopping for our honeymoon? She's going to need a week's worth of clothes."

"Honeymoon?" Kelsie gasps and turns around to face me. "What are you talking about?"

"You didn't think we'd get married and not go on a honeymoon, did you?" I look at her incredulously.

"Well, I... I didn't really think about it. You mentioned it to Trent's parents, but I just thought you were saying that to piss them off. I didn't know you were being serious." She glances over at Jordan, who's playing a board game with Tilly and Anna—Allison and Jackson's ten-year-old daughter— and I know exactly what's going through her mind.

"Jordan's coming with us," I tell her. "One day, once you're ready to leave her for longer than a night, I plan to take you away, just the two of us. However, this trip will be our first family vacation."

Her eyes turn glassy, and I hate that the most basic things—things that should be a given and are the bare minimum—cause her to become emotional.

"I've never been on a family vacation before," she admits sheepishly.

"Not even with your parents?"

"Nope, when they traveled, I stayed with the nanny or my grandparents, when they were alive. They have a vacation house we would go to during the holidays and a summer place we'd spend the Fourth of July, but it was more like a home away from home." She shrugs. "So, where are we going?"

"Now that's a surprise." I tap the tip of her nose then lean in and kiss her. "Try to find some clothes that will be better for being in warmer weather, though—for you and Jordan."

Her eyes light up in excitement, and I can't wait until they find out where exactly we're going. They're going to lose their shit in the best way.

We spend the evening eating, drinking, and discussing the upcoming wedding that we have exactly two weeks to plan. Since we're keeping it small, we're not doing a wedding party. Jordan will walk down the makeshift aisle first, then Kelsie. Allison has applied to officiate, and my family will be present when we exchange our vows.

We'll spend our wedding night at home—and Jordan will have a sleepover with Tilly. The next morning, we're flying out for our first family vacation-slash-honeymoon. I had fully planned to pay for it, but my parents insisted on doing so as our wedding gift.

"I really like your family," Kelsie tells me later once Jordan is tucked into bed and we're lying in ours. She's snuggled up into my side, her leg resting over mine.

"They really like you." I run my fingertips along her creamy skin, and she shivers in response.

"I didn't realize we were driving into the city to go dress shopping. Hopefully, we're back before—" Her sentence comes to a halt, and she shoots up into a sitting position. "Oh my God, Pierce. How am I supposed to get Jordan to school and pick her up?" She looks at me with eyes so wide, they're comical. "I can't walk her to school from here. What am I going—"

"Sweetheart, breathe," I say, holding back my nervous laugh.

I knew this was going to be an issue. Sure, I can take her, but she'd have to drop me off and pick me up on days that I'm working. So, I bought her an engagement present—one I've been putting off giving to her because I'm worried she's going to freak out.

"Pierce, I can't walk from here. It's too far."

"And if you truly believe I would ever let either of you walk, you've lost your mind." I slide off the bed and stand. "Come with me and please keep an open mind."

She looks at me in confusion but takes my hand, letting me guide her through the house and to the garage. When I switch the light on, the area is illuminated, showing my truck and a brand-new sleek black Chevy Tahoe.

"Pierce..." Kelsie says slowly, connecting the dots since she's seen and been in my truck dozens of times, but she's never seen the other vehicle—that has a red bow across the top of it.

"I bought it for you," I tell her, keeping her hand in mine but turning her around so she's looking at me, not the vehicle. "It's paid outright and is in your name. It's my engagement present to you."

Tears fill her eyes, and I have no clue if they're good or bad tears, so I continue. "You said you want to make sure if something happens that you and Jordan will be okay. Those assholes took your car from you the first chance they got, and I wanted to make sure you understand that there are no strings to this gift. It's yours."

"You... you bought me an SUV as an engagement gift?" she asks, disbelief in her tone.

"Yeah, well, you needed one. It's perfect for driving in the snow and—"

Before I can finish, Kelsie's jumping into my arms and then her mouth is on mine, kissing me like she needs me to breathe. It takes me a second to catch up with what's happening, but once I do, I hold on to her ass so she doesn't fall and push her against the side of the SUV, kissing her back.

When she breaks the kiss, she pulls back slightly, and I notice her eyes shining with emotion. "Thank you, Pierce," she chokes out. "For not only buying me a beautiful vehicle but for listening, and understanding, and being so amazing and patient with me." She tightens her arms around my neck. "I love you so much."

"I love you," I tell her back. "Now, how about I show you all the bells and whistles this SUV has?"

"I just need to know one thing," she says with a mischievous twinkle in her eye. "Is the back seat big enough for us to christen it?"

"Hell yes, it is."

"I THINK MOMMY WOULD LOVE THIS." JORDAN PICKS UP a bright pink and black checkered scarf and grins up at me.

"You do, huh?" I smirk. "Or do you think that's something you'd like?"

I raise a brow, and she shrugs. "We could share it."

I chuckle, and we continue walking around the store.

When Kelsie called freaking out because they were still in the city shopping, and she was afraid she wouldn't make it back in time to pick up Jordan from school, I told her I'd handle it. Since we live in a small town, all it took was her calling the office and letting them know, and I was able to pick Jordan up.

When she got in the truck with a frown on her face and confided to me that today was Christmas shopping day at school—everyone who brings in money can go to the makeshift school shop and buy presents for their family members—and that she couldn't buy her mom a present, I asked if she'd like to go to the mall and she excitedly agreed.

"How about this?" Jordan asks, pointing at a pink bottle

of perfume. I have a feeling that whatever she ends up buying her mom will be pink.

"Oh, this is a beautiful scent," the woman at the counter says.

"Really?" Jordan asks. "Can I smell it? Please?"

"Only if it's okay with your dad," the woman replies.

Jordan blinks several times at the woman's words, then glances up at me, her features displaying confusion and hope.

"Sure," I tell her without correcting the woman.

The woman sprays the paper and hands it to Jordan, who presses it to her nose and inhales deeply. "That smells so good. Like a princess! Smell it!" She lifts the paper toward me, and I lean down and take a quick sniff. Thankfully—because I have no doubt if Jordan gets this for her mom, she'll wear it every damn day regardless of the scent—it smells really good.

"It does," I agree. "Is this what you want to get for your mom?"

"Yes, please!"

"All right, then that's what we'll get her. One bottle of pink princess perfume, please," I tell the woman.

"Great! I'll ring you up over here." She leans down to Jordan's level. "If you want to buy your dad a prince cologne, come back and see me," she whispers, followed by a playful wink.

After we're done checking out, I surprise Jordan by getting us a couple of pretzels with icing. We're eating them at the table in the food court when she brings up what the woman said.

"Are you my dad now?"

I knew there was a chance she'd ask me this since I didn't correct the saleswoman, but I was hoping she'd let it go. Maybe I should've corrected the woman, but I've never been in this situation, and the truth is, I'd like nothing more than to take on the role of being Jordan's dad. Kelsie and I talked about it, and after we're married, we're going to look into me legally adopting Jordan.

"Trent is your dad…" I begin, but she cuts me off before I can finish my sentence.

"He's not here. He's in heaven, and I want a dad *here*." She crosses her arms over her chest and falls back with a huff. "It's not fair. Everyone's got one but me."

Kelsie and I had agreed we'd talk to Jordan together, but with how upset she is, there's no way I'm going to let her continue to feel this way.

PIERCE

Jordan's upset about not having a dad. Can I talk to her, please?

KELSIE

Is she okay? Of course you can!

PIERCE

It means telling her I can be her dad.

KELSIE

I know. I love you. Thank you.

After texting her back that I love her, I drag my chair closer to Jordan, who's back to eating her pretzel in silence.

"Trent is your dad," I start again. "But if you'd like, I'd love to be your bonus dad."

This gets her attention. "What's a bonus dad?"

"It's a special dad. Trent will still be your dad forever, but since I'm here and he can't be, I'll be your dad too."

"Can I call you Dad?" she asks softly.

"Yep, if you want to."

"Can you go to the dance with me?"

"Of course I will."

"Okay," she says nonchalantly. "You can be my bogus dad."

"Bonus, not bogus," I say with a chuckle.

"Okay, Bonus Dad."

"MOMMY! DADDY!" JORDAN YELLS FROM HER ROOM. I grin at Kelsie, loving the way Jordan took to calling me dad so easily. "How do you spell baby?"

Kelsie yells back, "B-a-b-y."

We go back to what we're doing: me, watching Monday Night Football, and her, reading a book, then a few minutes later, Jordan yells again, "Mommy! Daddy!"

Kelsie snorts and shakes her head. "I swear she just wants to say Daddy."

"I'm okay with it," I say to her, then to Jordan, I yell back, "What's up, Princess?"

"How do you spell brother?"

Kelsie chokes on her laugh, and we both get up to go see what Jordan's up to. In her room, she's sitting at her little table, writing on a piece of paper.

"What are you doing?" Kelsie asks as we walk farther into her room.

"Writing my letter to Santa."

"I thought you already wrote it?" I ask.

"I did. But I need to change it 'cause I asked for a daddy, but now I got a bogus one..."

"Bonus," I correct, while Kelsie laughs under her breath.

"Yeah, bonus," Jordan says. "So now I don't gotta ask for one. So I'm asking for a baby brother like Tilly's gonna have."

I glance at Kelsie and waggle my brows, then lean over and whisper, "You know, if she's asking for a baby brother, we should give her one or she might stop believing in Santa."

Kelsie snorts again, then whispers back, "Keep banging me in every part of this house and it will happen."

"Noted."

Twenty-Five

KELSIE

As I stare at myself in the full-length mirror, dressed in an off-the-shoulder ombre—fading from black to a beautiful Christmas red—floor-length gown and black stilettos, I feel like a different person. Obviously, I'm still me, but the person I'm staring at is a happier version of myself. I guess falling in love will do that to a person.

My thoughts go back to this past week... Aside from when Pierce was at work, every morning has been spent with me making breakfast and taking Jordan to school.

While she's there, we've been planning the wedding. Not only did I buy my wedding dress and Jordan's flower girl dress, but I also found a dress for the charity ball. The stores didn't have many summer clothes, so Pierce had me order stuff online and got it all rush delivered. We picked out our cake and what we'll have catered for the dinner afterward, and we even went to the courthouse and applied for our marriage license.

The afternoons have been spent with Pierce and Jordan: horseback riding, taking Cinder for walks, and hanging out while Jordan plays on the swing set that Pierce surprised her with.

In the evenings, I cook dinner—and Pierce helps by grilling or keeping Jordan entertained—and we eat as a family. On the night he worked, he surprised me by having food delivered to the house with a dozen roses and a note that read: **Since I can't be there... xoxo Pierce**

After Jordan has had her bath and is in bed, Pierce and I spend the rest of the evening wrapped up together—talking about everything and nothing—which always leads to us getting lost in each other. And on the night that he had to work, we had a crazy hot sexting session that still gets me horny when I think about it.

With each day that passes, I fall more in love with Pierce. With his thoughtfulness and selflessness and the surplus amount of patience he possesses. And the way he handled the dad situation with Jordan... Sigh.

"Holy shit," a masculine voice whispers, making me spin around in my heels. Standing in the doorway is Pierce, dressed in a sharp charcoal gray tux, complete with a red tie that matches my dress. His face is cleanly shaven, and his hair is styled in his signature messy way.

"Back at you," I say, sauntering over to him with an extra sway in my step. The way he looks at me and touches me and talks to me makes me feel like the most beautiful woman in the world. "Is this a preview of how you'll look on our wedding day? Because if it is, I'm not sure how long I'll be able to last without jumping your bones."

Pierce grins wide, and his dimple pops out, adding to his appeal. "The tux for our wedding is black, but I'm not opposed to you jumping my bones tonight." He leans in, sliding his arm around my waist, and kisses the corner of my mouth so he doesn't ruin the lipstick I just put on. "But with the way you look in this dress, I'm not sure I'll be able to wait until then." He peppers kisses along my neck, and I shiver in response.

"Mommy, Daddy!" Jordan calls, popping our intimate bubble. "I'm ready!"

She runs into our room, dressed in the most adorable pink snowflake dress with fluffy boots that she convinced Pierce to buy her while he was watching her the day my shopping trip ran longer than expected.

"Look at you," Pierce says. "Like a beautiful snowflake princess."

Jordan grins at the compliment and twirls around in her spot. I pull out my phone and snap a few pictures of her, getting a bit choked up with emotion because she's growing up way too fast.

When we arrive at the Firemen's Ball, several people Pierce has either worked with or knows due to his family stop him. Whenever someone does, he introduces me and Jordan as *his girls*.

"There you are!" Marta wraps her arms around me for a hug. "You look beautiful. And, Jordan, you're like a pretty pink princess in that dress."

"Daddy got me pink boots, too." She lifts her foot to show off the boots.

"Wow," Marta coos. "Why don't you guys stand together so I can take a picture of the three of you?"

Pierce hands her his phone, then wraps his arms around me as Jordan moves to stand in front of us. We say cheese and Marta snaps several pictures.

As I look at them, I can't help smiling at the sight of the three of us. At how happy we look. It's not that Jordan and I weren't happy before. My little girl is my entire world, and if it were us against the world for the rest of our lives, I'd be okay with that.

But there's just something about sharing your life with another adult. To share the ups and downs and have adult conversations I can't have with Jordan. On top of that, Jordan loves Pierce and Cinder and our new home. Without the stress of trying to make ends meet, it's easier to be more carefree and enjoy each other as well as the moment.

"Mommy, can I go dance with Tilly?" Jordan asks.

"Of course. Save a dance for me."

"Okay!" she says, grabbing Tilly's hand and running to the front of the stage where the D.J. is playing the music.

We spend another hour or so walking around talking to everyone, and then when a slow song comes on, Pierce asks me to dance.

My arms encircle his neck, and he holds me tightly against his body as we sway to "Bless the Broken Road" by Rascal Flatts while Pierce softly sings the lyrics to me with such emotion you'd think he wrote the song himself, just for me.

When the song ends, he cups the side of my face and looks at me with unshed tears in his eyes. "You are my North Star, Kels. For years, I was lost. I wasn't sure if I would find someone to spend my life with. But now I know it's because I was waiting for you."

He leans in and his mouth descends on mine. It's not a long kiss, yet it's one filled with passion and love and promises of forever.

The kiss ends, though his mouth lingers on mine. "I want that to be our wedding song," he murmurs against my lips. "I want to dance with you to that song after we say I do, and I want to dance with you to that song every day for the rest of our lives."

"For the rest of our lives," I repeat. "I love the idea of that."

After we reluctantly break apart, dinner is announced, so we find Jordan and make our way to our assigned table. It's a delicious four-course meal that is spent chatting with two other families—some high-powered attorney and a CEO of some fancy company I already forgot the name of. The point of the ball is to help raise money for firefighters since the tax dollars that pay them aren't enough. The money goes not only toward pay but for gear and housing. Every plate costs thousands of dollars (firefighters and their families don't pay), so to thank them, a firefighter sits at each table with the donors.

"Can I have another apple juice?" Jordan asks, showing us her empty glass.

Pierce glances around for a server, but with the plates

already cleared, they must be in the back, getting dessert ready.

"I'll go grab it for her at the bar," Pierce says, giving me a kiss on my cheek. "Be right back."

PIERCE

"There he is!" George Robertson says, slapping me on my back. "How have you been, son?"

George was the one who hired me in Boston when Tanya begged for me to give the city a try. As much as I didn't like living in the city, George is a good man, and I enjoyed working under him. I learned a lot from him during my short time at his station.

"I'm good." I glance at Kelsie and Jordan and grin. "Damn good, actually." I grab the bartender's attention. "Can I get an apple juice, please?"

"I heard...and saw," George says with a smile, sipping his drink. "It's like one of those fairy tales my girls read. The hero saves the day and gets the girl. I'm happy for you, Pierce. You deserve to get the girl."

"What the hell are you talking about?" I laugh in confusion.

"You saving Kelsie and her daughter..." He says it slow, like it's obvious.

"I'm not sure paying for her groceries would be considered

saving them or deem me hero worthy." I chuckle and shake my head, but George doesn't laugh.

"Pierce," he says, his voice serious. "Are you telling me you don't know who they are?"

"Who, *who* are?" I ask, starting to get annoyed. The guy isn't making any sense. "Kelsie and Jordan? Of course I know who they are. We're engaged and will be married on Christmas."

"I'm talking about the house fire. The one you ran into and single-handedly saved a mother and her daughter."

The bartender hands me the apple juice, and I thank him, then turn back to George. "I've saved a lot of people over the years. You'll have to be a bit more specific than that."

"Holy shit," he mutters. "You really don't remember. I guess it makes sense. You were in rough shape that night, having just discovered Tanya was cheating on you."

"George, what the fuck are you going on about?" The last thing I want to discuss is my cheating ex.

"The woman you're engaged to and her daughter. You saved their lives. You're the reason they're still alive. The night you found out Tanya cheated, you went into that burning house without any gear on while you were off duty and carried them both out of the house before the guys even made it there."

Visions of that night come back to me.

Catching Tanya giving the married attorney head behind his desk.

Driving around for hours, trying to figure out what to do next.

Seeing the house that was on fire.

"The house is on fire!" the elderly next-door neighbor yelled. "There's a family who lives there! A young couple and a little girl."

I acted on instinct and ran inside, not thinking clearly.

"Someone, help, please."

The plea was coming from upstairs. The fire was already spreading through the house.

I ran up the stairs and found the mom—who had passed out—with her little girl. The smoke was thick, but I was able to lift and carry them out of the house.

When we got outside, the ambulances and firetrucks had arrived. I handed them off, and Keith, the fire officer, insisted I get checked out because of the smoke inhalation.

I was taken in one ambulance and the girls were taken in another.

I saved their lives.

Kelsie and Jordan were the mother and daughter I saved.

"Wait," I say as the reality of the situation hits me. "If I'm the one who saved them..."

Fuck, fuck, fuck, fuck. I left in one ambulance, and they went in the other. But there was one more person in the house that night. I remember George mentioning the mother wanted to sue because her son had died, but he was dead before they arrived. And because I was off duty, she couldn't sue me.

Oh God. "If I'm the person who saved Kelsie and Jordan... then I'm also the reason why Trent is dead."

Twenty-Six

KELSIE

It's been four days since the charity event. Since my life went from feeling like I was living a fairy tale to... I don't even know what. A nightmare, maybe?

One minute, Pierce was kissing me and the next, he was saying there was an emergency at the station he needed to deal with. He dropped us off, and with a soul-crushing kiss, he left.

I haven't seen him since. He never came home on Sunday. Then he was scheduled to work a shift the following two days. He should be home now, only he's not. I woke up feeling nauseous, and I'm praying I haven't caught a bug less than four days before Christmas and our wedding. But what I'm more concerned about is my fiancé.

Did he get cold feet?

Did he realize taking on me and Jordan was too much?

Does he want someone who can bring more to the table?

These questions and many others have been plaguing my mind since he didn't come home Sunday and has barely texted me back. Still, no matter how many doubts my brain is riddled with, deep down, I feel like there's something wrong.

I know Pierce wants to marry me.

He loves Jordan and me with all of his heart.

He doesn't want me to be anything other than who I am.

Which is why I'm currently pulling into the station, so I can find Pierce and speak to him in person. I don't doubt his love for me, which means there's something else going on. And after all the times he's been there for me, it's time for me to be there for him.

As I walk through the main area, looking for Pierce, several guys smile my way, but there's a nervousness in the air. Something is definitely going on.

When I get to the bunk room, I don't find Pierce, but papers on a desk catch my attention before I can go looking for him in another part of the station.

A picture of me but younger.

I slide the papers around and find a picture of Jordan—but younger as well.

Curious about why pictures of us from several years ago are on the desk, I lift the papers up and try to make sense of what I'm seeing. It's a report and as I read through it, it hits me that this is the report from the night of the fire. I flip through several pages and stop when I'm met with a picture of Trent. It's the one from his driver's license. I remember it because I was there the day he got it.

I'm flipping through more of the pages, trying to figure

out why, what looks to be the official report from the fire, is on the desk where Pierce works, when the man himself walks out of the bathroom with a towel wrapped around his waist. He pauses at the sight of me, and I take a moment to stare at him. His hair is wet and messy, his body is hard, and he's sporting almost a full beard, telling me he hasn't shaved since the night of the charity event.

Our eyes meet, and he takes a step forward as if he's going to bridge the gap between us and take me into his arms. But then he suddenly stops, like there's an invisible wall preventing him from getting to me, and I find myself wrapping my arms around my torso, the room cold without his embrace.

His eyes are bloodshot with dark circles underneath, as if he hasn't been sleeping, and his shoulders are slightly hunched over. His lips are downturned in a frown that breaks my heart. Something is *very* wrong.

Then he notices the paper in my hands. I expect him to explain, but without a word, he turns his back on me and leaves the room while I stay rooted to my spot, wondering what the hell is going on.

When he returns, now dressed in a work shirt and jeans, he puts his socks and shoes on, then stands and takes the papers from my hands. Still remaining silent, he guides me out of the firehouse. Once he opens my vehicle door, he finally speaks. "I'll meet you at the house."

I nod, the lump of emotion caught in my throat preventing me from speaking. Something is more than wrong, and the more I try to figure out what it is, the more confused I get.

Back at home, we both park in the garage. Once we're

inside, Pierce lets Cinder out in the fenced-in backyard while I sit on the couch, unsure of what to do with myself.

A few minutes later, Pierce joins me, but rather than sitting next to me, he sits on the coffee table across from me.

For several minutes, he just stares at me as I silently pray that whatever's wrong won't mean losing the man I love. That it won't prevent us from getting married. I can handle anything that's thrown my way. I'm strong and resilient. No matter how tough shit gets, I always fight my way through it the best I can. But I don't *want* to handle losing Pierce.

When the silence becomes too much, I speak. "Pierce, you're scaring me," I admit. "I'm drawing a million conclusions, every one worse than the last. Please tell me what's wrong, so I can help you figure out how to fix it."

"That's the problem," he rasps. "It can't be fixed. What I did can't be undone."

The first thought that pops into my head is that he cheated, though I immediately push that thought away. Pierce isn't a cheater. He was cheated on and would never do that to someone else.

"Pierce, please." I reach out and cradle his hands in mine. "Talk to me."

With his head hanging, he says the last words I'm expecting. "I'm the reason Trent is dead."

I let the words soak in, trying to understand why the hell he would shoulder the blame for Trent's death, but when nothing comes to me, I say, "You're going to have to explain so that I can understand."

He releases a harsh breath and looks up, his bloodshot

eyes meeting mine. "The night I caught Tanya cheating on me, I was driving around to clear my head. I didn't want to go home, didn't want to face the reality of my situation. I left my family and job to move to the city with her, and she was fucking another guy."

I have no idea what that dumb woman was thinking, stepping out on a man like Pierce. However, her loss is my gain. If she hadn't done what she did, Pierce never would've moved home, and I wouldn't have met him. I never would have fallen in love with him. It's crazy how life is so similar to a game of dominos. One move can set off an entire series of events...

He clears his throat, and I pull myself out of my thoughts. "I saw the flames, so I stopped. She said a young couple lived there with a little girl."

"Who is *she*?" I ask, trying to put the pieces together.

"Your neighbor," he confesses. "She was standing outside, yelling. When I went inside, I heard you scream for help."

His words bring me back to that night—knowing no one was there to save us. I screamed for help anyway since it was the only thing I could do.

But I was wrong. Someone was there: Pierce.

"You saved us?" I choke out, tears filling my eyes at the thought that the man I love is the same man who saved my little girl and me three years ago.

"I didn't have any gear with me. I just ran in and up the stairs, following where the scream was coming from. You were passed out, and Jordan..." He chokes on a sob, and I can't help but fling myself into his lap, needing to hold him and touch him. "She was coughing and crying, but it sounded weak. Had I gotten there a few minutes later..."

"We would've been dead." I cradle Pierce's face in my hands. "It's like it was kismet. You saved us, and now we're together."

A humorless chuckle escapes his lips. "You're so focused on us that you're forgetting a huge piece to that puzzle. Yes, I saved you and Jordan, but Trent..."

Oh shit. The first thing he said. *I'm the reason Trent is dead.*

"No." I shake my head. "You are not the reason Trent is dead."

"But I am," he argues. "As I carried you and Jordan out, the firetrucks and ambulances arrived. They started assessing the situation, but I didn't know... Fuck!" He drops his head against my chest, shaking it back and forth for several seconds before lifting it back up and looking at me with eyes so sad, my heart cracks.

"I didn't know," he repeats. "I didn't follow proper protocol. I just went straight for you and got you guys out. When they asked if anyone else was in there, I told them I didn't know."

"Because you didn't," I say, lifting his face to look at him. "You couldn't have known Trent was in there—"

"She said a young *couple*!" he hisses. "That's two people. But once I had you and Jordan, I only thought of getting you two out. I didn't think! I just acted. If I had followed protocol, I would've checked the downstairs bedrooms first, and he'd still be alive."

"Is that why you're upset? Because you didn't check? You can't blame—"

"No." He shakes his head. "No, I feel guilty because the truth is... I'm thankful I didn't check. Had I checked, I would've found him asleep..."

Trent had taken a high dose of sleeping pills that night—they were found in his system. He had been stressed about finals and was popping caffeine pills to stay awake then taking melatonin to sleep at night.

"And I would've carried him out," he admits. "But I wasn't in gear, and there was no way I could've gone back in after getting him out."

He reaches for my hand and entwines our fingers together, then presses a kiss to my knuckles before speaking again. "You would've had to wait for the firefighters on duty to arrive, and instead of Trent, it would've been you and Jordan who died that night."

When his eyes finally meet mine, they're red-rimmed and puffy, and I hate how much he's hurting over this.

"I hate that you lost Trent," he whispers. "But if I had to do it over again, I would choose you and Jordan every time. When I found out that it was you, I was afraid... I *am* afraid you'll hate me for not saving Trent as well."

Oh, God. This beautiful, selfless man. Just when I don't think I can love him any more than I do, I fall that much harder for him. "Pierce, I could never hate you. What happened was a horrible, tragic accident. I'm so thankful that you drove by when you did and saved me and my little girl, but you are not responsible for Trent's death.

"There was so much that went wrong that night: The faulty wiring, Trent taking sleeping pills. The alarm not sounding upstairs. My cell phone wasn't with me. The fire and smoke... The bars on the windows. A million factors led to Trent's death, but none of them include you. You only get to take responsibility for saving me and Jordan. Because of you, instead of three people dying, two of them lived."

I cuddle closer into Pierce and wrap my arms around his neck. "I love you and I'm so thankful that you saved Jordan and me. I refuse to focus on the negative. We both went through something horrible that night, but you saved me. Then three years later, standing in the grocery line, you saved me again. It's kismet, Pierce. Every broken road we took led us to each other. It's like the Rascal Flatts song we danced to the other night. After that tragedy, we were both lost, living with the ugly truths of our reality. But we've taken that ugliness and morphed it into something beautiful."

"Fuck, I love you so damn much," he says, scooping me up and carrying me to our bedroom, where he makes love to me over and over again, showing me just how much he loves me. And in return, I show him how beautiful we are together.

"Merry Christmas, sweetheart," Pierce murmurs as he kisses along my neck, gently waking me up while he tugs on my nipple from behind.

"Mmm." I tilt my head slightly to give him a better angle.

As I reach back and stroke his cock, totally on board for some morning sex, a bout of nausea hits me. I fling myself off the bed and barely make it in time to throw up in the toilet.

Pierce joins me in the bathroom, concern etched on his face. "This isn't the first time you've thrown up, Kels. Do you think you've caught some kind of bug? I hate to say this, but do we need to postpone the wedding?"

I take a few seconds to catch my breath then quickly brush my teeth, rinsing out my mouth. "I could be wrong, but I think the only bug I've caught is one that lasts nine months and ends with me giving birth."

I smirk up at Pierce, and his eyes go wide. "Holy shit, you're pregnant?"

"I don't know."

I pull out the box of tests I bought a few days ago, when I realized my period was late. Not wanting to take it without Pierce, I hid it under the sink to wait for the right time. Only it never came. We've been a little busy between the last-minute Christmas shopping, getting ready for the wedding, attending Jordan's adorable Christmas show, and having Christmas Eve dinner with Pierce's family. And if I'm honest, I was afraid I was wrong and would be disappointed if it came back negative.

"I kept waiting for my period to come, but it's pretty late now. So I could be."

"Well, let's find out." Pierce rips the box open and hands me a stick. After taking the test, we stare at it, both of us silently watching and waiting for something to happen. Not even two minutes later, the word PREGNANT illuminates the screen.

"Fuck!" Pierce lifts me gently onto the edge of the counter and kisses me with fervor. "I can't believe it." He drops onto his knees and lifts my shirt, exposing my flat belly. "There's a baby in here," he murmurs. "A piece of you and me." He glances up at me with shimmering eyes. "Thank you."

"I think before we tell anyone, we should see a doctor first to confirm everything is okay. I wouldn't want to get Jordan's hopes up, and then something goes wrong."

Pierce stands and nods in understanding. Then a huge smile stretches across his face. "She might not know it, but Santa brought her a baby brother, after all."

"Or a baby sister."

Epilogue
PIERCE

"ARE YOU READY?" ALLISON ASKS AS WE WALK OVER TO where Kelsie and I will be saying our vows, and she'll be officiating. The barn has been transformed into a winter wonderland. My family is sitting in chairs on either side of the makeshift aisle, and my mom and sisters have just sat down, confirming Jordan and Kelsie are ready.

"More than ready," I admit truthfully.

This has already been the best Christmas I've ever had— between finding out Kelsie is pregnant and spending the day with my two favorite girls. I haven't told them where we're going on our first family trip, but I have a feeling it'll be the perfect end to today.

"Bless the Broken Road" by Rascal Flatts starts to play, and everyone turns to where Jordan and Kelsie will be walking down the aisle. Jordan's first, and she looks so adorable in a light blue princess-style dress. She's tossing flowers all over the ground and giggling as she does it.

When she gets to me, she dumps whatever she has left in the basket and grins up at me. "I threw them all."

"Good job." I kneel in front of her. "You look beautiful, like a real princess."

Her smile widens. "Thank you. Mommy looks like a princess, too."

She turns around to stand with me and a few seconds later, Kelsie appears, looking beyond gorgeous in her white, sparkly dress. My dad lifts his arm, and she smiles softly up at him, hooking her arm in his elbow.

Thanks to her parents being too stubborn to admit they fucked up and are missing out on both their daughter's *and* granddaughter's lives, Kelsie was set to walk down the aisle alone. Only the second my dad heard, he insisted on walking her, saying that she's family and he would be honored to give her away. Her parents might've disowned her, but she has a family here who love her.

When they get to me, I shake my dad's hand then lean in and kiss the corner of Kelsie's mouth. "You look beautiful."

She smiles a watery smile, and I wonder, not for the first time, how I got lucky enough to share my life with this woman.

We decided to say our own vows, so I go first. Resting my hand on the side of her face, I recite the words I wrote about our love.

"Kelsie, since the moment I met you, I knew you were the one for me. The first time I met you, you were down on your luck, but your strength showed me the type of person you are: strong, courageous, and determined. Since then, I've gotten to meet the many parts that make you who you are: the mother, the friend, the lover... and I've fallen in love with every part of you.

"You once asked what you could possibly bring to the table, worried that our relationship would be one-sided, but what you didn't realize is that you've already given me the two greatest gifts I could ask for: you and Jordan."

I glance down at the beautiful little girl beaming up at me. "I'm not sure there's anything in the world I could give you that would equal what you've given me. But I promise to love and cherish you both every day.

"My promise to you, as your husband, is to love you for who you are. When you are happy, I will be happy with you. When you are sad, I will make you smile. I will encourage you to grow as an individual, and I will be there by your side every step of the way. I promise to love and honor you and to respect you every day as we follow our dreams and grow old together."

I take her hand and push the wedding ring onto her finger, then place the engagement one back onto the same finger. She sniffles back her emotions, and I catch a falling tear, wiping it carefully so her makeup doesn't get smudged.

"Pierce, it wasn't until you that I got to experience true love," she begins, grinning up at me with a watery smile. "Before you, every person in my life loved selfishly, with terms and conditions and stipulations. Everyone always had an agenda. But then you came along and showed me that it's possible to love someone unconditionally. You accept me and love me the way I am, and I promise to always do the same. I promise to love you during the good times and bad, happy and sad, and to always be by your side. I promise to love you selflessly and unconditionally as we go through this journey of life together."

She takes the ring from Allison, slides it onto my ring finger, then raises it to her lips and kisses it. "I love you, Pierce."

Allison announces us husband and wife, and then I take my *wife* into my arms and kiss her with every ounce of love I have in me.

When we separate, instead of walking down the aisle, I turn toward Jordan, who's smiling at her mom and me. "Before we celebrate, I have one more vow to make."

I kneel in front of Jordan, and Allison hands me the box I asked her to hold. "Since the moment I met you and your mom, I knew you two were meant to be my family. The first time you called me Daddy, my heart felt like it would burst in my chest because I was so happy. I vow to take care of you, to guide and protect you, and to be there for you every day for the rest of our lives. You might not have my blood flowing through your veins, but you own my heart, and you are and will always be my daughter."

I open the box, and nestled inside is a small bracelet with a heart charm dangling from it. I already showed it to Kelsie, and she agreed Jordan could wear it tonight, but afterward, she wants to put it away for when she's a little older and won't lose it.

"I love you, Jordan, and I'm so happy to be your dad."

I latch the bracelet on, and she grins down at it for a few seconds before she looks at me and wraps her tiny arms around my waist. I lift her into my arms, shifting her so she's on my hip, and tug Kelsie into my side.

We face my family, and everyone stands and claps while Sara takes pictures of us since she's deemed herself the wedding photographer.

KELSIE

"ARE YOU READY, MRS. ADLER?" PIERCE ASKS, SCOOPING me into his arms bridal style. "Once we cross over this threshold, there's no going back."

I laugh at Pierce's dramatics, on a happiness high from the amazing day and night we've had. From opening presents with Jordan, to saying our vows, to spending the day celebrating our marriage with Pierce's family, to enjoying delicious food, and I don't even know how long we were dancing on the dance floor. The wedding wasn't big, with only his family in attendance. Compared to most weddings, it was low-key, but it was perfect, and I'll remember today for the rest of my life.

"Do it," I tell him, playfully kicking my feet out. "Cross over that threshold and then make love to me as your wife."

His eyes meet mine, twinkling with love as butterflies flutter in my chest. "I plan to make love to you every chance we get for the rest of our lives."

He pushes the door open—since his brother Jackson is watching Cinder, the house is quiet—and steps over the threshold, carrying me through the house and straight to our bedroom.

When he steps into the room, I'm momentarily taken aback by the dozens of candles placed on the various surfaces. A better peek tells me they're electric, and I breathe easier knowing there's no chance of a fire. On the bed, rose petals make out a heart, and next to the bed, there's a bucket of ice with a bottle of what looks like champagne inside.

I imagine he wants to start with the champagne and work our way to the bed, but it's been almost a full day since Pierce has been inside of me, and with all the kissing and touching and dancing today, all I want is for him to make love to me.

Since the dress is strapless and zips from the side, I gently pull the zipper down until it's loose enough to fall to the floor. The beautiful material pools at my feet, leaving me standing in front of Pierce in my white lace, strapless bustier, matching thong, and heels. I step out of the dress and saunter toward Pierce, who's frozen in his place, watching me intently with lust-filled eyes.

"You're so fucking beautiful," he rasps when I reach him. "And all mine." He bends down and gives me a tender kiss. "I want you to crawl onto the bed and lie down at the top for me," he gently demands.

Knowing he's asked me to do that so he can watch me walk across the room and crawl on all fours in my lingerie and heels, I do as he said, swinging my hips seductively as I go.

By the time I make it to the top of the bed and turn

around, he's stripped himself of his jacket and tie, with his shirt completely unbuttoned, showing off his muscular chest and torso.

I lie back on my elbows and watch as Pierce shrugs off his shirt then unbuttons and unzips his pants. He toes off his dress shoes then pushes his pants down his muscular thighs, and I wonder how the hell the guy can make undressing look so damn sexy.

"Can I take a picture of you like this?" he asks, stepping closer to the bed. "I want to say the way you look, in that sexy lingerie, in the middle of our bed will be ingrained in my brain forever, but I really want a visual."

I nod in understanding, and he grabs his phone to take a couple of pictures. Once he's done, he tosses the phone to the side and crawls onto the bed. When he gets to me, he removes one of my heels and kisses the instep of my foot. He does the same to the other, and then he spreads my legs and trails kisses up the inside of my thighs, playfully nipping and licking along the way.

He bypasses the apex of my legs and places a soft kiss to my belly. "I can't believe next year we'll be a family of four," he says in awe. "It's a good thing we're going away now."

"And where are we going?" I ask, hoping he'll tell me since he's made it a point not to give a single hint away.

"You'll see... tomorrow."

He kisses my belly once more, then ascends to my breasts. Pulling the cup down, he licks my nipple and then the other one.

It might be because I'm pregnant or extremely turned on,

but when he sucks a nipple into his mouth, my back arches and I release a loud moan of pleasure. I'm damn near close to coming before he's even had a chance to be inside me.

He moves back down my body, trailing fiery kisses along my flesh until he reaches my sex. He tugs the panties off my body and then he delves between my legs, eating my pussy with such expertise I come within minutes.

"So damn perfect," he murmurs, climbing up my body carefully so he doesn't put any weight on me. He shifts from one knee to the other, and his boxer briefs come off. His hands cradle my face, and he guides himself slowly into me until he's so deep, we've become one.

"And all mine," he mutters just before his lips descend on mine, and he makes love to my mouth with the same amount of passion his body makes love to mine for the first time as husband and wife.

When we've both found our release, Pierce carries me to the bathroom and into the shower so we can rinse off. Once we're clean, he insists I wear his shirt from today, saying the only thing sexier than the lingerie I was wearing, is me in his clothes.

When I climb onto the bed, ready to get comfortable, Pierce walks over to the bucket. He grabs the two flutes sitting on the nightstand and after popping the top, he pours us each a glass.

"It's non-alcoholic," he says with a wink when he hands me my flute and climbs into the bed next to me. "Sara had a bottle on hand."

"Thank you."

"To a lifetime of love and happiness," he says, raising his glass.

"May we live and love every day like it's our last," I rasp, getting choked up with emotion.

We clink glasses and take a sip.

"So, are you gonna tell me where we're going tomorrow?" I ask, hoping he'll give in and tell me this time.

"You truly want to know?" he asks, taking my glass and his and setting them on the nightstand.

"Yes, I'm dying to know."

"All right. I'll tell you." He sidles up next to me, and I cuddle into his chest, getting comfortable. It's still early, but we're leaving early, so I'm going to need all the sleep I can get.

"Disney World," he murmurs. "We're going to the most magical place on Earth for a week."

He glances down at me, and I sniffle. Of course he'd pick the place our daughter has dreamed of visiting—the place I dreamed of being able to take her—where princesses and princes and fairy tales exist.

We came to Christmas Valley on a whim, hoping for a fresh start from the tragedy we'd experienced. Not only did Jordan and I get that, but we found our Happily Ever After.

Extended Epilogue

PIERCE

ROUGHLY EIGHTEEN YEARS LATER

"Hey, Trent, this visit is long overdue, but as I'm sure you've seen, I've been a little busy."

I sit on the grass in front of the headstone and get comfortable, unsure of how long this visit will take. After the first time Kelsie and Jordan brought me to "meet" Trent, I've been coming back whenever I'm in the city.

Some might think it's weird that I'd want to visit a man's grave I've never met, but I look at it differently... The fire that took Trent's life is what led Kelsie and Jordan to me. I hate that he's gone, but I feel so blessed that by some miracle they ended up in Christmas Valley. And for the rest of my life, I get to be here on Earth with Jordan and Kelsie, while Trent is forced to watch from above. I just need him to know that even though they're with me, he'll always be a part of them—especially Jordan.

"As I'm sure you know," I continue, "Jordan got married last month. I wanted to hate him, but Blake's a good guy. I truly believe he'll treat her like the princess she is." I glance around and when I don't see anyone, I lean in and add, "But don't worry. I'll continue to look after her and protect her. She might have taken his last name and moved in with him, but she's still *our* daughter."

"And that's never going to change." Jordan sits on the grass next to me and grins a watery smile. "I thought I might find you here."

"More like you searched my location on the phone."

"Hey, you guys are the ones who always insisted we share our location." She nudges me playfully. "You can't get mad when I use it too."

"I didn't know you guys were back from your honeymoon."

Jordan met Blake during her senior year of college. Blake proposed the day of their graduation, and I'm not gonna lie, I thought she'd tell us she wouldn't be coming home.

Instead, she sat us down and asked if there was any room on the ranch for them. She told us they'd love to help run the ranch since my brother is ready to retire and my nephew moved to the city. Plus, Blake grew up on a farm not far from Christmas Valley.

My parents had planned to hire a manager, so they were ecstatic for Jordan and Blake to want to learn the ropes. And of course, they offered to pay for them to build a home on the property.

They were married a couple of weeks ago and then took off for their honeymoon. I knew they were due back soon, but I didn't realize they were already back.

"We arrived earlier this morning, and I came looking for you. Works out well," she says with a small smile. "I planned to come talk to my dad as well." She nods toward the headstone, and I wonder what she needs to tell us. It must be big for her to drive out here.

"I know I've said it before, but thank you for loving me." She glances my way and her glassy eyes have me pulling her into my side.

"You never have to thank me for loving you, Princess. Loving you, your mom, and your brother is as easy as breathing."

Unfortunately, when Kelsie gave birth to Josh eight months after we were married, there were complications, and she was forced to have a hysterectomy that would prevent us from having any more kids. Instead of focusing on the negative, we thanked God that she and Josh were okay and that we were blessed with a family of four.

"So, what did you come all this way to tell your dads?" I ask curiously.

"I wanted you both to know"—she turns her body so she's facing me—"that you're going to be grandfathers. Blake and I are expecting a baby." Her hand goes to her belly, and her expression looks like a mixture of nervousness and excitement. "It wasn't planned, but..." She shrugs.

Sure, she's young, and they've only just started their journey, but isn't that how life works?

"Sometimes the best things in life come from the unplanned," I tell her. "Look at you, your mom, and your brother. I wasn't expecting any of you, but you three turned out to be the best part of my life." I take my hand in hers and squeeze it. "And I have no doubt that this baby will be the best part of Blake's and your life."

About the Author

Reading is like breathing in, writing is like breathing out.
– Pam Allyn

Nikki Ash resides in South Florida where she is an English teacher by day and a writer by night. When she's not writing, you can find her with a book in her hand. From the Boxcar Children, to Wuthering Heights, to the latest single parent romance, she has lived and breathed every type of book. While reading and writing are her passions, her two children are her entire world. You can probably find them at a Disney park before you would find them at home on the weekends!

Milton Keynes UK
Ingram Content Group UK Ltd.
UKHW021405151124
2882UKWH00065B/624